DAUGHTER OF ANKOU

DAUGHTER OF ANKOU

KIM PRITEKEL

SAPPHIRE BOOKS

SALINAS, CALIFORNIA

Editor - Heather Flournoy
Book Design - LJ Reynolds
Cover Design - Fineline Cover Design

Sapphire Books Publishing, LLC
P.O. Box 8142
Salinas, CA 93912
www.sapphirebooks.com

Printed in the United States of America
First Edition – October 2023

This and other Sapphire Books titles can be found at
www.sapphirebooks.com

Kim's other books

Standalones
1049 Club
After Shadow
Blinded
Connection
Damaged
Shadow Box
Swann Song
The Gift
The Plan
Wild
Zero Ward
Control
Unmasked Desire

Dance with Me Series
Curtain Call
Encore Performance

The Traveler Series
The Traveler - The Hunted
The Traveler - The Hunter

The Wynter Series
Finding Faith
Taking Liberty
Justice Won
Keeping Hope
Showing Mercy

The Destiny Series
She Who Would be King

Dedication

I dedicate this book to Allison and Teresa. Two ladies who took one heck of a journey with me in the one hundred days it took me to write this series. You ladies are awesome!

Note to reader:

Cateline's name is pronounced: cat-ay-lene. It's the French version of the name, Catherine.

Bahutha's name is pronounced: bay-hugh-thay.

Prologue

Sursha, 1370

L ip tucked into her mouth, the four-year-old raised her kid-sized bow, just like her daidí had shown her. With arrow nocked perfectly and one eye squeezed shut, she released it. Her eye opened as she watched the projectile fly through the forest. To her great disappointment, it didn't land center of the knot in the tree as she'd been aiming for. Instead, to her horror, she heard the nightmarish squeal of a struck rabbit.

Gasping and tears instantly coming to her eyes, she dropped her bow, little quiver of arrows still strapped to her back, and took off. Leather shoes pounded the earth beneath her long tunic that covered leather trousers as she tried to get to the wounded animal. She slowed as she reached it. The beautiful little rabbit lay on the ground, the arrow protruding from its middle. The length of the arrow was much shorter than the ones her brother and father used, which might be the only reason the little creature was still alive, she thought.

She lowered herself until she knelt next to the creature. She looked into its large, black eyes. "I'm so sorry," she whispered, tears streaming down her cheeks and falling onto the gray fur. She touched it, so soft.

The rabbit stopped squealing, but it was breathing hard, side billowing with its quick, frightened, and no doubt pain-filled breaths.

"What would you like to do, child?"

Big, tear-filled green eyes looked up, stunned. Before the kneeling child was a woman in a deep blue cloak, gold stitching finishing off the brilliant blue color. It was unlike any colored garment she'd ever seen. And the woman who wore it was unlike any woman she'd ever seen.

As she knelt down to be more on her eye level on the opposite side of the rabbit, pale hands appeared out from under the cloak and gracefully pushed the hood back. The face that was revealed captivated the young one. Her hair was light blond and, to her surprise, short. She'd never seen a grown woman with short hair before.

But, even at such a tender age, it was the woman's eyes that struck the girl. They were the color of the shallowest ocean waters at the calm. With the paleness of her skin, the blue seemed to glow. She was captivating.

"What would you like to do?" the woman asked again, her voice soft. The words were Gaelic, but they were accented in a way she'd not heard before.

The tears returned as she looked down at the rabbit. "I didn't mean to hurt it."

"It's okay, Roishin," the woman murmured, giving her a sweet smile. "Give me your hand."

Stunned this stranger knew her name, she held it out to her. The tears increased when her little hand was placed upon the wound, the hot stickiness of the blood on her palm.

"What do you want for this creature?" the

woman asked, her soft voice flowing over her like honey.

Large, deep green eyes looked up to meet those of the ocean tide, and she said simply, "I want it to live."

A beautiful smile spread across the woman's lips as she reached a hand out and gently used a fingertip to wipe away tears from Roishin's eyes. She brought that fingertip down and dipped it into the animal's blood. The little forest critter gasped, then calmed. It lay there as though it had decided to take a rest for a moment.

"Pull your arrow, *karantez*," she instructed.

Roishin forced her eyes away from those of the woman's and back to the rabbit. With one final sniffle, she did as she was told and wrapped a small hand around the arrow's shaft. As though pulling a spoon out of warm lard, the arrow slowly slid loose from the animal's body. She gasped to see there was no blood on the deadly tip.

Looking up with wide, confused eyes, she was met by a beautiful smile. The woman reached that hand back out and lightly tucked wild, long dark hair out of Roishin's face. "We will meet again," she promised in a soft murmur.

"Roishin!"

The child gasped as her head whipped to look over her shoulder toward the frantic voice. She knew she had to go. Looking back, she found herself alone. She stood, looking everywhere for the woman in the cloak, but she was nowhere to be found. Something at her feet caught her attention.

The rabbit had pushed up to sit. It slowly raised itself to its haunches, little nose twitching as it studied her. Without a sound, it darted off into the lush forest. She stood there staring after it, the spent arrow still gripped in her hand.

"Roishin!" The voice was closer now, that of her older brother, Garratt.

"I'm here," she called out, her gaze still staring after the rabbit. She wondered if perhaps she'd imagined the whole thing.

Chapter One

Sursha, 1378

A bracer-clad arm shot out, and a large, tanned hand slapped down on a bopping knee.

"Sorry," was muttered in response.

Fallon said nothing, simply squeezed the offending knee for a moment before removing her hand. She had to remember back to when she and Cateline had first married and it was clear their family was growing. Her father had warned her that, no matter how good a parent she and her wife were, it was the curse of the gods to make children twice as ornery as their parents ever were.

Lord, was that ever true with their youngest, Roishin. A twelve-year-old spitfire, that one was. She redirected her attention to Roishin's grandfather, who was Fallon's father and, of course, King of Sursha. She so wanted to turn to see her daughter's expression as King Carthac read over his youngest granddaughter's request.

No doubt she was about to chew her lower lip to shreds. When the tip of her thumb wasn't at her disposal, that was usually what got gnawed to pieces. Finally, the king cleared his throat. He brought a hand up and ran his fingers over the long, snow-white goatee he wore with his heavy mustache. His thick head of hair was just as stark white, worn long like

Fallon's, with warrior braids along the sides.

Dark eyes raised to take in Roishin as Carthac rested the parchment on the desktop. "So," he said, deep voice resonating in the large room that acted both as his bedchamber and the solar, where more informal business was dealt with. Fallon had tried to get her father to address his granddaughter's petition in the throne room, but Carthac had refused. "You wish to petition the Crown to allow you to wear your trousers in public."

"Yes, Daideó—" Roishin began, but cut herself off at Fallon's nudge with her leg. "Your Highness."

He nodded, studying the youngster with an intense stare. Fallon had to admit, she was impressed that her father, who absolutely adored Roishin, was managing to keep the ever-present twinkle from his eyes. He was looking the young hopeful over like he would anyone else who came before him with a serious request. It was so serious, in fact, she'd written it out herself.

"And, why do you think this is necessary for you, Roishin?" he asked.

Roishin cleared her throat and sat up even straighter than she already had been in the chair. "Because, dresses interfere with my riding, with my archery, and frankly, with my life."

It was Fallon's turn to bite down on her lower lip as amusement and just plain *pride* flowed through her.

"Do they, now?" Carthac asked, heavy eyebrows raised.

"Yes, sire," Roishin said with a nod. "They absolutely do."

"How don't they get in the way of the lives of

your mamaí or your sister?"

Roishin's dark eyebrows fell. "Because, their life is being a girl, Your Highness. My interests go further than just that."

"I see," Carthac said. Fallon could see he was now absolutely struggling to remain stoic. Clearing his throat, the king said, "Your proposal is well drafted and well thought out, lass. Give me the night to ponder this, and I will give you my verdict on the morrow."

"Yes, sire." Roishin popped up from her chair in her excitement but immediately fell back into the chair when Carthac raised that eyebrow again. Contrite, Roishin bowed her head in deference as the king stood.

"You are both excused."

Fallon pushed to her feet, her daughter doing the same. Immediately, she draped a protective arm around Roishin's shoulders as the two headed out of the King's chambers. Together, they walked down the long hall, Fallon's booted steps echoing off the stone. Though she was no longer head of the Elite Guard or fully armed on the regular, she hadn't lost her flair for the uniform of the soldier.

Well, that and the fact that she had little choice in what she wore anywhere but in the sacred space she shared with Cateline. Unlike what was seen as customary for royal or noble couples, the two women shared a bedchamber. To that end, and to make sure that their secret was kept hidden, Fallon assumed male garb whenever she left their chambers, and was commonly known to the kingdom as Carthac's son. Fallon adored Cateline more than life itself, and to not have her by her side at night was to cut her own heart out.

Once they hit the stairs that would take them to lower levels in the castle, Fallon looked to her daughter. "I cannot even begin to tell you how proud I am of you, Roishin," she said.

Her hand moved from the girl's shoulder to lightly tug at a strand of dark hair that had come loose from the updo that had been so carefully put into place for her that morning by Elsie. She was a young Scottish lass brought into their household to help Cateline. She also often traveled with them to help manage the chaos.

Though only sixteen, she was bright, mature, and extremely disciplined in her duties. She had quickly become a trusted member of the small circle of servants that worked closely with the family. Fallon had to laugh. Honestly, she had no idea how Roishin managed to do it. Her hair could be perfect, every dark strand in place, but turn around and suddenly it was trying to run as wild as the girl herself.

"Really, Daidí?" the girl asked, question in her tone.

"Absolutely." Fallon dropped her hand from the dark hair and guided them to the dining room where she knew lunch would be waiting for them. "That took a lot of courage, Roishin."

"Do you think he'll decree it?" She waited as Fallon pulled open a door for her, passing before her and into the smaller, more intimate dining room meant only for the family. Rather than a table that could seat half an army, this one could comfortably seat ten. Though certainly larger than the two of them needed, it was better than the formal hall.

"I know not," Fallon responded. In her heart she knew her father would want to, but he had to think outside of his role as a grandfather. Whatever he decided here would set precedent. What she *did* know was that the following day, before they began their journey home to Caisleán Thíar, they were going to take a very special detour. There was a place she wanted to introduce to Roishin, as it was time she knew.

⁂

Once night had fallen after Fallon had taken her daughter to the training fields to work on her archery, they'd shared a good dinner with Carthac the grandfather. Roishin had regaled him with tales of that day's exploits. Six bullseyes in a row! Exhausted after a long and exciting day, Roishin had all but dropped in bed.

Making sure her daughter was tucked in and given a kiss good night to the forehead to send her into sweet dreams, sheshe'd headed back to her father's chambers. Carthac reclined near the fire with a mug of ale in hand. Fallon joined him, smiling as she took the seat next to his and the mug of ale waiting for her. "Thank you, Daidí."

"You know," Carthac said conversationally. "I was just sitting here thinking that I cannot believe it's been thirteen years since Cateline joined our lives." He looked from the flames to the eyes of his daughter, already looking at him. "Seems like it was just yesterday in one way, but then seems she's been here forever, doesn't it?"

Fallon nodded as she sipped from her mug. "It does. And," she added. "I love her more with each passing day." She met and held her father's gaze. "I know it wasn't an easy decision you had to make, Daidí, with Fergus. And now, especially as a parent of three children myself, I can't even imagine. But, I'll be grateful until the day I die that you did."

Carthac was quiet for a long moment as he stared into the flames but finally said, "I've never questioned that I made the right decision, Fallon." He shrugged. "Yes, I lost my son, but I gained so much more in Cateline." He smiled. "I gained a daughter, three grandchildren I adore, and even Livia I can include in that." He raised his heavy brows as he shook his head in wonder. "She's become quite the advisor to you."

Fallon nodded. "That is a true statement." She chuckled. "Once she was given a chance at education, she was a sponge. The way she learned our history, our laws." She shook her head. "The world was truly her oyster."

She smiled, considering the young woman who had come to them at the age of sixteen. An orphan pitied by the local monastery, the monks had given her shelter in a shed if she tended the orphanage garden. In her usual, almost otherworldly understanding of people, Cateline had been drawn to the girl and had brought her into the castle. Trained as her lady-in-waiting, she'd quickly become a cherished member of the household.

After Fallon and Cateline had married, Livia had asked for more responsibility and a larger stake in her adopted country, as she was Italian born. Fallon and Cateline had jumped at the idea, and Livia had begun an intense education. She'd thrived, and thrived still as a woman of twenty-nine. She was Fallon's most trusted advisor.

"So proud of her," Fallon murmured softly.

"Which," Carthac said. "Brings me to Roishin's request."

Fallon grinned and shook her head. "Oh, my dear, dear Roishin." She glanced to her father. "I had nothing to do with that petition, I swear. I just got her here. But, I felt that if it was something she felt that strongly about, she needed to have the courage to ask for it." She shrugged. "If her petition is accepted, she can feel proud that she fought for what she wants and believes in. If not, it's a lesson in acceptance and that sometimes in life, you don't get what you want."

Carthac nodded. "What does Cateline have to say about all this?"

"She feels as I do. Trust, she'd love nothing more than to throw on a pair of trousers than have to deal with all the nonsense women are forced to. But, she understands her situation is quite different from Roishin's." She ran a hand through her hair. "And honestly," she added quietly. "Neither of us wants to see her have to go through what I have just to be herself."

"So," Carthac said. "You think she's like you?"

Fallon shrugged. "I think she has her own mind, Daidí. I think she knows who she is." She chucked. "Sometimes I look into her eyes and I don't see a twelve-year-old girl, but a two-hundred-year-old woman. Sometimes it's downright intimidating."

They shared a laugh at that. "You know," Carthac said after a moment. "She has the exact same color eyes as your mother did."

"Really?"

"Aye." Carthac nodded, his gaze drifting away for a moment as if looking back to another time in his heart. "The first time I saw those deep green eyes,

I knew I'd fall on my own sword for Roishin." He smiled. "*Both* of them."

"Yes, she's had you wrapped around her fingers since the day we brought her home. But," Fallon added, her eyebrow drawn in thought. "There's always been something about her, something I can't put my finger on. Now, you know I love all my children with all that I am, but that little girl..." She shook her head, trying to figure out exactly what it was she was trying to say. "You say she has the same color of eyes as my mother, and yet when I look at her, I see both Cateline and I." She looked at him. "How is that possible?"

Carthac shook his head as he took a drink. "I don't know, but I see it, too."

"She sees things," Fallon said quietly. "In her dreams. More than once I've had to rock her back to sleep. Wakes up absolutely petrified."

Carthac was quiet for a long moment, so long Fallon thought perhaps he hadn't heard her. But, when she looked over at him, she saw a very strange expression on his face. He set his mug aside and pushed up from his chair with a grunt of exertion. A man in his early seventies, he was beginning to wear his age.

Fallon remained where she was but glanced over her shoulder to see where he was going. For all she knew, he was headed to his garderobe to do his business after a bit too much ale. Instead, he walked to his bed and the small gold chest that was always nearby. It was the very same chest that had housed the amulet Fallon was to wear when her brother Fergus had sent her on a death mission to Brittany thirteen years before. It was a mission that had changed all their lives.

Closing the chest after he fished something out, Carthac made his way back to his chair and sat down again. He held out his hand to Fallon. Looking down at it, Fallon realized it was yet another medallion-type necklace, though the pendant was much smaller than the serpent-wrapped crystal skull that was Fallon's.

On a silver chain was a silver triangle slab. At the center of the triangle was an eye made of a deep, opaque blue stone with little gold flecks in it. The small pupil was onyx. The triangle was perhaps only two inches high and across, at best. She looked to her father for explanation.

"Your mother's," he said. "She once told me that she didn't remember many details of her childhood, but that this had been with her from her earliest memories." He gave her a rueful smile. "I don't know why, but that popped back into my mind when you said that about Roishin. I feel she should have that."

"Oh, Daidí," Fallon whispered, touched. "We've spoken to her about Mamaí." A sad smile crossed her lips as she studied the pendant. "What I know of her, anyway." She wrapped her fingers around it, the silver chain dangling down from her clasped hand. "She'll love this."

Carthac nodded, a look of satisfaction on his grizzled features. "So, about this petition." He smiled, the youthful spirit inside the elderly body clear in his dark eyes. "What would you do?" he asked, a heavy brow raised. "If you were king."

Fallon chuckled. "Well, pushing aside that it's my daughter, Sursha has been a progressive paradigm for women for a long, long time now." She shrugged. "What other country do you know of where soldiers— good, hardened fighters—would be executed or punished for the mistreatment of women?" She paused to let that sink in. "And, we have women who own property. Look at Millie," she said as an example. "After Burke was killed, she was given ownership of their property as his widow."

Carthac sipped his ale, staring into the flames. "You think I should decree this, you're saying." It was a statement.

Fallon shook her head. "Nope. Do I think it should be allowed? Absolutely. I think it's absurd women have to be so uncomfortable, and for what? Propriety?" She waved off the notion with a hand. "But, ultimately, I'm not the king, Daidí."

ॐॐॐॐ

This time, they *were* in the throne room. King Carthac of Sursha was in his finery and sitting atop his throne. Fallon stood back with those who were there with somebody asking the king's favor on this or that, as this was not her petition. Watching her daughter step up to the bottom of those stairs all by herself, Fallon's heart hurt.

She so badly wanted to step up beside her, arm slung around her shoulders as it always was, but she was pleased to see Roishin standing her ground in her dress of light blue with a tunic draping the garment. Her hair was still pinned atop her head, Fallon making sure she hadn't run off to do whatever and destroying Elsie's handiwork in the process.

"I have received and read your petition, child," the king stated, his deep voice booming through the throne room. "A petition for women and girls in this country to be legally allowed to wear trousers in a public setting."

A common gasp went up around the room. Some began to chatter at the astonishing audacity of this child, but a look from the king quelled that immediately.

"As you stand before your king," he continued. "I'd like you to summarize your argument on why I should decree this as law."

Fallon nearly held her breath. She knew this could go one of two ways: either Roishin would be that two-hundred-year-old woman and blow them all away with her reasoning and logic, or she'd drop the filter right out of her mouth and get herself thrown into her own grandfather's dungeon.

"Well," Roishin said, standing straight and looking every bit the lady with her hands clasped in front of her. "Men and women are not the same, Your Highness. This is a statement I often hear, and certainly a reason stated by man for the difference in what we wear."

Okay, Fallon thought. So far, so good...

"But, women do a heck of a lot more work that requires them to crawl around and get wet than men, Your Highness."

Fallon groaned inwardly.

Carthac raised an eyebrow. "Oh? Care to elaborate?"

"Who does the laundry, sire? Who does the cooking, who runs after the children and bathes them?" Her words hung in the air, heavy and pregnant. "Why on earth should a woman have to run after a little one with all that extra material, let alone chance tripping over her skirts while carrying something so precious as a newborn babe?" Hands on hips, she added. "I'd like to see a man try that."

Fallon *did* hold her breath. She thought half of those gathered would carry her around on their shoulders cheering while the other half would tie her to the rack. She spared a glance to her father, curious what was running through his mind in that moment. She didn't have to wait long, nor did anyone else in the chamber.

"Your petition was compelling, young lass," he said, holding up the rolled parchment in question. "And, your argument here today is equally so. However," he quickly added. "We do have norms and we do have customs." His gaze bored into hers from across the expanse. "Those are important. Wouldn't you agree?"

"Yes, Your Highness," Roishin conceded. "However—"

Fallon's eyes fell closed as her daughter continued.

"'Customs' and 'norms' didn't originate from laws. Those are simply things people have gotten used to over time. Your Highness, there are cultures in history where men wore robes and togas." She glanced over her shoulder at those gathered. "Essentially, a dress." She looked back to the king. "So then, why do the men here wear trousers? Surely, at some point, we decided that appropriate clothing should be dictated by what the wearer is doing and that practicality in performing those tasks is the most important. It seems to me that logic applies here as well. I know no man who would agree that hunting or riding a horse or building a house would be easier in a dress, therefore robes and togas were a custom and a norm...until they weren't. Wouldn't you agree?"

A heaviness fell over those gathered, the king leaning over as one of his advisors leaned down to speak to him quietly. The two men went back and forth, words unheard by those gathered. Fallon was almost rocking on her heels, no clue how this one was going to end. All she knew, however, was that she was proud as hell of her daughter. Win or lose, she'd fought hard and had the guts to try.

The advisor stepped away and King Carthac looked back to the petitioner who stood at the bottom of the throne dais. "Petition granted!"

Chapter Two

L ooking down at her, Fallon raised an
eyebrow. "Ready?"

Roishin looked up at her, arms crossed over
her chest. "You know," she said. "If Mamaí had seen
fit to provide me with a pair of trousers for this trip
and I weren't stuck in this waste of material"—she
uncrossed her arms and tugged out the skirt of her
dress—"I'd be able to hop over this with no problem,
Daidí."

Fallon eyed the girl. "So, are you telling me that
back when you were little and we let you roam around
in breeches, you could have jumped this?" She indicated the small body of water. Though no problem for
her as an adult and tall for a woman, with long legs
that could easily span the watery gap, it was a challenge for a child, or even a twelve-year-old.

Roishin looked down, eyeing the moving stream.
Tucking her bottom lip in, she looked up at Fallon
with those big, deep green eyes and simply raised her
arms to be picked up. Fallon chuckled, gripping her
underneath the arms and lifting her easily. The girl's
feet left the ground, but Fallon didn't set her down
right away. Instead, she hugged her youngest child to
her.

A smile graced Fallon's face when Roishin's
arms wrapped around her neck, the hug returned.
"Don't grow up too fast, little one," she said into the

hug, cradling the dark head against her shoulder. "You'll leave your mark, I assure you." Leaving a kiss to the side of her head, she set her down on the other side of the water.

"Through there?" Roishin asked, indicating the small opening in what appeared to be the outside wall of a cave.

Fallon nodded, excited to see what her little girl thought of the hidden gem that lay within. Since living at Caisleán Thíar for so long, she didn't get to come to her special place all that often, and until now, she'd only shared it with Cateline. Something told her that Roishin would appreciate it.

Besides, she felt it was the right time to share her true identity with her youngest, and there was no better place to do so. The girl disappeared inside the enclosed space and a loud curse burst from her. Fallon grinned but quickly turned on "parent" mode. "Roishin!"

"Sorry."

Following, Fallon saw the beautiful and magical waterfall that had been her escape her entire life—until she'd met and fallen in love with Cateline. Well, that is to say, until Cateline had fallen in love with *her*, then her wife had become her escape and greatest passion.

Once part of a cave system, her waterfall was what was left after erosion had opened up the ceiling and let the rain and sunlight in to allow vegetation to flourish. A pool of water at the bottom constantly gurgled from the waterfall that circulated the pool so it never grew stagnant or mossy,

Fallon stood back and watched. It was such an amazing feeling to share this with Roishin. Much like her mother, Roishin was an extremely sensitive soul. She could be brash and certainly speak her mind—also like her mother—but at heart, she was in awe of the land and creatures that skittered upon it.

Roishin had found the large, flat rock that Fallon had always sat or laid upon when she spent time there in her younger years. Fallon stepped up to stand beside her. She wasn't entirely surprised to see emotion well up in those deep green eyes, a young soul overwhelmed by the beauty around her. There was something about the little hiding spot that was nowhere else on Earth, and Fallon had been all over the place during her years with the Elite Guard.

"Beautiful, isn't it?" Fallon murmured. Roishin nodded, obviously trying to blink the tears out of her eyes. Fallon wrapped her arm around the slight shoulders and gently pulled the girl into her side. "Do you know what's the most beautiful thing about you, child?" she whispered into her hair after leaving a kiss atop the dark head.

"Mamaí says my eyes," Roishin muttered.

Fallon smiled and nodded. "Yes, they are. But more than that is your heart, the beauty you see in so many things." She left another kiss, then removed her arm as she lowered herself to sit. Roishin sat next to her. "Don't ever hide that about yourself."

The girl didn't say anything as she tucked her legs up under her skirts, but Fallon saw the soft smile that crossed her lips at her words. "What did Garratt say about this place?" she asked, referring to her brother, nine years older.

"He's not seen this," Fallon said, bringing her own legs up to sit cross-legged.

She looked up at her, eyes wide. "Why?"

Fallon shrugged, looking out over the magic of her waterfall. "Your brother is a warrior, *mo leanbh*," she said simply, the term of endearment for her daughter easily rolling off her tongue. She smirked. "He tends to see beauty in things such as a new blade or people of the female persuasion.'

Nodding, Roishin grinned as she rested her chin on her knees. Her arms were wrapped around her raised, dress-draped legs. "True." She turned her head so her cheek rested upon them instead as she looked up at Fallon with adoring eyes. "Thank you for bringing me here, Daidí."

"Of course." Her stomach was in knots as she tried to garner the courage to say what needed to be said. Though she'd already done this three times, with her older daughter and son and also with Livia, it didn't get any easier. "I brought you here because, yes, I wanted to share this with you," she began. "But I also want to talk to you about something."

Roishin changed her position so she was fully facing Fallon. It was unnerving, how intense that green gaze was at times, like the girl was looking into her very soul. Clearing her throat, she began her tale.

"I discovered this place when I was just a bit younger than you with your Uncle Ailfred. It became my special place. I'd come here alone so I..." She swallowed. Damn, why was she so nervous to say the words to this child? Swallowing again, she continued. "So I could be me."

Roishin's gaze was unwavering, even as it was clear wheels were turning behind her eyes. She nodded, letting Fallon know she was listening.

"You see, as a child, well..." She smiled. "In a lot of ways, I was just like you." She met those penetrating eyes. "In a *lot* of ways."

"You were curious about everything, Daidí?" Roishin asked.

Fallon nodded. "Aye." She smiled. "Very."

"You liked to run around and be free, chasing whatever crazy idea entered your heart?" she pushed.

Again, Fallon nodded. "Definitely."

"And," Roishin said slowly. "You were also a girl?" She held Fallon's gaze. "*Are* a girl." She rolled her eyes. "Woman."

Fallon could only stare at her. "Did Laigen tell you?"

Roishin's eyes opened wide. "You told *Laigen*? And the whole country doesn't know by now?"

Fallon raised an eyebrow in challenge. "She didn't tell you, did she?"

"No," Roishin muttered in concession. She shrugged a shoulder and looked out to the gurgling pool. "I saw it in a dream," she said softly. "I was about seven."

Fallon was stunned. That was five years ago. "And, you believed what you saw in your dream?" she asked gently, not to scold or accuse, but to understand.

Roishin nodded. "Always."

Fallon nodded. "And," she said quietly. "You're okay with it?"

Roishin quirked a dark eyebrow as she tugged on the skirt of her dress. A bark of laughter erupted from Fallon's throat, part amusement and part relief. She hugged the girl to her. "I love you."

"I love you, too," Roishin murmured against Fallon's chest.

"I do want to explain, though," Fallon said, releasing the hug. "I didn't do this," she said, indicating herself and the false torso that was still part of her everyday wardrobe, "because I hated dresses. It was far more complicated than that."

"Because Uncle Fergus was such a bastard?"

Fallon stared at her. "Where on earth do you get your language, child?"

"Garratt."

Fallon let out a heavy sigh and shook her head. She'd definitely be having a talk with that boy. "But, yes, that was part of it. Ultimately, my father, acting as king, felt it was more important to have an heir than a daughter at the time."

"And now?" Roishin asked.

Fallon shrugged. "He has both." She smiled. "And I have your mamaí, and Garratt and Laigen, and you." She shook her head. "None of which would have happened if I'd been just a girl named Fallon."

Roishin looked down at her knees, though Fallon knew that wasn't what she was seeing or thinking about. She remained quiet, letting the child sort through her feelings and thoughts. Finally, she looked up at her and spoke, her voice quiet and unsure.

"So, you and Mamaí must both like girls, then. Like them in love, I mean."

Fallon nodded. "Yes."

"Did you always know that, Daidí? Wait, can I still call you 'Daidí'?"

Fallon nodded, laughing. "Please do. I can't imagine being called anything else. And yes, I always knew." She shrugged. "I may not have exactly understood what it meant, but you have to figure, I already knew I was very different from any other girl that I'd ever known. In a way, I thought I was cursed, stuck in a land between male and female. I *knew* I was female and was fine being female, but I also knew that wasn't all there was to me." She gave the girl a sad smile. "It was very confusing. So, I figured liking girls was just part of that confusion for me. Maybe I was both a male and female accidentally squished together by the gods."

"Do you still think that?"

Fallon shook her head as she brought up a hand and brushed some long strands that had, yet again, managed to escape Roishin's updo. "No. I now know I'm exactly what I need to be to be happy yet still keep our country safe. I also now know there are others, both male and female, that love the same gender as themselves."

Roishin's eyes grew wide. "Boys, too?"

"Boys, too."

Roishin looked out to the water once again, seeming to mull over what she'd been told. Finally, she nodded and looked back to Fallon. "Thanks, Daidí," she said. "I feel quite enlightened."

Fallon smiled. "I'm very glad."

ぷ.ぷ.ぬ.ぬ

Their home at Caisleán Thíar was a two-day ride, and by time they got there, it was late. Fallon and Roishin had been dropped off at the door, the driver and a small pack of guards heading off to unload the carriage and take care of the horses. With a "good night" and "congratulations, *again*" hug, Fallon had sent her daughter off to her room to get some sleep.

Now, she was on the top floor of the castle where the bedchamber she shared with Cateline was located. She was quiet as she walked into the massive rooms, the very rooms where her brother had taken his last breath thirteen years before. Not a soul in the kingdom missed him, except perhaps their father during a moment of reflection. He had been his son, after all.

But now, Fallon was the legal heir to the throne and lord of the manor, as it were—even though everybody knew that the lovely woman asleep in the bed truly ran things. Fallon smiled at that thought as she disrobed. The woman she'd first met had been a stunningly beautiful yet deeply inexperienced and naïve twenty-one-year-old woman, just barely more than a girl.

Now, she was an even more stunningly beautiful woman of thirty-four who, to Fallon, was deeply sensual and endlessly exciting. To her people, she was beloved by all. Her kindness and generosity were legendary, and many already saw her as their queen, even as Carthac was still alive and their sovereign.

Now, Prince Fallon of Sursha was tucked safely away into the locked trunk at the foot of the bed, and Fallon, wife of Cateline, climbed nude into bed. The fire was still burning well in the massive fireplace to warm the chamber, so the covers that covered Cateline's body had been pushed down in slumber.

Fallon had to smile. When she was home, they slept naked—whether they made love or not was irrelevant. When they were apart at night, usually because Fallon had to deal with a military matter or go see her father, they slept in nightclothes. Sleeping naked was something just for each other.

The fact that Cateline was naked now told Fallon she was very much awaiting the arrival of her spouse back in her bed. For Fallon, the feel of the warm, soft skin of the woman she loved was the only way for her to find peace at night. Years of battles won and lost, lives taken and saved, haunted her dreams.

For whatever reason, since their first night naked together—the night Fallon had held Cateline's hypothermic body against her own after Fergus had tossed her into the tower to freeze to death—Fallon had only been able to find peace in slumber with Cateline by her side. It was the warmth of her skin, the scent and feel of her hair, her very soul, that let Fallon rest.

Now, Cateline lay on her stomach, her long, curly auburn hair spread out over Fallon's pillow like a wave of flame. The smooth skin of her back was licked by the dancing gold and orange light of the fire. The covers started at her lower back, covering the rest of her, but it wasn't hard at all for Fallon to fill in the blanks in her mind.

The thought of Cateline's exquisite backside and the pale softness of her thighs and calves made her heart beat faster. Pulling the covers back just enough to climb into the bed they'd had made specifically for them, her eyes fell closed as she eased her body over to that of her sleeping wife. Though she'd absolutely loved the week's time alone with Roishin at the king's castle and would cherish it, she had missed Cateline so much.

Unable to stop herself, her fingers trailed over the soft warmth of Cateline's back, dipping beneath the covers to caress the swell of her lovely behind. She smiled at the little sigh released in slumber, Cateline's body moving just a bit as the touch registered in her subconscious.

Moving her body so she hovered over the prone

form, she gently thrust her hips against the very body part she'd just been touching. The little sigh from a moment ago issued again, but this time in pleasure rather than a body beginning to wake. Fallon smiled when Cateline pushed up into Fallon's pressing hips.

"I missed you," Fallon murmured into soft, auburn hair.

"I can tell," Cateline whispered, amusement in her tone as she pressed her behind even more into Fallon's hips to emphasize her observation, Fallon's hips beginning a gentle thrust against her.

Fallon chuckled deep in her throat. "Not my fault you've been on my mind all day."

"Just today?" Cateline asked, turning over to her back once Fallon lifted herself just enough for clearance. The beautiful princess accepted Fallon's body atop hers again. The two shared a slow, sensuous kiss hello as Fallon insinuated a muscular thigh between Cateline's. She was exhausted and didn't have the energy for a lot, but she needed the woman beneath her.

Fallon grinned when the kiss broke as they began to slowly move together, each pressing their need against the other's thigh. "I had our twelve-year-old with me," she murmured. "I had to be good."

"Poor baby," Cateline murmured, words a bit breathy as she trailed her nails down Fallon's strong back, sending a delicious shiver through the warrior.

Fallon nodded as she initiated a deep, sensuous kiss as her hand found a soft breast. Arousal speared through her at the soft little whimper earned as she tugged on a hard nipple. Releasing the breast, her hand slid down Cateline's body to grip Cateline's thigh. She urged it upward, trailing her nails along the underside as Cateline raised it up to rest against Fallon's hip.

It didn't take long before they were breathing too hard to keep kissing. She was held tightly to Cateline as they continued to move together, Fallon's orgasm imminent. Fingernails gripped the back sides of her shoulders as Cateline came with a loud cry. A moment later Fallon fell over the edge, her cry muffled in a warm neck, her hips grinding against those pressed against her.

Finally, her body stilled and she lifted her head. She couldn't help but smile at the absolute love she saw aimed at her from Cateline's beautiful gray-blue eyes, so often the color of incoming storms.

"So beautiful," Fallon murmured, caressing a soft cheek with her fingers.

"I love you," Cateline said softly. "I missed you both so much."

"I love you, too, baby." Fallon hugged her to her for a long moment before moving off her. "I missed you, too. Daidí says hello."

"We need to go spend some time with him, Fallon," Cateline said, cuddling up into Fallon's arms with her head resting on her shoulder. "Family time, not business."

"I agree."

"How'd it go?"

Fallon smiled. "You know better than that," she murmured, exhaustion easing in around the edges again. "If I don't let Roishin tell you, I'll never hear the end of it."

Chapter Three

It was hard having a crush on an older woman. Sadly, the sixteen-year-old Elsie didn't even know Roishin was alive—other than when she was wrestling with her hair, that is. She'd never tell, but half the time Roishin's hair was running wild was because she knew Elsie would have to try and tame it. A little pull here, little tug there, an updo was destroyed.

The twelve-year-old was fully and completely aware that this was manipulative behavior because, as a servant, what was Elsie going to say? *"Um, no. This time figure your own damn hair out, Roishin!"* Nope. She had to play along, though at times Roishin was pretty darn sure the young woman knew *what* her game was all about, just maybe not *why*.

No doubt she thought the little princess was being a rich, spoiled pain in the butt. Perhaps that was true, to a point. The truth was, Roishin thought Elsie was the most beautiful girl she'd ever seen— except for the angel she saw from time to time in her dreams. Elsie, with her blond hair and blue eyes, kind of reminded Roishin of her.

She knew she was an angel because the first time she'd come to her was when Roishin was four years old and wide awake. In the eight years since, she'd come to her a handful of times in her slumber, but never again while awake. Roishin tried to see her face in every blonde that passed her way. Maybe it was her, just maybe this time? It never was.

So, as she was doing currently, she'd just enjoy watching Elsie. Roishin was lying in bed still, Elsie puttering around her bedchamber doing her morning duties for the young princess before moving on to other duties on the family levels of the castle. So many mornings, Roishin feigned sleep so she could watch her.

Her flaxen locks were bound atop her head, of course. Roishin often wondered how long Elsie's hair was when it was down. Her face was lovely with big, blue eyes, though hers were a darker blue than those of Roishin's angel. She didn't mind, though. They were still beautiful. Elsie was slight, with delicate features and small hands.

Her figure was womanly, and of course that caught Roishin's attention. She herself was still mostly shaped like a girl at this point, and she wondered when she'd have a bosom like the one she admired upon Elsie. Ironically, Roishin's older sister Laigen was an even more beautiful version of Elsie, with her long, flowing blond hair and bright blue eyes.

There wasn't a suitor in the kingdom and beyond that hadn't sent interest in Laigen's hand, as her beauty was legendary. At seventeen, she was getting to the age when their parents would give serious thought to her potential mate.

What Roishin found absolutely strange was that Laigen welcomed the male attention. Oh, that one knew how to play the game well, Roishin thought. Her own little attempts at getting Elsie's eye for two seconds was mere child's play compared to Laigen's little giggles and side-eyes to unsuspecting men.

Roishin had seen more than one fully armed and armored warrior fold like parchment at her feet.

Obviously, she didn't look at Laigen as anything other than her sister, though she certainly recognized her beauty for what it was. Their mother was absolutely stunning, and Roishin could only hope someday she would be even half as beautiful. Even more so, she hoped she would be the amazing person her mamaí was. Cateline was adored by all her siblings, as well as all the people of the kingdom.

Deciding she'd done enough thinking and enough watching—for now—Roishin yawned and pretended to stretch into wakefulness. Elsie, who was gathering all the dirty clothes from the week-long trip across the island to add to the wash, glanced over at her. She gave the girl a polite smile and a curtsey.

"Good morrow, milady," the servant greeted.

"Good morrow, Elsie," Roishin said, sitting up. She braced herself back on her hands on the mattress behind her as she looked around. As much as she loved visiting her grandfather, she was glad to be back home and in her own bed. "What's the weather like this morning?" she asked, mostly for something to say that the lovely young servant had to respond to her. Oh, she was a naughty little imp, she knew.

"'Tis cloudy out today, milady," Elsie said. "Tad chilly."

Roishin nodded. "Thank you."

Nodding, the young woman turned back to her task, the basket she held loaded with more clothing. She ignored the dark green eyes that followed her around the chamber, following the trail left by the princess the night before. She knew her daidí would scold her for leaving such a mess, and yes, she knew better.

She sighed as she climbed out of bed. She certainly needed to find something else to occupy her brain than watching Elsie bend over to pick up yet another article of clothing. She ran a hand through long, dark hair that was pretty much ratted like a rosebush atop her head. She sighed in frustration.

"Elsie?" she muttered, walking over to the door that led to her garderobe.

"Yes, milady?" the young woman asked, gathering the last of the clothing.

"Today, after my bath, would you please remove my hair?"

Elsie paused, and her blond eyebrows, just a shade darker than her head hair, shot up. "Uh…if that's what you wish, milady."

Oh my, you're so adorable when you're flummoxed! Roishin spared her a glance just before she stepped inside the tiny room to do her morning business. "If only," she muttered. "Braids today will be fine."

Looking beyond relieved, Elsie nodded. "Yes, milady."

☙ ☙ ☙ ☙

The princess's bedchamber had initially been intended for just that. However, the prince and princess of Sursha were also naughty little imps, and they insisted on sharing a bedchamber. That, of course, was the larger of the two, so the one Cateline had inhabited until she'd married Fallon had been turned into an area for the family. It was lovingly called the "family chamber."

The bed had been removed, in its place a table for the family to share meals. The raised dais beneath the windows—including the "rose window," so called for the stained glass rose center of it—was a game table. Upon that was an everlasting chess game. All three children had been trying for years to beat Fallon, yet none had succeeded.

Livia, who had been far more like an aunt to the three children than merely Fallon's advisor, was the closest to beating her. Bathed, dressed in trousers, and hair put into tight braids upon her head and snaked around her crown to get it out of her way, Roishin bounced her way into the family living space. She was excited to share her great triumph with her siblings, Livia—if she was there—and especially, her mamaí. She knew she'd be proud of her.

"Good morrow!" Roishin bellowed as she entered the chamber. She was the last to enter, done on purpose. She was darn proud of what she'd accomplished, and now, dressed in her favorite pair of trousers and sleeveless tunic tugged on over her long-sleeved shirt, she felt like she could fly. Every eye in the large chamber on her, she strutted around like a little peacock, proud of her skirtless feathers.

All conversation stopped. Though all of them were used to seeing her in trousers within the castle walls, it was clear something had changed. As if on cue, everyone—except a rather proud-looking Fallon—burst into cheers and congratulatory cries.

Cateline popped up from her seat at the table and rushed over to her youngest. Taking her in a tight hug, she held her close.

"So proud of you, *ma chérie*," she murmured in French. Theirs was a household that spoke in both

French and Gaelic, depending on the mood, speaker, and audience.

Roishin beamed, hugging her mother just as tightly. She adored the woman holding her, and nothing pleased her more than earning the pride of both her parents. "*Merci.*"

Cateline pulled out of the embrace but cupped her daughter's face in her hands. She gave Roishin one of her stunning smiles. "So proud, my love." She left a kiss to both cheeks. She brushed the backs of her fingers along her cheek in maternal affection. "We will celebrate."

Roishin nodded, but then dark eyebrows drew. "Did Daidí tell you?"

"No," Cateline said, shaking her head with a laugh. "Your face did."

"What have I missed?" Garratt asked. He was dressed in his military garb, following in Fallon's footsteps into the Elite Guard. It was a rare treat for him to be able to join the family for breakfast, so Roishin was excited that, of all days, this was the one he was there.

"Our dear little sister," Laigen said, eyeing the twenty-one-year-old warrior, "has taken it upon herself to speak for all females in Sursha."

Confused, Garratt looked from her to Fallon. "What?"

Fallon said nothing but indicated that Roishin should explain for herself. The youngest of the family pulled out her chair at the table and sat down, scooting herself in.

"You act as though my petition to the king forces all females to wear pants, Laigen," she chided, glaring at her sister across the table.

Garratt's eyes opened wide. "Wait, what? Pants?"

Roishin laced her fingers and rested her chin upon them. She gave him a charming smile. "Yup. I hate, loathe, and detest dresses," she said, smiling a thanks to the servant who placed a plate of breakfast before her. "So, I petitioned the king—"

"Our grandfather," Laigen muttered.

"The *king*," Roishin continued, "that it wasn't fair for us to have to wear dresses all the time when they're big, bulky, uncomfortable, and frankly, make our lives miserable."

Garratt's eyebrows shot up. "So, now you can wear pants?" he asked. "Anywhere?"

"Almost," Fallon said, tugging a thick piece of bacon off the slab that was on her plate. She sipped from her watered-down wine before explaining. "The king made a concession with a stipulation."

Roishin nodded, picking up the story. "We can wear them in public if we're working. But, on special occasions or at Court or leaving Sursha's boundaries, we must wear a dress."

"I think that's fair," he said, glancing at the glare from his oldest sister. He looked to Cateline. "What do you think, Mamaí?"

Cateline sipped from her wine which, like Fallon's, was watered down for the morning meal. She seemed to be considering the question and situation at hand. Finally, she looked to her son and responded.

"I think it is vital that women, and girls," she added, nodding to Roishin, "be able to be their best selves, no matter what that is. I think they should have choices and not be forever beholden to men who are threatened by their strength. This has been a struggle since the beginning of time, and will be until the end.

Not every girl or woman fits in the box built for them by men, and that is okay. Not every *boy*," she added, "fits, either. And that, too, is okay. And then, there are those who feel safest in conformity and tradition." She nodded. "That is okay as well."

Roishin listened, in awe of her mother's understanding and wisdom. She rested her chin in an upturned palm, looking over at the beautiful woman with the adoration she felt. Fallon was looking at her pretty much the same way.

"Now, in my position," Cateline continued. "I understand I'm in a bit different situation." She gave her youngest a sweet smile. "I must be what our people expect, and I'm fine with that. But," she added, looking over to her husband and taking her hand. "I'm profoundly proud to be part of a family where love and acceptance is part of our rule." She looked to Garratt. "How's that?"

He smiled. "Well said, Mamaí."

☙☙☙☙

Roishin and Laigen joined their mother in the rose garden later in the day when the son had decided to come out. It was late spring and Cateline's favorite time of year. When Roishin had been just a baby, Cateline and Livia had single-handedly created the gorgeous gardens they strolled through now.

The only thing marring the perfection of the day was the inclusion of Fiona. She was a prickly woman of twenty and Cateline's lady-in-waiting. The household was populated largely with servants taken from Sursha's orphanages. Rumor had it that Garratt, his blood sister Laigen, and teenager-at-the-time Livia had been the first of the princess's many rescues.

Of course the children had become her own. But now, and over the last dozen years, if a job could be handled by a child and grown into, that was what she demanded. Many of those who had been brought in as children were now grown adults. And, though servants, they'd been given a family to grow up with.

Many, many times children's laughter had been heard tearing through the halls of Caisleán Thíar, Garratt and Laigen giggling as they were chased by servant children, taking a moment to be just that before getting back to work.

After putting in ten years of paid service, these servants were given a choice by Fallon and Cateline: they could be relieved of duty and go on to marry or work beyond the castle walls, or they could stay on. Most remained at the castle, moving the families they'd made as adults inside its protective walls. Many of the orphaned children married each other upon maturing.

Fiona had been one of those young brought in. She'd worked her way up to lady-in-waiting, and though she was quite good at it, she irritated Roishin. But then, Roishin mused as she strolled with the two ladies in her family, she wasn't Elsie. Perhaps that was it. Her attention was garnered by her mother's voice, speaking to Laigen as they sat.

"I want you to have your choice," she was saying. "And, I do not want you to rush things. You are young," she said to her pointedly. "You have time, love." The two sat on a stone bench, Cateline's hands taking both of her eldest daughter's in her own and resting them on her skirt-clad leg. "You must make a choice, yes, but we want it to be of love."

"But Mamaí," Laigen said. "Why must I get married right away? Why can't I choose a man and be courted for a long time?"

Eyebrows drawn, Roishin turned and looked at the two from where she was messing with the water in a beautiful birdbath carved of marble. "What does he get out of that arrangement?" she asked.

Laigen glared over at her but said nothing as she turned back to their mother. "Is that not possible?" she asked.

It was clear Cateline was skeptical of the idea. "I think what we should do is have a gala for you," she said, reaching up and lightly brushing aside one of the tendrils of blond hair that had purposefully been left to bounce around her lovely face. "Your daidí can send word to the suitors we feel may be the best options for you to choose from."

"All here at the same time?" Laigen asked, eyes aglow in seeming delight at the idea.

"*Oui.*"

"Oh, thank you, Mamaí!" Laigen exclaimed, hugging her mother to her in excitement. She hopped up. "I must tell Celine!" Laigen's best friend worked in the castle and was her personal servant.

Roishin watched her go, shaking her head. She heard her mother pat the bench next to her. Roishin moved away from the birdbath and took her sister's vacated seat.

"I do not understand that one," the girl muttered.

Cateline chuckled, leaving a kiss to the side of her head. "Your sister is unlike you, Roishin."

"No kidding."

Cateline smiled. "My sweet, sweet Roishin. You and your sister are very different, my love. And, there is nothing wrong with that. But," she added. "You have similarities, too."

Roishin stared at her like she'd lost her mind, earning a smile. "How?"

"You are both very strong young women. Eager to make your own way, in your own ways."

Roishin looked at her. "But Mamaí, she wants to find a man and marry him so he can tell her what to do."

Cateline grinned down at her. "And you want to wear pants." She playfully tapped the tip of Roishin's nose. "You mistake Laigen's excitement to marry as weakness. I see it in her eyes. She wants to be the lady of the house, make her mark through her husband. This is why your daidí and I will make sure she finds the right man."

Roishin thought about that for a moment. It had never occurred to her to think of it that way. But then, all she had to do was look at her own parents' marriage. Wasn't that exactly what her mother had done in a lot of ways? Just in their household, Fallon was more than happy to step aside and let her shine.

"Daidí told me," she said quietly, changing the subject. They were alone, but she knew it had to remain a secret. She looked up at her mother. "But I already knew."

Cateline's eyebrows rose. "You did?"

Roishin nodded. "We went to the waterfall."

"I'm so glad she took you there," Cateline murmured. "Of anyone, I think you could truly appreciate it."

Roishin nodded. "That's what Daidí said, too." They shared a smile, but Roishin was troubled.

"Are you upset?" Cateline asked.

"No. No matter what, she'll always be my daidí."
She smiled at the small hug that earned her. "Why
can't she just be who she is?"

Cateline gave her a sad smile. "The same reason
that I cannot wear pants, *mon petit chou*." She pushed
to her feet. "Come. Let's walk and enjoy the day."

Chapter Four

It was so beautiful. She could hear the sound of the waterfall roaring over the side of the wall that was left of the cave. She watched as it fell to the pool near where she sat. If it were a bit warmer, she thought, she'd go swimming. Perhaps once the hotter months began after the summer solstice—which was her birthday.

She smiled at that thought. She'd be thirteen, almost a woman. Her mother told her that the bleeding should begin soon. No, she wasn't at all looking forward to that, but it would at least mean she was no longer a child. She hated being a child.

"Why?"

Startled, she looked up from the water to see a figure literally stepping out from behind the waterfall. Her smile grew slowly as she realized who it was. The blue cloak with gold stitching that was usually wrapped around her was not there. Her angel wore white, flowing robes. With her short, light blond hair and pale skin, she looked ethereal. Beautiful.

That stunning, almost unsettling cerulean gaze was focused on Roishin as she made her way around the pool and to the flat rock where the girl sat, legs pulled up against her chest. She lowered herself to sit next to her. All Roishin could do was stare. Her heart raced, her palms sweating where they rested on her legs, her arms were wrapped around them.

"*You came,*" Roishin said, *her voice small as she felt so small next to this woman who had literally haunted her since she was four years old.*

The woman smiled at her, taking Roishin's breath away. "Of course," *she said in that same soft, soothing tone that she always used.* "I told you I would."

"What's your name?" *Roishin asked, stunned she'd been so bold as to ask.*

"I am Enori."

"Enori," *Roishin whispered, almost as if to taste the name on her tongue. She was so happy to have a name, now, something to think about when this woman wasn't near.*

"I've left something for you, Roishin," *she said, pushing to her feet again.*

Feeling panicked, Roishin also stood. "Wait," *she said.* "Please don't go."

Enori smiled at her as she brought up a hand and rested it against Roishin's cheek. She bent down and left the softest of kisses to her opposite cheek. "I'll be back," *she murmured against the soft flesh.* "Soon."

"No!" Roishin gasped, shooting up in bed. "Don't go!" Chest heaving, she looked around to see that she was in her bed in her bedchamber. To her eternal embarrassment, Elsie was doing her morning duties.

"Are you okay, milady?" she asked, hurrying over to the bed. She sat next to her, concern on her lovely face. "You're crying."

Really feeling stupid now, Roishin looked away, but what would have at one time been a delight filled her with such confusing feelings as Elsie wrapped her in a warm hug. Part of her wanted to play it up to prolong the hug and the feel of soft breasts against her, but she just couldn't. She felt utterly devastated but had no idea why. It was a sense of loss that she couldn't define.

"Are you all right, milady?" Elsie asked again, softly. When Roishin nodded, she pulled out of the hug but remained on the bed. "Bad dream?"

Roishin nodded, though somehow she knew that wasn't the cause. She sniffed, using the sleeve of her sleeping gown to wipe at her eyes. She met the kind blue eyes of the young woman sitting next to her.

"Thank you for your kindness, Elsie," she managed.

The young servant nodded and smiled. "Of course, milady." With a small squeeze to Roishin's shoulder, she pushed up from the bed and continued her duties. "Oh, is this yours?"

Roishin glanced over. Elsie was holding something in her hands where she stood near the desk Roishin used for her studies.

Sniffling one last time, Roishin climbed out of bed and walked over to her. She saw a small leather pouch cinched with a leather cord resting in the open palm. There was a symbol burned into the leather that she'd never seen before. She met Elsie's gaze, surprise in her own.

"Looks like protection," Elsie whispered, indicating the symbol. Elsie was a Scot and of a pagan background, so Roishin figured she must know what she was talking about.

Though she'd never seen it before, it was in her bedchamber and therefore must be meant for her to see. Nervous butterflies batted at her rib cage with iron wings as she took the pouch, and she carefully opened it.

She dumped the contents into her own palm, and a small silver ring fell out. Upon it was a hooded skull, as though just the head of a cloaked skeleton. Its grinning face and sightless eyes looked up at her. In the sockets were two tiny sapphires—and they were the exact color of Enori's eyes.

❧ ❧ ❧ ❧

She glanced down at her ring. Again. She grinned, so happy that it fit so perfectly on the middle finger of her right hand. She'd never owned a ring before. The strange thing was, as frightened as she'd initially been when she'd realized it was a skull, somehow, someway she knew it had been from her angel, Enori.

Now, she and her daidí were riding to one of the villages to visit the cobbler. She needed a new pair of boots—so said Fallon—to go along with her trousers. Plus, she was outgrowing all her shoes again. Her mamaí said she was growing like a weed. This was true. She was outgrowing everything seemingly overnight, and, to her delight, some other things were beginning to grow, too.

Fallon rode her now retired war horse Toirneach while Roishin rode her own mare, Gaoth, who could run like her namesake. The pair raced down the lane, in the backroad Fallon had guided them to. Roishin glanced over at the warrior, seeing the absolute joy on her face as her midnight hair streamed behind her. Fallon of Sursha was so beautiful. Roishin often wondered just how exactly anyone believed she was a man, anyway.

Sure, her beauty was not traditional beauty at

all, not like Laigen or Cateline. It was a unique beauty in a league all its own. But, she figured people saw what they wanted to see, and in her daidí's case, it had worked to her benefit. For now, she knew darn well Fallon was holding Toirneach back, as that giant black stallion could leave Roishin's mare in the dust in a heartbeat, and they both knew it.

It didn't matter. Roishin and Gaoth gave it their all. Roishin cried out in victory as "suddenly" the war horse fell back and the dappled gray and her rider crossed into the village first. She slowed her mare and pulled off the road where Fallon joined her. Grinning like a fool, the warrior raised her bracer-clad arm for Roishin to slap her hand in camaraderie, which she did.

"Nicely done, lass."

The two made their way to the community stables and dismounted. Fallon paid the stableboy handsomely to care for their horses before she placed an arm around Roishin's shoulders and the two made their way to the cobbler's stone cottage.

"Daidí?" she said, as they walked. "I'd like to wear my hair down, in warrior braids."

Fallon looked down at her with a quirked eyebrow. "You would, would you?"

"Aye." She shrugged. "Maybe at least when I'm dressed to work?" she offered, indicating the trousers she wore.

"Well, don't you have to be a warrior to wear warrior braids?" Fallon asked with a small grin touching her lips.

"I can wear my quiver."

Fallon threw her head as a loud bark of laughter erupted from her lips. Her laughter was cut short as they both started at the thunderous crash that rent the morning air. Fallon instantly placed a large hand on Roishin's upper chest to stop her advance as she reached back and drew one of her double blades mounted to her back whenever they were out.

The cry of an injured horse and a woman crying for help got the two running. Fallon yelled for her to stay put, but there was no way she wasn't going along, too. They reached the tree line to see a horrible accident. It looked as though a horse had gotten spooked and had run for it, pulling the wagon with its occupants and goods along with it.

The crash through the woods was catastrophic. The majority of a man's body was pinned beneath the wagon and was clearly dead, his eyes open yet eternally unseeing. A woman was partially pinned, her entire right leg trapped. She also had a horrible head wound that was bleeding profusely and her right arm was broken, twisted behind her back.

"My baby!" she was screaming. "Find my baby!"

Fallon turned to see that Roishin had followed her to the crash. "Go!" she bellowed, pointing back to the village proper.

"No!" Roishin bellowed right back. "I want to help!"

Other people from the village had also begun to run over to the crash site. Roishin wasn't sure what to do or where to go, so she went to the woman as it was clear the men were going to team up to try to lift the wagon. Lowering herself to her knees next to the crying woman, Roishin brushed bloody hair out of the woman's face.

Pain-filled brown eyes looked up at her, pleading. "Find my baby," she whispered.

Roishin nodded. "Okay." She gave her as encouraging a smile as she could before she began to crawl around in the dense foliage and spilled belongings. Her heart was racing as she heard no baby cries. She was so worried about what she'd find.

She grunted as she used all her strength to push on a barrel until it finally, stubbornly rolled aside. Beyond it she saw a debris trail. She saw cabbages and bundles of sticks and even some clothing scattered where it had been thrown. When she pushed aside a large wicker basket, her heart stopped.

It looked as though the baby had been inside the basket in the wagon. The infant, a tiny babe, looking to be no more than six months old at most, was lying face down. It was unmoving and made not one sound. She made her way over to it and, on her knees, grabbed for the child. Rolling it over, the baby looked like it was asleep, with its face relaxed and eyes closed.

As she scanned its body, she saw a substantial wound to its chest. It looked fatal. Her gaze took in the rest of its body, and she surprisingly saw nothing else of concern, just the rags the baby was still wrapped in from the waist down acting as a diaper. Looking back to its beautiful face with its cherubic features and tiny little lips, she felt tears sting the backs of her eyes.

"Oh, little one," she whispered. She sat down on her behind and cradled the baby in her arms against her chest. She looked into its face. She brought up a hand and stroked the impossibly soft skin of its cheek.

Looking down at it, she wanted nothing more than for this little one to be spared such an early death and have a chance at life. Her tears began to fall, rolling slowly down her cheeks in grief for a little life she'd never know, and for a mother who had not only lost her husband—she assumed—but also her child.

Shaking her head, she sniffled. "No. It's not fair."

Her gaze went to the chest wound again and, closing her eyes, she bowed her head over the baby's body and began to silently pray. She had no idea where the words came from, but her lips moved with each word:

Father Ankou, please. Please give this child back her life, her chance.

Opening her eyes, twin tears fell from her eyes and into the wound, mixing with the blood. Then two more fell, and two more, and two more. She gasped softly as she watched the wound begin to glow, softly at first, but then brighter and brighter until she had to squint to continue looking at it.

A breath blew across her face and the body of the child in her arms. The vegetation around them danced in its wake, ending in a distant hum that drifted off with the breeze. In its place was a bundle that was moving, a tiny face screwed up as tiny fingers balled themselves into fists. Roishin's eyes widened and her mouth fell open. A little grunt, then another as little lips bowed then puckered as a cry was let loose.

Fresh tears were rolling down her cheeks, but these were tears of fear. She pushed to her feet and nearly threw the wailing baby, terrified at what had just happened. There was no sign of injury, the baby's skin pristine save for a small birthmark on the right side of its abdomen.

"No,"

She turned to see Fallon behind her, who scooped

the baby from her. "I'm sorry," Roishin whispered, crying. She was afraid: afraid of what she'd seen, what she'd done, and what would happen now.

"I've got her," Fallon said, looking her in the eye. Roishin could see so much in their violet depths, though she could tell the warrior was keeping her emotions buried to get them through the situation. When she looked down at Roishin's hand and saw the ring, the careful mask of focus cracked. Eyes widening, Fallon's gaze bored into hers. "Where did you get that?" she demanded, cradling the baby to her chest.

"The lady at the waterfall," Roishin said through her tears, truly upset now from the entire situation. "Enori."

Fallon turned away as the voices of concerned townspeople crowded into their private bubble.

No idea what to do, Roishin tried to get her emotions under control. She used her hands to wipe tears from her eyes and the sleeve to wipe at her cheeks. She was scared, she was confused, and she was deeply disquieted by everything. Raising her hand, she looked at the ring that seemed to have so unsettled Fallon.

For a moment, she considered taking it off and throwing it into the woods. Something inside her told her not to. So, she cradled her other hand around it and took a very deep breath before going to join the others.

Chapter Five

W hat do you think, Millie?" Cateline asked, a finger tugging on her bottom lip as she concentrated on the list she'd made.

Millie, who had been the closest ally of Cateline and Fallon's marriage and one of Fallon's greatest champions to help hide her secret her entire life, stepped over to the princess. She was also the longtime cook at the castle. Cateline reached up to brush blond strands that had escaped her updo out of her face as she looked down at the parchment laid out on the cooking surface Millie used to roll out her bread dough.

"I figure," Cateline said, glancing to the woman who was about ten years older than she. "One of these three entrées."

Millie chewed on the inside of her lip as read the proposed menus over. "I don't see why any of these should be a problem," she said, sparing the princess a glance. "And," she added with a grin. "I think fish is appropriate since this is the 'fishing for a husband' dinner."

Cateline playfully nudged her with her shoulder. "You worry about the cooking, I'll worry about the fishing."

They both glanced up when they heard some commotion in the great hall, which had to be passed through after entering the front doors to get anywhere else in the castle. Cateline recognized Fallon's voice, raised. It was incredibly rare to hear her lose control of her emotions in any sort of way.

She and Millie glanced at each other again before Cateline hurried away from the kitchens and toward the noisy voices.

"Where is she?" Fallon was demanding to a passing servant.

"I know not, Your Highness," the poor man was saying, eyes wide as he took in this most unusual version of Fallon. The entire kingdom knew just how deadly a warrior Fallon could be, and this man looked as though he were about to lose his bladder.

"Fallon!" Cateline called out, shocked by her display of anger. She smiled at the frightened servant and softly sent him on his way. She turned her ire back to her spouse. "We never treat our people that way," she chided in French, to keep it just between them. Very few in the castle spoke Cateline's mother tongue fluently except herself, Fallon, and their children.

Fallon's gaze met hers, the violet depths nearly black with whatever was going on inside her. She hurried over to Cateline and grabbed her hand. "Come with me," she growled, tugging her behind her and toward the upper floors.

Fallon's legs were much longer than her own, and Cateline nearly tripped over her skirts. The princess yanked her hand from his. "Stop this!" she exclaimed.

Turning, Fallon looked at her, surprise in her eyes. "I said—"

"I do not care what you said," Cateline said, chest heaving from trying to keep up with Fallon as well as growing irritation and, frankly, fear. "I will not take another step until you stop treating me like one of your spoils of battle!" She looked the other woman over, noting that she had blood smudged on her face and dried blood under her fingernails as well as upon her tunic. "What happened? Where is Roishin?"

For a moment, Fallon just stared at her. She looked lost or like she had no idea who Cateline was. The princess walked up to her, truly concerned. She cupped the side of Fallon's face that had no blood.

"*Ma chérie*," she whispered. "What has happened?"

"I need to go to Brittany," Fallon said, not making much more sense, but at least she'd calmed down.

"Why? Where is Roishin? She was with you today, yes?"

Fallon nodded, taking several deep breaths. "She is in the bath," Fallon said. She ran a hand through her hair. Meeting Cateline's gaze again, she said, "Come upstairs with me?"

"Of course."

Fallon held out her hand to Cateline, who took it, her smaller hand cradled lovingly by the woman she knew and loved, as opposed to the dark, sinister stranger from moments ago. As they continued up the final flight of stairs, she was still very disquieted by what was happening.

Though she'd calmed, she could still feel an underlying energy in Fallon that was so unlike her. The last time she'd seen Fallon like that was many, many years ago when Livia had been brutally attacked by one of Fallon's men and left for dead.

Reaching their bedchamber, Fallon closed the door behind them and turned to Cateline. She took her into her arms and held her. She said nothing for long moments, so Cateline kept quiet. Though Fallon was larger and technically enfolded the smaller woman, they both knew in that moment who was truly holding whom, Cateline keeping Fallon together until she could do it on her own.

Finally, Fallon pulled away just enough to rest her forehead against Cateline's, a hand cupping the side of the princess's neck. "I'm sorry," she whispered.

Cateline covered that hand with her own, turning her head just enough to leave a kiss in the palm. "What happened, my love?" she asked softly, pulling her head back to look into Fallon's face.

Fallon left a lingering kiss of apology on Cateline's lips before stepping away from her. "We both knew from the start that Roishin was special," she began, unbuckling her back scabbard for the two blades that crossed her back.

Cateline watched, knowing how cathartic it was for Fallon to disarm and disrobe from the false torso. She enjoyed watching, to be perfectly honest. "Yes," she acknowledged.

Fallon looked down at her hands for a moment before she started to unlace her bracer after setting the blades atop the trunk where her torso would be stowed along with other such equipment of a personal nature. She seemed deeply lost in thought before shaking herself out of it. She removed her first bracer, tossing it to the bed before beginning on the second.

"When we were in the village today," she said, her voice quiet. "There was an accident. A man lost control of his horse and it caused a wagon to overturn."

Cateline took a few steps closer, her gaze never leaving Fallon as she wrapped her hands around one of the thick poles of the four-poster bed, which held up the wood canopy. As horrible as that was, she knew that wasn't what had upset Fallon so profoundly.

"The man is dead, and I'm not positive the mother will survive." She tossed the second bracer. "She lost so much blood." She swallowed, taking a deep breath. Releasing it, she looked to Cateline, who was riveted by her quiet tone. "There was a child."

"Did the child die?"

Fallon nodded, looking away again. Thinking that was it, Cateline began to walk over to her, but Fallon held up a hand to stop her advance. Swallowing again, Fallon's next words were so soft Cateline struggled to hear them. "Roishin brought her back to life."

Struck dumb for a moment, the princess shook her head as she hugged herself. "What do you mean?"

"I mean," Fallon said, looking over at Cateline. "That baby was d*ead*, Cateline. A wound to the chest like I've seen on a battlefield." That somewhat crazed look returned to her eyes. "Dead."

Cateline met her gaze for a long time, her brain trying to process what she was being told. "And, Roishin brought her back to life?" she asked slowly, repeating the words Fallon had initially said. "From such a wound?"

Fallon nodded. She walked over to Cateline, her hand placed on the same bedpost just a bit higher than where Cateline's had been. Cateline met her gaze, so many questions in her mind, but she remained quiet.

"She held that child," Fallon said, her voice soft, almost as if afraid of being overheard. "She cried and..." She looked away as though she were searching for the words. "The wound began to glow, like a thousand candles." Looking back to Cateline, she concluded. "It was gone. The wound was gone, and the baby began to move and cry."

Absolutely no idea what to say, Cateline turned away from her, hugging herself tighter. She felt a chill go through her, but she had no idea why. "Where is the baby now?"

≈≈≈≈

Cateline made her way to the room on the second floor where the mother and her baby had been brought, along with the castle healer. One of the servants was on standby, a young mother who offered to breastfeed should she be needed. She knocked on the closed wood door, ribbed with iron. A moment later, it was opened.

"Good eve," she said to the aged man in robes who stood on the other side.

"Milady," he said, stepping aside.

She entered the small room, which had once belonged to a servant. There was a narrow bed, a stand for a chamber pot and water pitcher, and a chair near the small fireplace. The book left face down upon the chair was likely where the castle physician had been seated before her arrival.

Upon the narrow bed was an incredibly pale woman. Her eyes were closed and her face was riddled with cuts and bruises, and a wound had been bandaged on her head. Her body was covered in a blanket. In a wicker basket lying on the floor near the bed was the sleeping babe.

Walking over to the bed, the princess looked down at the young woman, who looked no older than twenty. She reached out and took a pale hand in her own. Sadness ebbed through her as she had a feeling this poor woman wouldn't last the night.

"What say you?" she whispered to the physician, who stepped up beside her, never taking her gaze off the pale face.

"I'm afraid she'll likely be gone by morning, Your Highness," he said, his voice weak and whispery.

Cateline nodded. "My fear, as well." Bending down, she left a soft kiss on the woman's forehead. "May you go in peace, *chére*, if it is your time. Your child will be taken care of, I promise you."

As if on cue, the baby began to whine. Looking over at it, Cateline moved over to the basket and squatted down next to it. A smile instantly spread across her lips as she looked into the face of the beautiful little one.

"This child is hungry," she said, knowing that little cry all too well from raising Roishin from the time she was a day old. She began to softly sing in French as she picked up the baby to calm her as she looked to the man who watched. "Can the mother breastfeed?" she asked him. "Even if she is not conscious?"

"Aye, milady."

"Can you help me turn the mother to her side, please?"

Together, they were able to get the woman braced back against the wall so she lay on her side, making enough space on the bed for the baby to feed. Cateline looked to the healer.

"Will you give us some privacy?"

Left alone, Cateline cradled the baby in one arm as she sat on the side of the bed and gingerly pulled the woman's garment aside enough expose a breast, which was swollen with mother's milk. She lay the baby, whom she gauged was about three months old, into position. With careful touches to the warm breast, she helped the process begin.

The baby latched on and nature took over. Cateline remained seated to ensure the baby got what she needed. She looked to the woman and rested her hand upon her head. "A last gift for your daughter," she whispered.

As she watched, she was awed all over again by the wonder of mother and child. No, she'd never given birth to her own, nor breastfed any of them. But all three of her children, granted to her at ages four and eight years and one day, she loved with all that she was. She could not even imagine this young mother thinking her baby was dead.

Did she know of her baby's second chance? Was she conscious when Roishin performed the miracle? Was this young mother able to die in peace, knowing her child would be loved and taken care of all the rest of her days?

She caressed the side of the woman's face, the skin so soft where it wasn't injured from the accident. "I am so sorry," she whispered. "For my daughter to give yours a second chance, I swear to you here and now, she will be raised by us. We will keep her safe, we will keep her warm and she will always have all that she needs."

Leaning over, she left a kiss on the side of the woman's head. When she sat back up, she watched the baby take her fill, tiny lips suckling for all they were worth. It was almost as if she knew she had a limited amount of time to get this last, precious gift from her mother.

After a time, it was clear the baby was finished

and was falling asleep. Cateline gathered the little bundle in her arms and eased the woman's still body over until she was on her back again. She covered her exposed chest with her garment. Aa Cateline was about to stand from the bed, a long, slow breath eased from the woman's mouth, then all was quiet.

Cateline studied her as she cradled the baby against her own chest. "May you find your peace now, *ma chérie,*" she whispered, a tear slipping from her eye and slowly rolling down her cheek.

❧ ❧ ❧ ❧

The castle physician had officially declared the young mother dead, and Cateline had taken the baby to the servant just to get them through the night. On the morrow, they'd bring in a wet nurse and prepare a more permanent situation. For now, Cateline desperately needed to see Roishin.

She lifted her skirts enough for clearance as she hurried up the stairs to the floor where her children's bedrooms were. Knocking on the closed door, she got no response, so she let herself in. Roishin was already in bed and asleep. From the glow of the firelight in the fireplace, she was able to make her way to the bed in the otherwise darkened room.

Roishin was curled up on her side, hands together and tucked under her chin. Cateline smiled, as it reminded her of how the girl used to sleep when she was a baby. Carefully, so as not to wake her daughter, she climbed onto the bed. Remaining atop the covers, she scooted herself over until she lightly spooned the girl.

Holding her, she kissed the side of her head before resting her head on the pillow. This had been their miracle child, she thought. She remembered so well that Summer Solstice day when she'd been sent into their lives. Fallon had known from the first that the newborn had been meant for them. Felt it in her gut. Cateline, on the other hand, had always worried they'd left a mother heartbroken out there, somewhere.

She'd been found in a blanket that was a deep, rich blue with golden stitching, which Fallon had explained was just like the cloaks she'd seen while in Brittany, as well as on Head Priestess Enori, who had then married them. She held Roishin closer to her, the twelve-year-old snuggling back into her in her sleep. Cateline smiled at that.

"My little one," she whispered. "What gifts have you?"

As she lay there, a sense of foreboding began to gnaw at her stomach, but she couldn't place where it was from or why it was there. She'd always sensed something about Roishin, something different. At times she'd look into her beautiful green eyes and see an ancient soul looking back at her.

All too often, she felt Roishin was simply playing at being a child, when in fact she was a grown being simply humoring them all. Roishin seemed so confused by rules and laws of the land. Not in the way of somebody like Fergus, her first husband and Fallon's dead brother. Fergus had had the same queries, but it was because he felt he didn't need to abide by any law or rules but his own and for his own benefit.

No, that wasn't her daughter. It was like Roishin had a higher level of understanding and thought so much of what happened in Sursha—or on Earth, for that matter—was quaint and unnecessary. Her thoughts were interrupted when she heard a soft snort, as though Roishin were coming into wakefulness.

"Mamaí?" she asked sleepily.

"I am here, my love," Cateline murmured, holding her tighter. "I wanted to make sure you're okay."

Roishin nodded. "I think so. I think Daidí is angry with me."

"Oh, no, no, *ma chérie*." Cateline left a kiss on the side of her head. "Fallon was startled by what happened, and she's afraid for you."

"Why?"

"I think she worries what this may mean for you. We want you safe, Roishin."

The girl was quiet for a moment before asking, "Will people want to hurt me?"

That was precisely what Cateline was worried about, but she wasn't about to say that to her child. "People do crazy things," she said instead. "So," she added softly, resting her chin upon Roishin's shoulder. "We must work as a family to keep you safe. To let you have a normal childhood." She smiled. "Even as you're getting so big. Don't want to face the fact that my baby is growing up."

Roishin was quiet for a moment, leading Cateline to believe that maybe she'd drifted back to sleep, but then she spoke. "Mamaí, do you believe in angels?"

"As in the kind in Christian beliefs?" Cateline asked. She and Fallon had decided early on that the religious beliefs of France and other parts of Europe would not be what their children were taught, so she was surprised by the question.

"I guess," Roishin said. "I guess, maybe a being that watches over you, visits you?" She shrugged the one shoulder that didn't rest upon the mattress.

"Sure," Cateline said. "I believe there are those that guide us, watch over us, as you said. Make sure we are safe."

"But that don't live here on earth," Roishin added.

"*Oui.*"

"Me, too," Roishin said softly.

Chapter Six

Exhausted, Cateline finally left Roishin when the girl drifted back to sleep. Feeling she was asleep for the night, the princess left her to get back to Fallon. Entering the bedchamber, she closed the door behind her and saw that Fallon was in the solar area of the spacious chamber. She sat in one of the chairs in front of the fire, clearly deep in thought.

Walking over to her, Cateline reached down and removed the hand that rested on Fallon's thigh, making enough room for her to be able to climb astride her. She was immediately wrapped up in strong arms, Fallon's head cradled against Cateline's breasts.

"The mother has died," she said softly. "The child is with Rose for the night, as she's already nursing her son."

Fallon, bathed and changed into fresh clothing, minus her false torso, nodded. "Is the baby okay?"

Cateline nodded. "Yes. She was able to feed one last time before the mother passed."

Fallon let out a heavy breath, which sent a little shiver through Cateline as it blew across her upper chest. "What do we do with this child?"

"Well," the princess said, moving back just enough to look down into Fallon's beautiful face. She used her hands to push thick, dark hair back before her fingers traced down along a strong, proud jaw. "If we find no next of kin who can or will take her, I want us to raise her."

"Nobody in that village recognized them," Fallon said, eyes closing as she leaned into the touches. Her eyes opened, looking up into Cateline's. "You really want to take this baby in?"

"I will not allow her to go to an orphanage, Fallon." Cateline shook her head. "I will not."

Nodding, Fallon let out a heavy sigh. "How's Roishin doing?"

"She's okay. She brought up angels again."

"I believe I know who this 'angel' is."

Cateline studied her, head slightly tilting to the side. "Who?"

"Enori."

Her eyebrows shooting up, Cateline asked, "The priestess?"

"The very one."

Thinking for a moment, Cateline let out a breath. "Why you said you need to go to Brittany." At Fallon's nod, Cateline climbed off Fallon's lap and walked over to the sleeping area to ready for bed. With she and Fallon sharing a bedchamber, she didn't have her lady-in-waiting help her at night, only in the morning. "Love?"

Fallon pushed up from the chair and walked over to her, helping her undress, as it certainly wasn't a one-person job. Normally, it was a task that Fallon rather enjoyed and took her time with, but tonight it was clear her mind was far away from making love or even teasing the princess.

She certainly didn't push the issue, but simply thanked her spouse for her help and grabbed her brush to brush out the long, curly auburn hair after it had been pinned up all day. Naked, she sat in bed doing her task, watching as Fallon mindlessly undressed herself, still seeming to be miles away. No doubt, still on a country road in the village.

Setting her brush aside, Cateline got herself settled in bed. She watched, admiring Fallon as she disrobed. The strength of her body excited Cateline. The sculpted arms and shoulders, a strong back that Cateline loved to run her tongue down. A stomach that could be used to wash the laundry. Yet, her breasts were magnificent, dark rose nipples wonderfully responsive.

Her gaze scanned over that marvelous body as Fallon climbed into bed, but then looked away. She knew it was not the time for that. She stayed on her side of the bed and let Fallon take the lead in terms of what she needed in that moment. Staring up at the underside of the canopy, Cateline thought of the baby that may be joining their family.

She at thirty-four and Fallon at thirty-seven... did they want to become parents again, start over? It was a big question, but she had made a promise to that young mother, and however she could, she intended to keep it. Looking over at Fallon, she saw that the warrior was already looking at her.

"Are you okay?" she asked softly. She smiled when a hand reached for hers underneath the blankets, fingers wrapping around her own.

"I'm worried about Roishin," Fallon said. "When I was in Brittany with my men, I saw things I'd never seen before, and I've been a warrior for a long, long time."

"Do you think they'd actually mean her harm, though?" Cateline asked, releasing Fallon's hand as she turned to her side to face her spouse.

"No, I don't think they mean her harm, but where did Roishin come from?" Fallon asked quietly, mirroring Cateline's position. "How does she possess such a gift?"

Cateline was quiet for a moment before she voiced a thought. "Is it possible it was just coincidence, Fallon? Perhaps the baby wasn't as injured as you thought? Maybe she had blood on her from her father, something?"

Fallon shook her head. "No."

Cateline knew Fallon was an incredibly logical woman and would have considered every possibility before settling on the most extreme answer, but she felt she needed to bring such things up, perhaps for herself, as she still had no idea what to think of all of this. "Do you think Roishin could save the mother, then?"

"I don't know. I'm honestly not sure how much she can control it. Think of all the times in her life she could have done that, Cateline," Fallon said. "John, our beloved gardener, died two years ago on the property. She was devastated, but yet..."

"Dead he remains," Cateline said. At Fallon's nod, she added, "Perhaps it was an emotional reaction today?"

"I know not." Fallon studied Cateline's face for a long time, seeming to be committing every feature to memory. "I'm going to gather some men, and we'll head out within a fortnight."

"Fallon," Cateline said, feeling a bit nervous by the soft declaration. "Perhaps they have nothing to do with this. Perhaps she's just a blessed child."

Still looking troubled, Fallon leaned forward and kissed Cateline's lips. "Let's sleep," she murmured against them. She urged the princess to turn to her other side, and when she did, Fallon spooned up behind her, holding her close.

⚜⚜⚜⚜

"No!"

Cateline nearly jumped out of her skin at the single word, yelled loudly beside her. She partially sat up, head whipping to the left to see Fallon gasping for air as she was wrestling with the blankets.

"Fallon?" Cateline reached a hand over to try to still her obvious panic. She cried out in surprise when Fallon's eyes popped open and, faster than a snake strike, she was on top of Cateline, a hand clenched around her throat.

"You will not take her," she growled, eyes wide and pupils enlarged, making her eyes look nearly black.

Cateline stared up at this woman she did not know. She gripped the hand that held her firmly to the bed. She tried to pull it from her throat, but it was an iron grip. "Fallon," she gasped. "Let go."

The vise tightened as Fallon lowered her face, now mere inches from Cateline. "You will not take her," she said again, the words more like a threatening hiss.

"All right," Cateline whispered, terrified. "I won't."

The hand slowly loosened, but the hard, penetrating gaze remained for a long moment before Fallon eased herself up and off her. The tears were instant for Cateline, who scrambled out of bed and away from the warrior who sat there looking dazed.

She brought a hand up to her neck, still able to feel the ghost grip of Fallon's fingers on her skin, warm to the touch.

Breasts heaving, Cateline backed away from the bed, trying to get herself under control. She tried to blink the tears away but they refused to desist, so she turned around instead. She covered her face with her hands for a moment, taking several deep breaths before they fell away. She walked to the boudoir and grabbed a robe to cover her nakedness. She felt entirely too vulnerable.

Belting the robe tightly, she looked to Fallon, who still sat where she'd put herself after moving away from Cateline. "Have you nothing to say for yourself?" she asked.

Fallon looked at her, though the movement of her head was slow, as though she were in a dream or under water. Her gaze fixed on Cateline, but she said nothing. Hurt and very confused, Cateline turned away. Yes, it was time to start her day. She left the bedchamber to alert Fiona she would be ready for a bath soon.

The lady-in-waiting occupied the small bedroom Marie first slept in when they'd arrived at Caisleán Thíar with Cateline after her marriage to Fergus. It had later been turned into a bedroom for Garratt and Laigen when they'd first been brought in, far too small to bunk in the servants' quarters.

The large boudoir already set up in Cateline's former chambers worked perfectly for her baths and her daily ablutions. It kept the bedchamber she shared with Fallon for just the two of them, and Fallon had the freedom and privacy to ready herself. Even their children knew as they got older that, unless it was an emergency or a particularly disturbing nightmare, once the bedchamber door was closed, it was Cateline and Fallon's time.

Once the couple was up and ready for their day, servants would enter to clean, make the bed, and gather laundry.

Cateline stood in the family chamber, waiting for the ladies to begin their duties after she'd awakened Fiona. She stood up on the dais where the table was set up with the ongoing chess game. She fingered one of the onyx pieces: the knight. It had always been her favorite piece, as to her it represented her very own warrior.

"Milady?"

Her head turned to see Elsie standing at the bottom of the three stairs that led to where the princess stood. Such a lovely girl, Cateline thought. Very sweet disposition as well. At times she almost wished she'd known the young Scot before Fiona as she would have made a much more pleasant lady-in-waiting.

"Shall I help with your bath before my duties in Roishin's chambers?" she asked. Cateline had stirred the young women early this day, so their routines were a bit off.

"Is Roishin still asleep?" she asked, taking the three stairs down to stand next to the young woman.

"She is, milady," Elsie said. Cateline saw her blue gaze drop to Cateline's neck. For just a moment, they registered surprise, then quickly looked away, back to the gaze of the princess.

This greatly alerted Cateline. Though she was still upset from her terrifying thrust into wakefulness that morning, she knew it was absolutely not Fallon's normal behavior. In thirteen years together, Fallon had never once laid a hand on her, never once. But clearly, she was wearing what had happened this morning around her neck like a band of shame.

"Let her sleep," she said. "Yesterday was trying on her."

Elsie bowed her head in deference, then quickly left the chamber to alert the servants who would help her bring in the water for the bath while Fiona would help her sort through her outfits to decide on the day's wardrobe.

As the morning activity went on around her, Cateline felt like she was just going through the motions, not feeling or thinking much of anything. She thanked her people, as she always did, certainly grateful for how well they performed their jobs. But the truth was, she just wanted to be alone. She was also deeply concerned that whispers would make their way around the castle about the light bruises forming on her neck, which she had seen were red fingermarks when she'd looked into the mirror in the boudoir.

Yes, they would fade, probably be gone by breakfast, but from the quiet looks she was getting from those around her, it was clear they were seen by all. Yes, she absolutely intended to have a stern discussion with Fallon when she saw her, but the warrior wasn't deserving of whispered concerns or gossip behind their backs.

No matter how beloved the prince and princess were, people were people, and people liked to talk—especially those around who were old enough to remember Fergus and his crazed abuse to just about anyone. She already hated that Fallon was in that man's bloodline, let alone that any other comparisons that may be made between the two.

·♫·♫·♪·♪·

Breakfast was a quiet affair for Cateline. She kept to herself as her family chatted. Laigen knew nothing of the events of the previous day, so she chatted on and on about the upcoming gala for her suitors. Honestly, it was fine with Cateline. She didn't have to add much to the conversation as Roishin and Laigen bantered back and forth about it.

Feeling eyes on her, she glanced over to see Fallon watching her. The look of unspoken concern was evident in her eyes, the eyes that Cateline had always known. Nowhere was the violent killer from that morning. She just couldn't hold the loving gaze as she felt pricks of hurt and confusion, forcing her to blink a few times for fear those pricks of emotions may show themselves down her cheeks.

Fallon reached over and took her hand in hers where it rested on the table. "What is it?"

All she could do was stare at her, incredulous. "Is that a serious question?" Cateline asked quietly, not wanting to garner the attention of their girls.

"Aye," Fallon said. "What happened?"

What was left of her appetite very much gone, Cateline pulled her hand out of Fallon's and pushed back from the table. "Forgive me, girls," she said to their daughters, who looked up at the sudden move. She walked over to Laigen and left a kiss on her forehead before doing the same to Roishin. "We'll talk today about the gala," she promised her eldest before hurrying from the chamber before she burst into tears.

She just barely made it to her own bedchamber before Fallon caught up with her. She was grabbed and swung around to face an extremely concerned-looking warrior. Cateline snatched her hand away.

"Don't touch me."

Fallon closed their bedchamber door before turning back to her. "What have I done?" she asked. "Please, Cateline. I cannot fix it if you won't tell me."

Looking up into those violet eyes, Cateline knew that Fallon truly had no idea what she was talking about. Was it Cateline? Was she going mad? No, there were marks around her throat, and she raised her chin to show Fallon.

Gasping, the warrior bent down a bit to get a better look. "What happened?" she asked, fingers coming up to ever so gently touch the fading marks.

"What happened?" Cateline exclaimed. "You attacked me this morning, *that's* what happened, Fallon!"

"What?" Fallon's eyes grew huge. "What are you talking about? When I woke up, you were already gone."

Unable to stop the tears now, they streamed down her face. "Because I was afraid of you!" She sobbed, pushing Fallon away as she tried to take her into a hug.

"No," Fallon said, shaking her head. Her own eyes were welling. "You know I'd never hurt you, Cateline. Never." She grabbed her wife with a gentle hold on her hand to stop her. She examined the marks on her pale skin more closely. Tears slowly rolled down her cheeks as she looked into Cateline's eyes, her own pleading. "I have no words," she whispered.

Able to see how utterly devastated Fallon was, Cateline's heart softened, just a little. "You woke up screaming," she explained. "I tried to comfort you and you grabbed me by the throat." Fresh tears broke her words. This time she allowed Fallon to cradle her against her. She clung to her, the upset and fear of that morning still so raw. "You told me I'd never take her," she finished in a whisper.

She knew all too well what Fallon was capable of as a warrior, yet it had always been something kept very separate from their relationship, and certainly their bed. The bridge between the two had been crossed, and she'd been left profoundly shaken. She was held tightly as she cried.

"I love you so much," Fallon murmured into the hug, emotion making her words thick. "I am so sorry, my love. So very sorry." She placed her hands on either side of Cateline's head in a gentle hold as she pulled away just enough to look down into her face. Her anguish was clear as day. "I have no memory of this, I swear. I would never hurt you. *Ever.*"

The words were as comforting as they were unsettling. In that moment, Cateline believed everything she was saying as Fallon's truth—at least as the warrior understood it. But what had happened for her to have no memory of such a thing?

"Please forgive me," Fallon pleaded softly, leaving a kiss on Cateline's lips, then another and another.

Somehow, their kisses deepened and Cateline was holding on to her desperately, her mouth almost ravenous against Fallon's. She needed *her* warrior, not the terrifying beast that had slain countless foes in her military years. Their kiss never breaking, Cateline was swept up in strong arms and carried to the bed.

Gently laid down on her back, she was hungry for Fallon's touch. She desperately needed to feel everything was okay, and their intense passion had always been their way of communicating when words just weren't enough.

Fallon left her mouth and moved to her neck. Though still passionate, she was gentle. "I'm so sorry," she murmured against the reddened skin. "So sorry."

As she kissed the earlier trauma away, one of her hands found its way up and under the layers of skirts to where Cateline was already wet and pulsing. Her head fell to the side, offering her flesh to Fallon even as her legs parted for her questing fingers. Fallon groaned into her neck when her fingers found the volcanic need between Cateline's thighs.

Cateline's breasts were heaving within the confines of her dress as those strong, knowing fingers found exactly where she needed them to be. They were ruthless as they rubbed against the hard, slick need which, mere moments later, made Cateline cry out as she came, hard.

After a moment, Fallon gently removed her hand, replacing the skirts before she gathered the princess to her, Cateline now crying for a whole different reason: relief.

Chapter Seven

Her breath escaped in steamed puffs as the early morning was bitterly cold. She stood next to Toirneach, ready to mount up, along with the three men she'd chosen to accompany her. A wagon with provisions had been sent the previous evening, so now it was just her and her men and their personal packs to head to the harbor and their awaiting ship.

It would be a two-day voyage if nothing went wrong, and she wasn't expecting anything to. She lifted her leg, about to place her booted foot in the stirrups, when she heard a voice shouting for her in the early morning darkness. Looking over her shoulder, she saw a figure.

Cloak fanning out like a cape behind her, Roishin was running over to her. Lowering her leg, Fallon nodded to the men to go on before she turned to face her daughter. "What are you doing?" she chastised. "Go back inside before you catch your death out here."

"I'm sorry, Daidí!" the girl cried, tears running down her cheeks.

Fallon caught the girl's forward progress with her hands on her shoulders to avoid being bowled over by her. Concerned, she looked down into her upturned face. "What on earth for?"

"I won't do it again, I swear!" she cried. "I didn't mean to make you leave."

"Oh, no, my sweet girl." Fallon wrapped the

crying child into her embrace. She cradled her head against her chest. "No, you didn't." She smiled when she felt Roishin's arms wrap around her back. "*Mo a leanbh*," she murmured against the top of her head. "Never would I leave you." She left a kiss there. "For any reason."

"I dreamt that you were going," Roishin said, voice thick with her tears. "You were fading away." The tears came faster. "I couldn't see you anymore."

Fallon stroked her hair, long around her shoulders and down her back as the child had clearly erupted straight from sleep. "I am leaving, my sweet girl," she whispered. "But only for a short time, I promise."

"It's because of me," Roishin said, a statement.

Sometimes, Fallon thought with a rueful internal chuckle, it was hard having a child who saw so very much. "Yes, but," she said, gently urging her daughter to look up at her. She used the edge of her own cloak to gently wipe away tear streaks from the girl's face. "But only so your mamaí and I will better understand this wonderful gift you have." Fallon pushed wild, dark hair back from her lovely young face. "Nothing more, child." She gave her the most loving smile she could.

Calming, Roishin nodded. She sniffled, using the sleeve of her sleeping gown to wipe at her eyes. "Daidí?" she said softly.

"Yes, my sweet?"

"Be careful of the shadow man," Roishin said sagely. "I saw him in my dream, too."

Fallon nodded, taking the girl's words to heart. She couldn't help but remember another early morning warning from a dream she'd received so long ago. "I promise." She left a kiss on Roishin's forehead. "Now," she murmured. "Go back inside and get warm."

The girl nodded. "Okay." Her face screwed up in concern. "You'll be back for the husband fishing expedition, won't you?"

Fallon's head threw back in a loud bark of laughter, Toirneach huffing from where he stood waiting next to the pair. He was clearly not amused. "I'm not sure who I'd have to run faster from if I did, your mamaí or your sister." They shared a smile. Fallon gave her one last tight hug and kiss. "I love you. Now go," she said softly, but sternly. "See you soon."

Fallon watched as her daughter did as she was told and scurried back to the castle. She waited until she knew she was safely inside before turning back to her horse to mount.

⁂

Wrapped in her cloak, Fallon stood on deck, watching as waves from the vast Celtic Sea pounded against the sides of their ship as they cut through the water. The sun was high and they should reach the shores of Brittany by early morning.

"Didn't think we'd be making this trip again."

Glancing over, she saw Eoin walking up to her. They shared a smile. "Neither did I." One of her most trusted men for nearly twenty years, she was glad he was with her.

Though she'd had to back off her military service, per the king's orders as she was now next in line for the throne, she still kept up with the happenings of the Elite Guard. She no longer went out on missions with them, as the kingdom would be profoundly damaged were she to be killed, but she maintained her training with them and kept in close contact with those she had appointed to take over.

"Garratt confirmed for me that he'd brought in five men to help cover Caisleán Thíar while you're gone," he noted.

Fallon chuckled. "Well, I guess I'd rather a little too much muscle than not enough." They shared a knowing smile. Eoin was around the same age as Fallon, a couple years older but had served a long time. They both understood how the young soldier could be a wee overzealous.

"I'm sure he's trying to impress you, sire."

"He already does," Fallon acknowledged. "Every single day."

They stood in companionable silence for a long moment before Eoin asked, "Are you expecting trouble, sire? It was pretty damn rough last time we were here."

"Well." Fallon smirked. "I have a strong feeling our arrival isn't unknown," she said cryptically.

"Well," the soldier said. "Lunch is ready if you're hungry, Your Highness."

She turned to him, looking into his dark eyes. "You call me Fallon when we're alone, Eoin. You know that."

The man smiled and looked down, as if to try and hide the expression. Nodding, he looked up again and at Fallon. "Aye." He grinned. "Fallon." With a playful punch to Fallon's shoulder, he headed back the way he'd come below decks.

Left alone, Fallon's gaze turned back to the ocean. Her dark hair blew back from her face with the sea breeze, the salty air filling her nose and her lungs. She had an unsettling feeling knotting her gut. She wasn't so much worried about being attacked or ambushed or anything like that.

Her concern lay with what she'd find out. Her hand reached up and she lightly plucked the medallion out from where it had rested against the sculpted cuirass beneath her tunic. She gripped it in her hand and absently ran her thumb across the smooth surface of the skull-shaped stone, the golden serpent wrapped around it.

When she'd returned from Brittany the first time, her father had told her to keep it when she'd tried to give it back to him.

Looking her dead in the eye, Carthac said softly, "This is part of your legacy and your destiny now, Fallon." The king took the proffered medallion from Fallon's hand and allowed the heavy pendant to fall, the gold chain falling taught along with it. He'd raised his hands that held the chain and placed the medallion back around Fallon's neck. "Keep this," he said. "You'll know when you need it again."

"I guess that time is now," she murmured.

▞▞▟▟

Of the four men she'd brought with her, only two would accompany her ashore. The other two and the small crew would remain with the ship. It was just as cold now in Brittany as it had been back in Sursha the morning they'd left. Fallon ignored the harsh temperatures as she sloshed through the shallow waters from the dinghy to the shoreline.

It was early, the moon still in the sky. They'd landed where they had thirteen years ago, sent on a suicide mission by Fergus. That had been an awful night, she remembered. Enori, the head priestess of the Order of Ankou, had asked that Gunther be left behind. Gunther, of course, had been Fergus's chosen man to try and assassinate Fallon.

"Now," Enori said. "We need to get you home. You and those who survived are free to leave, except the one called Gunther." She pushed up from the stool. "He brought corruption and murder to our shores." She made her way over to where Fallon sat, the warrior still weak. "The dead we'll give to Ankou to sort."

Fallon shivered at the memory of that long-ago time. She wondered what had happened to the soldier and would-be assassin. Had the Bretons executed him? Sold him into slavery? Set him free? She knew not, and likely never would. For now, it didn't matter, as she had only one mission, and that was to once again speak to the priestess.

Eoin and Donovan stepped up beside her as Fallon took in the beach. As had been the case the last time, cliffs off to the left, thick woods to the right, and the sea behind them. Obviously, their only route was through the trees. The last time, she'd been knocked out by the noxious fumes from whatever on earth had been glowing in the glass jars thrown at the beach. Fallon had been carried to Enori's cave, and she had no clue where that was, now.

On pure instinct, Fallon reached just inside the neckline of her tunic and brought out the medallion. As she held it in her fingers, about to release it to rest against the garment, she noticed that part of the skull began to glow. She glanced over to the two men beside her; they had also noticed. She looked back down at it.

She was partially facing the cliffs and the skull that was on the far right of the small crystal skull was glowing, which was more toward the trees. Curious, she turned slightly right, and sure enough, the more she faced the trees, the more of the skull began to glow.

"Is it guiding you?" Eoin asked.

"No idea," Fallon murmured. She turned a bit more toward the water, and sure enough, the glow moved with her, now just to the left edge of the skull. Okay, forward into the trees it was.

The three headed into the darkness, the woods so dense even the moonlight above couldn't cut through the canopy. She heard both men begin to pull a weapon, but she held out her hand.

"No," she said quietly, both of her own blades still sheathed.

The deeper in they got, the darker it got. The light emanating from the medallion was truly their guiding light. It wasn't enough to act as a torch, but she found that as long as they went in a direction that kept the light center of the skull, they ran into nothing. It cut a path through the dense foliage and between the massive, ancient trunks.

Her heart was beginning to race, but she couldn't discern for what reason. It wasn't exactly nerves, wasn't exactly anxiety or fear. It was almost a feeling of...recognition? Familiarity? She certainly felt she was being pulled.

She wasn't sure how long they'd walked, but it felt like miles. Finally, the trees began to clear a bit, just the slightest bit of moonlight trickling in. She stopped when she realized they were about to reach the stone face of more cliffs. The stone was pale in the dimness, almost looking like a giant sheet of bone protruding from the rich, dark soil at their feet.

"What are we supposed to do?" Donovan asked. "Climb it?"

Fallon craned her head to try to see if there was a ledge, anything. From left to right, it was just that sheer wall as far as the eye could see. Looking down at her amulet, she saw that it was pulsing, almost like a glowing, silvery heartbeat.

Walking up to the wall, Fallon placed her hands against the cool, smooth stone. She ran her palms along it, trying to feel for anything that would give her any sort of clue where to go next. She felt they were close, could feel that excitement within her gut growing.

Suddenly, her waterfall passed before her mind's eye. She saw herself heading into what looked like a cave entrance but instead was a drop down into the hidden area. It had been how she'd initially found it, literally falling and breaking her arm upon landing.

She immediately went in search. "You two stay here," she ordered absently.

Her fingertips grazed along the stone wall, which was smooth from eons of being sandblasted by the harsh saltwater breeze. Suddenly, she knew exactly where to go. Heading toward the sea, she slowed her pace, her eyes searching through the dimness until finally, the trees broke as she reached a tiny bit of rocky beach.

There it was. It looked like a shallow cavity in the wall, but she knew better. Looking back the way she'd come, she called out. "You two stay there. I'll be back."

Stepping inside the small space, she looked down at what the casual observer would see as a gaping maw in the stone floor, an unknown fate to he who would challenge its depths. But Fallon knew she had to go. Lowering herself to her knees, she tried to peer through the darkness, but it was impenetrable.

Reaching behind her, she unsheathed one of her blades and used its length to lightly poke around. The tip of the steel clinked lightly against stone about three feet down. She moved the blade a few inches and again poked against hard stone, but farther down. Stairs, or at least a couple different levels.

Sliding the blade back into its scabbard, she lowered herself down into the hole, her booted feet coming into contact with the stone ledge she'd initially felt. Moving one foot, she felt the next, then another and another. It was stairs. As she went down, she glanced up to see the last bright of the moonlight disappear.

She'd stepped down at least ten stairs when finally she seemed to reach the floor. It was blacker than black, but within a few moments, the skull began to glow again rather than the pulsing it had been doing since they'd reached the wall.

Glancing around, she saw that in the inky darkness, it acted like a guiding light. She was in a tunnel, stone walls curved up into a ceiling and down to the floor. It was just wide enough for a man to walk without hitting his head or brushing his shoulders against the walls. Fallon had plenty of clearance, so she continued onward, as it seemed there was only one direction to go.

Her booted footfalls echoed off the stone, but other than that, she heard no other sounds: no voices, no running water from an underground spring, not even the waves crashing above ground. The light of her medallion was only able to cut through the complete darkness so far, leaving the unknown ahead. Glancing over her shoulder, she saw the blackness swallowing the tunnel behind her.

It seemed she'd easily walked a mile when she came to a T in the path. She could go left or right or turn back. She looked down at the skull, but it was absolutely no help, as either way she turned, it remained aglow. About to choose the right-hand tunnel, she stopped. Looking to her left, she heard soft humming.

Taking a step in that direction, she listened. It was beautiful, a woman's voice. It almost sounded like a woman humming to a child as she rocked it to sleep. She figured that even if it wasn't whom she was looking for, at least it was a person that could perhaps direct her.

This tunnel was much shorter, and soon enough she saw another tunnel jetting off to the right, and from that one she saw the soft glow of firelight. The source of the humming also seemed to be coming from that direction. Heading that way, she saw an open room carved out of the stone. No real corners to speak of, as everything had smooth, rounded lines.

The room was small, nothing more in it than a small cutout in the wall, where the flames of a fire were dancing, a small hole at the top that pulled the smoke up into it rather than inside the room. There was a niche in the wall for sleeping, a bed pallet tucked inside of it, as well as a small table and stool carved from the stone.

To her confusion, there was nobody there and the humming had stopped. Her skull no longer glowed. She turned, about to head back the way she'd come, when she started. Leaning against the stone wall just outside the small room was Enori.

She wasn't wearing the vibrant blue cloak she'd worn the only other times Fallon had seen her. Now, she wore a flowing gown of white, which seemed to caress her every curve with every move. She was just as stunning as Fallon remembered, with her short blond hair and piercing blue eyes that, in the flickering firelight from the room to Fallon's left, looked gray.

What got Fallon the most was that Enori hadn't seemed to age a single day in the thirteen years since she'd seen her last. She still looked to be a woman in her mid twenties, at best. She was absolutely ethereal, but in that moment, Fallon could only glare at her.

"Welcome," she said. "We've been expecting you, Fallon."

"Oh?" Fallon said, arms crossing over her chest as she looked down at her.

"Oh, yes. However, I had hoped that you would have brought Roishin with you," Enori said, one delicately arched eyebrow quirked. "It's time for her to come home, after all."

"She *is* home," Fallon replied, voice low and dangerous. "She's home with her mother."

"Indeed." Enori pushed away from the wall. "Well, now it's time for her to return home to her father."

Chapter Eight

Stunned, Fallon just stared at her. "What are you saying?"

Enori eyed her before turning around and walking off down the tunnel, her white gown flowing around shapely calves with every step. Fallon followed, the two heading into the right-hand side of the T, which was where she'd initially intended to go before hearing the humming.

"Was that you humming?" she asked, surprising herself with the question.

"Yes," Enori responded, her words Gaelic though accented.

"Why did you lead me to the left, then?"

"Because I did not want you near my rooms if you were not alone," she said simply.

A few moments later, they turned down into yet another tunnel, Fallon nearly running straight into the wall before seeing a dim firelight glow off to the left. She followed, wondering how on earth she was going to find her way out of this place. The chamber where the fire was coming from was the same one where Fallon had woken up thirteen years before.

She saw the large stone slab, the table carved out of the wall and stools on either side. Another bedroll niche was in the wall, like the other room. Enori's space had a larger fireplace, the flames within warm, the golden glow reflecting off the stone walls. She noted that it looked like the bedroll had just recently been vacated.

"Would you like some?" Enori asked, walking over to the table and tapping a wine pitcher.

"No," Fallon said, standing at the center of the room with her arms crossed over her chest.

Enori glanced at her and smiled, turning her attention back to the pitcher. She poured the dark red liquid into a wooden goblet before grabbing a second from a small recess in the wall and pouring a second glass. She walked over to her, holding it out.

Fallon looked down into the cup, then decided to take it. "Thank you."

Enori sat on one of the stools, crossing one leg over the other as she sipped her wine. She studied Fallon as she did. Fallon remained standing, the goblet held in her hand. She honestly wasn't sure what to say, the priestess making her feel very unsteady. There was an aura to her, almost like an energy that made the warrior feel light-headed and a bit disoriented.

"It's you my daughter believes is her angel," Fallon finally said. "Isn't it?"

"She doesn't *believe*," Enori said easily. "She *knows*."

"Why?" Fallon asked, setting the goblet down on the stone slab. "Why are you bothering her?"

"I'm not bothering her, Fallon," the priestess said. "I've been watching her."

"Why?" Fallon asked again.

"Because," she said simply, sipping from her wine. "We needed to know when it was time."

"Time for what?"

"Time for her to come home," Enori said softly. "As I said to you, her father is ready for her. But," she added, uncrossing her legs and pushing to her bare feet. "More so, Roishin is ready.'

"*We* are her parents, Enori," Fallon said, hand splayed out across her chest. "Cateline and I."

"Yes." Enori agreed with a nod as she walked over to Fallon, looking up into her face. "You are. You both are her mothers, and you see that in her." She smiled, beautiful. "The perfect combination of you and Cateline. Physically." She grabbed the goblet from the stone slab and held it up to Fallon. "Drink," she said softly.

Fallon took it, looking into its scarlet depths before meeting the woman's eyes who stood before her. Never taking her eyes off her, she took a small sip. It was sweet, with just the tiniest bitterness from the fermenting of the grape.

Enori turned away from her and walked back to her stool and her own wine. "What did I tell you when I married you and Cateline?" she asked, seating herself again. "At the celebration after," she clarified.

Fallon looked down into her wine, a small smile gracing her lips as she remembered like it was yesterday. "You said," she began quietly. "'Tonight, love well and true. At the summer solstice, your family of four will grow to five for you.'" She looked up and met the priestess's approving gaze.

"And you did," Enori said, a little twinkle in her eyes. "And," she added, retrieving her wine. "I gave Cateline a red rose, and that red rose was in the bedchamber with the two of you as you made love that night." Her gaze was intense as she studied Fallon. "It gathered the true essence of the passion you and Cateline share for each other."

Fallon could only stare, no idea where Enori was

going with this. She took another sip from her wine, never taking her gaze off the seated woman.

"That rose was taken the following morning," Enori said, her chin slightly raised almost as if in challenge.

"By whom?"

"By me," she said casually.

Fallon felt anger beginning to grow, a violation of the very personal and precious space she shared with Cateline. "How?" she growled.

The smile that spread upon full lips was almost sweet, which only added to Fallon's anger. "By the door, of course." She smirked as she took another sip.

"Why?" Fallon asked, taking a step toward her. As a warrior, she'd had to learn early on how to keep the balance of emotions in check: anger versus fear versus battler rage versus profound grief. Whatever it was, she had lived that balance her entire life. But now, standing ten feet away from that woman, she felt she was losing that balance. It scared her.

"Because he needed that essence," Enori said. "To combine with his own to create the precious creature known as Roishin."

"Who?"

"Roishin's father, Fallon. You and Cateline are her mothers, but she is also the daughter of Ankou."

Fallon stared at her, her blood going cold. "What?"

"You have known this, Fallon," Enori said, setting her goblet down. She pushed to her feet. "You may not have known the exact details, but deep down, you always knew."

For a moment, she couldn't breathe. Fallon turned away from her, nearly dropped the wooden goblet in her hand, so she set it down on the stone slab again. Palms resting on the hard, cold surface, her head fell.

"Fallon," Enori said softly, walking over to her and placing a warm hand on her shoulder. "Your job is done. It is time for her father to take over—"

"Over my dead body!" Fallon raged, whirling on the priestess, who barely batted an eyelash. Her hand falling away from Fallon was the only indication she'd even noticed the outburst.

"If that's what you want," Enori said simply.

"How dare you!" Fallon bellowed. "How dare you haunt her mind. How *dare* you give her a ring without our blessing. She is too young to understand any of this!"

"Which is why she needs me!" Enori's eyes were blue fire as she glared up into Fallon's, not a shred of fear of the warrior. "It has begun, Fallon, and she must be trained. She must learn how to control her gifts. She may look like you and Cateline," she said, voice low and dangerous. "But I assure you, she *is* her father and all that entails."

Fallon couldn't speak, could hardly breathe.

"And, she needs to return here before she begins her bleed."

"That is none of your business," Fallon said, her anger returning.

Enori took a step closer, putting them nearly breast to breast. "You've seen what she can do with her tears," she murmured. "Imagine what she can do with her blood."

"You will never have my daughter," Fallon said, the words like a growl from deep in her throat. "You and your god can go to hell."

Enori smirked. "Ankou is the god of the underworld, Fallon. He's already there."

Fallon leaned forward, the two looking as though they were about to kiss. "You will never have my daughter," she said.

Enori didn't back down, didn't flinch a muscle. "You are a fool," she purred. "You'd sacrifice your own family, and for what? Stubborn pride? Ego, perhaps?"

"Love."

"Oh?" Enori challenged. "Is that why you're gathering men to sell off your oldest daughter to? Is that love also?"

Fallon's body was nearly vibrating now with rage. Without taking her gaze off the blue that held hers to the spot, she slowly reached up and eased one of her blades from its scabbard on her back.

"Do it," Enori challenged. Fallon placed the tip of the blade at the priestess's throat, but Enori reached up and gently eased the tip until it rested just above her left breast at her heart, her gaze unwavering. "Do it," she said again.

With a howl of frustration, Fallon raised the short sword and with speed that was barely seen, the wood goblet was split in two, cup to stem. As though bleeding for her fury, crimson slowly spread across the face of the stone slab.

Turning away from Enori, Fallon closed her eyes and brought the sword up, resting the flat of the blade to rest against her forehead. How had she gotten to this place? How had she lost control so badly?

"It has begun already," Enori murmured, as if to herself. "He's coming for you, Fallon."

Fallon glared at her over her shoulder. "Let him." She stared the priestess down. "I'll fight this."

"And," Enori said softly, stepping over to her. "You will lose. You are a warrior," she conceded. "One of the best the world has ever known. But," she added, reaching out and lightly taking Fallon's sword from her. Fallon was about to turn on her, but Enori gently urged her to turn her back to her. For reasons she'd never understand, Fallon did. Her blade was carefully slid back into its scabbard. "You cannot win the battle you are asking for."

Fallon turned around to look at the priestess, surprised to see understanding in her eyes. "I will die for my child, Enori."

Enori looked into her eyes for a long moment, then nodded. "Yes. Yes, you will." She stepped away from her, walking back to the stone table and grasping her goblet of wine. "You and your men may leave. But," she warned. "Watch out for the shadows, Fallon."

About to leave, Fallon stopped yet again, her blood turned to ice. She turned and looked at the woman who had taken a seat on the stone stool. She couldn't speak.

"There is someone around Roishin who can help keep her safe," Enori added, head slightly cocked to the side. "And, it is not you."

Gaze never wavering, Fallon reached up and took hold of the medallion and lifted the chain from around her neck. She placed it, curled around the medallion, on the stone slab, then turned and walked away.

❧❧❧❧

She was grateful she could see the light just barely beginning to stream in from above. It looked as though darkness were falling, the sun just barely hovering in the sky before another night's sleep. Tired and ready to head home, Fallon pulled herself out of the hole and back to ground level. Taking one last look down into that dastardly place, she hurried back toward where she'd left Eoin and Donovan who knew how many hours before.

To her shock, they both still stood exactly where she'd left them. She figured they'd at least go sit down. Perhaps they'd heard her? She raised a hand in a small wave.

"Didn't find anything, eh?" Eoin asked.

She looked at him. "What do you mean? Of course I did. Just got back."

Eoin and Donovan exchanged a glance before both looking back to Fallon. "Back?"

"Back from the caves below," Fallon said. She indicated the falling sun above. "Been gone all day, lads."

Again, the men exchanged a look. "You've been gone about three minutes, milord," Donovan said. "The sun is about to start rising."

Fallon looked to them both, about to crack a smile as they no doubt were fooling with her, but both were serious as mud. Running a hand through her hair, she turned away from them. Her head hurt.

"Well," she muttered. "I, uh…I got what I needed." Without another word, she headed back the way they'd come.

Though the men with her said nothing, to her or each other, she could feel their confusion. It made her feel confused, and that made her feel angry. Her pace picked up until she was nearly marching through the trees. Then, her pace picked up again until she was nearly running through the trees. She could hear the men behind her, trying to keep up with her unexpected increase in pace.

Finally, dodging trees, hair flying back behind her, Fallon ran. She barely heard her boots touch the forest floor as powerful thighs propelled her and her arms pumped. Her teeth were bared and determination roused as she flew through the ancient maze of trees on a foreign land that, for some reason, she felt she knew in her heart.

Enori's words bounced around in her mind, chasing her through the forest and back to the sea, back to her ship, and back to her family. She desperately needed to be with them. She needed to see Cateline's beautiful face. She needed to hear her voice and feel her touch. She needed to hear the unending chatter of her children and she needed the balm of their presence.

She needed the calm presence of Livia and her practical words of advice. She needed her son's big smile and a good day exchanging blades with him in the training yard behind the barracks. She needed to smell the horseflesh of the stables when she went in to pat her horse on his massive neck in affection before climbing atop his back and the two flying out for a ride.

She needed to be back on the land of her birth, her beloved Sursha. She needed to see the smiling faces of her people, to chat with the cobbler as he told her the latest gossip of the village and about his wife's latest horrendous attempts at cooking. She needed to see the robin's-egg-blue sky and the lush rolling green hills and the deep auburn of Cateline's hair.

Nearly in tears, it wasn't until she was splashing

in the waters of the Celtic Sea that she realized she'd just sprinted back to the boat. She was gasping, bent over with her hands on her knees as she desperately tried to fill her lungs with much-needed air. She felt the breeze off the sea on her face and, as it made her cheeks feel cold, she realized that she had been crying.

Panting heavily, Eoin and then Donovan caught up with her. Donovan's face was red from the intense run to try to catch Fallon, Eoin looking at her like she'd lost her mind even as he panted from the exertion.

"Milord?" he gasped, broad chest heaving.

She turned away from him, hands on her hips as she walked off the unexpected run that went for miles, her own lungs still burning. She desperately tried to get her emotions under control but just couldn't. Finally, she looked up into the sky as another day was being birthed in colors of gold, orange, and pink.

She needed to get home.

꒰꒱꒰꒱

Ship finally landed at the Surshan harbor and a horse under her, Fallon pounded her way home. She leaned over the neck of her mount, thighs pressed hard against the breadth of the animal's back as she urged him on faster and faster. Her cloak sailed behind her, as did her hair, as they flew across the land while darkness fell.

Her heart eased, as did her urging of the beast when the torches of Caisleán Thíar came into view. Toirneach rode hard, as if he, too, was happy to be home. Once the war horse was handed off to the stable boy, Fallon took off into the castle.

Pounding up the many stone stairs, she finally

reached the third floor and the family chamber. She felt like a drowning woman who was desperate for land. It was in sight. She nearly cried again when she heard the voices of those who grounded her, stabilized her, made her who she was.

Reaching the chamber door, which stood open, she just stopped. She was out of breath from her desperation to get there. Still in her cloak and muddy boots, she stood and watched. Livia sat at the chessboard with Garratt, both laughing at something one of them had done or said. Laigen sat with her personal servant and best friend, Celine.

The two were looking over swatches of material, no doubt for a new dress for her upcoming gala. They were giggling like little girls, bringing a smile to Fallon's lips just by virtue of knowing Laigen was excited about…something. Her gaze swept toward the fireplace to see Roishin curled up in one of the two matching chairs reading a book. She smiled when she saw her in trousers and that her hair was down.

But then, she saw Cateline. She sat in the matching chair to Roishin's, knitting, her gaze once in a while moving to the hourglass upon the mantel, the sand about to drain as the hour was coming to an end.

It was during one of those glances that she stopped, almost as though she'd heard something. Her gaze slowly moved over to meet Fallon's. Full lips parted just a bit as if in surprise. Without taking her gaze from Fallon's, she set her knitting aside and rose from the chair and walked over to the warrior.

Without a word, Fallon gathered her to her, holding her close as Cateline wrapped her arms around Fallon beneath her cloak. She buried her face in her neck, the two just holding each other.

Chapter Nine

So soft. They were so incredibly soft. Never in her wildest dreams did she think they would be. But, as they pressed against her own, she was getting lost. Her fingers found themselves in long blond hair that was equally as soft as the lips she was kissing. She sighed. So soft...

Her eyes popping open, Roishin breathed hard. She was lying on her back in her bed and was shocked to find herself alone. Well, no. She was alone in the bed, but as she glanced to her right, she saw that she was not alone in the bedchamber. Elsie quietly went about her business, absolutely no idea that mere moments before she'd been on a grassy hillside with her charge, kissing and lightly touching.

Roishin's eyes squeezed closed as her hands slapped down to cover her face. Her stomach was in knots and her body was suffused with all sorts of warm sensations that she didn't understand. She also felt super guilty.

Turning her head, she peeked between her fingers to see Elsie picking up the trail of clothing left behind the previous night. She was as lovely as ever. Her hands fell away from her face and back to the bed as she watched the young woman. She had to wonder if Elsie's lips actually were that soft. She blushed at the mere thought.

Looking away, Roishin's eyes closed as she groaned inwardly. What was wrong with her? Blowing out a breath, she sat up, taking a moment before glancing back over at the young servant who was just turning to look at her.

"Good morrow, milady," Elsie said, her arms full of clothing.

"Good morrow, Elsie. How are you today?" she asked, pushing the covers off her legs.

"I am well, milady. And you?"

"Living the dream," Roishin muttered, slipping her bare feet into warm slippers as the stone floor was awfully cold in the morning, even with rugs laid out everywhere. She walked over to the door of her garderobe, hand on the iron handle for the thick plank door when she turned at her title. "Yes?"

"Will you be wanting help to ready for the gala this eve, milady?" Elsie asked, looking over at her.

Roishin cursed under her breath. Right. Gala. "Aye," she said with a nod, meeting the young woman's eyes. Her gaze fell to the soft-looking lips, which made Roishin blush all over again. Muttering to herself, she turned and entered the small chamber.

It was a narrow stone space with two stone steps up to the thick wood plank with a hole cut out of it. An arrow slit in the stone wall served for ventilation as the user sat upon the plank over the hole and did their business, which would fall into the moat far below.

Stepping up to the seat, Roishin turned and tugged the skirt portion of her sleeping gown up until her nether regions were exposed to relieve her morning bodily needs. She started as the cold seat touched her bare bum. Getting settled, she brought her hands up and covered her face again as her head fell. Dark hair fell like a curtain.

It had been so real, so incredibly vivid. She was so confused. Clearly, her parents were two women who liked to be kissed by another woman, but weren't they the only people in the country that were like that? In all the world? She thought about her sister and brother. Laigen was completely boy-crazy, that much she knew. She *thought* Garratt was into girls, but mostly, he just seemed to be into his work in the Elite Guard.

From what she'd been told and remembered, he'd wanted to be a soldier all his life and had idolized Fallon since he and Laigen had come to live in the castle. Laigen, it seemed, had pretty much liked boys since she knew what a boy was.

And then there was Roishin. The only interest she'd ever had in boys was beating them up or competing against them with her bow. The dream she'd had about Elsie kissing her...she'd never, ever had a dream like that about anyone, certainly not a boy. Nor had she wanted to or wondered about doing such a thing with boys while awake.

It wasn't the only issue. Not only was Roishin a girl, but she was also only twelve. Well, she'd be thirteen in a matter of weeks, now—six of them, to be exact. Elsie was sixteen, and though they were only three or four years apart in age, at this stage, it may as well have been thirty.

As she ran her hands through her mass of hair, she had no idea what any of it meant. She just knew that Elsie made her feel all gooey inside, much like her angel, Enori. Instantly, a smile came to her lips at the thought of her. Then, a frown curved her expression. Maybe she just had a thing for blondes. Older ones.

"I have no idea," she muttered, finishing her business.

❧❧❧❧

Roishin was all gussied up, as was the law for an official event—plus it would have been sororicide had Laigen seen her wander into her big night in trousers and crazy hair. She'd bathed and put on one of her finest dresses. Elsie had been her usual quiet, efficient, helpful self to get her ready. Honestly, Roishin had no idea why she even had to be there. It certainly wasn't *her* looking for a future husband or betrothed.

But alas, she'd been asked to be there, so there she be. In the great hall of the castle, people wandered and mingled. Minstrels entertained with their joyous songs from the gallery above meant just for such a thing. Vast quantities of food were available for consumption, as Millie and her staff in the kitchens had been preparing around the clock for days.

Many, many barrels of wine and ale had been brought in for the event. Roishin stood off to the side by herself watching. Her parents looked wonderful, both in garbs befitting their station as Prince and Princess of Sursha. Fallon looked handsome in her uniquely beautiful way. Cateline, of course, was stunning.

But, Roishin thought, the true belle of this ball was Laigen, as was the point. She was utterly beautiful in the gown she, their mother, and Celine had been working on for weeks. Her hair was styled in an intricate updo, looking much like spun gold atop her head.

Their mother had lent her jewels for the important

event, but even the sparkle of the sapphires upon her neck and ears couldn't compete with those of Laigen's eyes. Roishin hated such gatherings, and she and Laigen butted heads on many a topic, but watching her now, she couldn't be more proud to call the lovely young woman her big sister.

As different of a future as they wanted for themselves, it genuinely made Roishin happy for her sister to have such a special night. Laigen was glowing with the attention of the myriad handsome young princes and noblemen who had journeyed from near and far to see the Beauty of Sursha. She was gracious and kind, talking to any of the men who wanted her ear.

Honestly, Roishin was impressed. Once in a while she heard some of the closer conversations Laigen had as she drifted around the room. She was intelligent, insightful, and not just some vapid princess looking for a wealthy man to take care of her. She asked pointed questions, more than once seeming to throw a young man off guard.

Grinning, Roishin took a sip from the watered-down ale she was nursing. Noting that yet again it looked as if some of the suitors were looking her way, she once again moved. She had no desire to be involved in conversations with young hopefuls that might see her as a consolation prize should Laigen choose otherwise.

"And, where do you think you're going?"

Startled, she turned to see Livia staring at her with a knowing look on her face. Busted. The Advisor to the Prince of Sursha looked stunning, her raven locks in an updo revealing the pale skin of her face and graceful neck. Her equally dark eyes were filled with the little twinkle that always seemed to be in them when speaking to Roishin.

The princess adored Livia, who was far more like an aunt than someone who was part of the royal court. There had always been something about Livia that made Roishin feel both shy and at peace. At peace because she trusted the woman, just a bit younger than her own mother, with her life, but shy because Livia always seemed to see right through whatever little scheme was rolling around in Roishin's overactive brain.

"I was moving my ship out of enemy range," Roishin muttered, eyeing the older woman standing next to her, who burst into laughter. Roishin grinned.

Shaking her head, Livia raised her glass of wine and took a sip. "You, my dear, will either rule the world someday or wander forever."

Roishin raised an eyebrow. "Can't I do both?"

"Oh, *fanciulla*, if there was a way, it would be you that would find it." She playfully nudged Roishin's shoulder with her own.

They were both quiet for a moment as they watched. "Why are you not married, Livia?" Roishin asked, a question she'd always wondered.

The advisor was quiet for a moment before she said softly, "The want for me to ever have a husband was beaten out of me years ago, Roishin."

Roishin looked at her, noting the lovely face— and also the scar that was clearly old but still very noticeable that ran across her left cheek. "Your scar?" Roishin asked.

Livia met her gaze, understanding what Roishin was insinuating with that simple question. "*Si*. It was a bad night."

Roishin wrapped her arm around the other

woman's waist and rested her head against Livia's for a moment. "I'm sorry."

"Don't be." Livia hugged the girl to her. "My heart is with your parents, you and your siblings, and the kingdom and her people. Only love I've ever known."

Roishin smiled. "Well, I for one can say selfishly that I'm glad you're with us."

With a squeeze, Livia released her after Fallon waved her over to join the conversation she was in with the Duke of Rothesay. She raised her glass in acknowledgment before murmuring to Roishin, "Stay out of trouble."

Amused, Roishin simply smiled noncommittally before the older woman left, chuckling. Left alone again, Roishin was about to wander through the large room again to find a new spot to lurk when something caught her eye.

Above the great hall there was a huge balcony-type level that overlooked the goings-on below. It was a place where the entertainment was, as well as where some had wandered to chat amongst themselves. It was up there that Roishin saw just the flash of bright blue. She realized it was the flowing material of a cloak.

Quickly setting her glass down upon the tray of a passing servant, she grabbed the skirts of her dress so she wouldn't trip and hurried toward the stairs. Oh, what she wouldn't do to have her trousers in that moment! She went as fast as her clothing and footwear would allow, reaching the second level and looking around, as the figure had disappeared.

Standing there, she saw that neither the minstrels nor those visiting even noticed her, let alone anyone else. Her head whipped to the right when just on the edge of her vision she spotted movement. Back on the trail, she hurried in that direction, which took her down a second-floor hallway. She passed a corridor that would take her to the servants' area of that floor, which she'd been to before, but was being led down another one she wasn't familiar with.

She thought it led to the wing of the castle that was where the Elite Guard were bunked, but she wasn't entirely sure. Fallon had made it very apparent from day one that the children stay out of these areas. So, one of the few times she'd actually listened, Roishin now found herself to be lost.

The stone corridors all looked the same: large, thick stone blocks made up the walls, ceiling, and floor. Unlike the more traversed hallways of the castle, this one had no rug runner to help with cold and noise. There were also no hanging chandeliers with candles to light the way. Here, there were mounted torches every twenty feet or so, leaving large pockets of shadow.

Unfortunately, in those pockets of shadow were the doors to the soldiers' rooms. Yes, it was a hard and fast rule in the Surshan military: you hurt a woman, you pay dearly. But, as evidenced by Livia's physical scar and the one upon her psyche, it didn't stop all. The soldier who had attacked Livia so long ago had lost his life, but Livia would forever live with that pain and fear.

Roishin felt nervous, very nervous, as she had no idea where she was being led or frankly, why she was following. Perhaps it was a trap? Perhaps it wasn't meant for her at all. She slowed her pace, glancing over her shoulder as she considered heading back. She was nervous enough that she was beginning to miss the comfort of the masses at Laigen's gala.

Chewing on her lower lip, she was about to turn around when she heard footfalls just up ahead. They seemed to belong to someone who had been waiting for her to catch up and now was on the move again. Taking a deep breath, she decided to continue.

The end of the corridor came, giving her two choices: one was a hallway to the right, or a very narrow, winding set of stairs off to the left. The hallway to the right looked exactly like the sparse, torch-lit one she'd just walked down. Her head whipped to the left when she heard footfalls growing distant.

She turned that way and began to climb. Much like the hallways, a torch—now tucked back into a recess in the stone wall, as there wasn't enough clearance for them to jut out—lit the way every ten feet or so. With the winding nature of the stairs, it was impossible to see what was around the bend.

Roishin felt her nerves building with her anxiety, as she felt suffocated in the narrow space with no idea where it led nor who was in there with her. Heart racing, she quickened her steps. No matter where she ended up, she needed to get out of that staircase. She almost couldn't breathe as she couldn't escape the feeling that someone or something was hurrying up behind her, round and round and round they went through the shadows to reach her.

She was almost in tears when she finally reached the top step. With a whimper of relief, she shot out of the staircase and pressed her back to the sturdiness of the stone wall just to the right of the mouth. Her chest was heaving as she desperately tried to catch her breath. Hand to heart, she closed her eyes, taking several deep, slow breaths.

She started, eyes popping open when she heard the squeak of unused hinges as a door was opened. Looking around her, she found that she stood in a rounded area. Initially confused, she realized that she was likely up in the tower. Just to her left was the entrance to the staircase she'd just come out of it, to the right was an iron-ribbed door, and from the smell, she figured was likely the garderobe for the men downstairs.

But, it was the door across the way and just a bit to the left—directly across from the stairs—that caught her attention. It was slightly ajar, almost as if to beckon her forward. Pushing away from the wall, she took one final glance into the dark maw that was the staircase before making her way to the door.

Placing a hand on the cool wood of the thick plank door, she gently pushed. It made the same squeak she'd heard moments before. She poked her head inside to see it was, in fact, a tower room. There was a single bed, though it was just the bedframe, no mattress.

Clearly nobody used the room anymore, so the mattress had likely been removed so pests couldn't nest inside it. There was a set of stairs that went up to a door that was closed. She assumed it led to a walking path among the turrets. She figured this must have once been the bedchamber for a military man, perhaps captain of the guard?

Pushing the door open a bit more, Roishin stepped inside. The room was bitterly cold. With the stone walls, it would either keep the cold in or, if the small, domed fireplace had been lit, no doubt the small, rounded room would have been nice and cozy, the heat bouncing off the face of the stone.

What caught her attention the most, however, was a trunk tucked into a so-called corner. It was a plain, flat top wooden trunk, and the lid was open. Curious, she went over to it. Expecting to find an empty container, cleared out long ago by the last tenant of the room, she was stunned to see that not only wasn't there a bottom to the trunk, there were stairs leading down from the inside of it.

A small bit of firelight flickered just beyond the stairs. Was it finally her guide waiting for her? Heart about to leap into her throat, Roishin carefully lifted her leg and stepped over the edge of the trunk, cursing softly when her dress caught on the edge of the wood box. Picking it free, she raised her other leg until she was standing on the top stair.

Watching her step, she carefully made her way down inside the trunk and down the stone staircase. She realized that the light she'd seen was a single lit candle in a holder set on the floor just beyond the stairs. Reaching the floor, Roishin looked up, still stunned that she'd just stepped through a trunk that was actually a secret door.

Shaking her head, she reached down and grabbed the candle, grateful for the light. She was in a narrow tunnel, stone walls rounding up into the ceiling. A large man, or one that was fully armored, would be brushing his shoulders on either side. She hurried through the long, straight path, dark as death, her little flame only showing the immediate way.

Finally, she reached a door. Grabbing the iron handle, she turned it, wincing at the loud squeak, but it easily turned and the door easily pushed forward. Absolutely no clue where she could possibly be in this maze of a journey, she stepped through the door and gasped. She was completely stunned to find herself in the family chamber.

Closing the door behind her, she saw that it had always been there, hidden behind a large tapestry, which had been pulled up and out of the way of the door, pinned in place. Relieved yet very confused, she looked around, gaze scanning for anything out of place. It was then that she noticed a figure was sitting in one of the two comfortable chairs set before the huge fireplace, which was currently cold and dark.

Swallowing hard, she walked over to the chairs, candle still held in hand. As she reached the occupied seat, the back of it visible to her, she saw a forearm draped along the arm of the chair, a pale hand casually resting upon the rounded wood end.

"I've been waiting for you, Roishin," came the soft, soothing voice that the princess had heard in her dreams her entire life.

Chapter Ten

Gasping, Roishin could only watch as the figure stood from the chair and faced her. The blue cloak was draped over her shoulders, gold stitching glinting in the candlelight, her gown of white just barely be seen beneath it. The draping neckline showed the pale creaminess of her upper chest as well as her throat and neck, revealed below the short hair.

The somewhat wavy blond hair just barely brushed over the tops of her ears and her forehead. Those beautiful eyes that Roishin had seen and thought about so many times looked down at her. In the candlelight they looked gray, but she knew better. She couldn't speak, she was so moved by the actual presence of this woman, her angel.

"Enori," she whispered.

The blonde nodded, the smile upon her beautiful lips soft. "Yes." She reached up and lightly cupped Roishin's cheek. "I told you I'd come."

With tears in her eyes, Roishin looked up into her face. It was the strangest feeling. She felt like she was looking at somebody so familiar to her, almost like a family member that she'd yearned for yet had no idea who they were or why. She felt a longing to be with this woman, to go with her wherever "with her" was, even as her feet wanted to stay planted where they were.

Without saying another word, Enori stepped

forward and wrapped her arms around Roishin. She held her tightly to her, such a gentle touch as she cradled Roishin's head against her chest. She felt a soft pressure against the top of her head, like a kiss.

"Am I going with you?" Roishin asked into the hug, surprised the words had tumbled off her lips.

"No," Enori said softly. "I cannot take you, Roishin."

Roishin was deeply confused by her feelings. She felt profound disappointment yet also profound relief, in equal measure. "Then," she said. "Why are you here?"

Enori pulled out of the hug but didn't release the physical connection. One hand resting on a shoulder, her other lightly caressed Roishin's jaw before it fell away. "To bring you something." She reached inside her cloak and produced a small gold brooch. It was in the shape of the ancient triskelion. "Keep this on you," she said quietly, her gaze boring into Roishin's. "Keep it safe."

Taking it, Roishin noted that it was warm. She held it in her fingers, turning it this way and that, the trio of connected spirals beautiful. Nodding, she looked back to Enori. "I will."

"Good girl." She moved away from her. "I must go."

"Do you have to?" Roishin asked, feeling panic wash through her.

"Yes," Enori said, turning to face her again. "I must." She hesitated just a moment before taking her into another hug. "I'll see you again," she promised. A final squeeze, then she released her. "Walk with me?"

"Aye."

Roishin expected to head to the door of the

chamber but was surprised when the beautiful woman headed for the door from whence they'd come. Neither said anything, nor was Roishin's candle taken with them, but left on the table.

It was strange, she thought. But, as they walked down the passage toward the tower room, she felt so safe with Enori. Again, that strange feeling of familiarity. Yes, Enori had been coming to her for years now, but to her knowledge this was the first time since she'd been but four that she'd seen her in the flesh.

She didn't feel awkward, didn't feel shy. However, when they stopped at the foot of the stairs, she did know that she'd never forget the incredible beauty of this woman. Roishin was taken aback by it, and it was something she *felt*, not just something she saw with her eyes. She didn't understand it nor had time to contemplate it as Enori turned to her once more.

"I must go," she said again. Smiling at Roishin, she lightly touched her cheek before soft fingers fell away. "Be good."

Roishin grinned. "Livia basically said the same thing."

Enori quirked an eyebrow. "Perhaps because Livia knows as I do."

"Knows what?"

Enori's smile was broad. "That *you* are trouble." She tapped the tip of Roishin's nose with a fingertip before she turned and began to climb the stairs.

Roishin watched her go, not sure if she was supposed to follow. As the older woman stepped out of the trunk, she turned and looked down at Roishin. With a small wave, she eased the lid of the trunk closed.

The broach held in her hands, she felt the metal

begin to warm against her fingers. Realizing she had no idea where and how she was supposed to wear it, Roishin shot up the stairs and palmed the underside of the lid, easily pushing it open. Stunned, she saw that the room was empty.

Fully climbing out of it, she nearly stumbled to get to the closed door of the small tower room. Pulling it open...nothing. No footfalls, nothing. She knew, somehow, someway, Enori was gone. And strangely, she felt that part of herself had gone with her.

⁂

There was no way in heck Roishin was going back to the gala the way she'd come to the family chamber. She'd scurried back through the trunk and the passage to the family chamber, blown out the candle, then headed downstairs. Truth be told, she'd wanted to just stay upstairs and go to her bedroom but knew that wasn't an option. As it was, she was worried she'd be missed.

She nearly took a header down the final set of stairs, past the minstrels and talking groups and to the ground floor. So worried the gala would be over or nearly over, she slowed her steps as she looked around. She was utterly confused. As she watched, Livia walked over to Fallon, who stood with the Duke of Rothesay, the two clearly waiting for her to join them.

Looking around, every single person was exactly where she'd remembered them being when she and Livia had finished their conversation. She blew out a long, slow breath, her thumb absently rubbing against the smooth metal of the broach she clutched in her hand. It was like she'd never left.

If she didn't feel the warm, hard metal against her palm, she'd think she'd imagined the whole thing. She glanced to her left to see servants standing in a line against the wall, waiting for the slightest indication that anyone needed anything. The family's personal servants were also helping out for such a large event.

Elsie was standing in that line, and though she faced forward like the rest of them, her eyes were on Roishin. There was something in the blue depths that Roishin couldn't quite read, but it was an interesting expression. She looked away, once again, focused solely on her duty.

❧❧❧❧

The gala had been a roaring success, but Roishin was infinitely glad it was over. She was tired, her feet hurt, her back hurt, and frankly, her brain hurt. She was ready to be away from people and alone. She needed to think.

In her bedchamber, she walked over to the vanity where she'd sit once Elsie arrived, and the servant would unbraid and unwind her hair before brushing it out to a brown, shiny wave. She looked forward to that. She was pretty sure that was part of why her brain hurt, her hair being wound so tight. Such was the pain of beauty, she supposed.

She stood there and looked down at her hands, which held the broach given to her. It didn't have a stick pin as other broaches she'd seen her mother wear had, but instead just a little metal arm that jutted out from the back of the center where the three spirals emerged from. How would it stay on? Perhaps it was meant to go in a pocket?

The door to her bedchamber opened and Elsie appeared. She gave Roishin a polite smile as she always did. "Good eve, milady," she said softly. "Forgive my being a few minutes late. Celine asked me to help her with Lady Laigen's gown."

"It's okay," Roishin said. "I understand." She grinned. "That thing looked pretty complicated."

Elsie gave her a shy smile and a nod. "Aye." She walked over to Roishin at the vanity, her gaze falling to the broach in the girl's hands. She looked into Roishin's eyes, a question in her own. "Did you find that?"

For a moment, Roishin considered lying and saying that yes, she had, but she decided to be honest. "No. 'Twas given to me." She smiled sheepishly. "Though, I have no idea how to wear it." She held it up, showing the strange little stem.

"You trust this person," Elsie asked, gently taking the broach from Roishin's fingers. "Who gave this to you?"

Though the words were in Elsie's usual soft, beautiful voice, the look in her blue eyes was not. It pinned Roishin to the spot. It made her question the gift for a moment, but then she saw Enori's face, her eyes, and her smile. Nodding, she said, "Aye. Why?"

"You were told to wear this?" Elsie asked. "Always?"

At Roishin's nod, Elsie began to explain. "This," she said, "in this form, is meant to bond the giver with the person this is given to, as well as a third. It's an eternal bond."

Roishin swallowed. Hard. Who was the third? She nodded slowly. "All right. How do you wear it?"

Elsie held the broach in the fingers of one hand while those of the other showed that the center part of the little stem could be pushed out so it was parallel to the broach, held fast between the remaining two little posts of the stem. Roishin's eyes widened in surprise.

"How do you know all this?"

Elsie handed Roishin back her broach before she tugged off her tunic, shocking Roishin. Beneath she wore a simple servant's dress. She used deft fingers to unbutton the first few buttons, just enough for her to pull back one side to reveal her chemise beneath. Roishin wasn't sure if she'd combust where she stood from the sudden warmth of her skin, or run. This was especially true when she saw just the barest bit of cleavage in the neckline of the chemise.

Swallowing, she forced her gaze away from that and focused on what she was being shown. Sure enough, a smaller example of the triskelion was pinned to the garment, this one a bit more crude and crafted in silver. Her eyes wide, she looked up into Elsie's.

"Where did you get that?"

"My mam," the young woman said, rebuttoning her dress. "Before she died back in Edinburgh, she gave this to me. For her and me Athair, who died when I was but a girl."

"I'm so sorry, Elsie," Roishin said, wanting to give the young woman before her a hug. For the first time in the years Elsie had been attending her, she saw the young woman and not the young servant. She felt like a horrible human being, as she didn't even know her story or how she'd come to be in Sursha. She intended to find out.

Elsie simply gave her a small smile but said nothing to that. "I can create a tiny hole in your chemise as I have mine," she said. "Give it a border so it won't tear, and you can place this there." She placed a warm hand over that of Roishin's that held the broach. "These are to be personal, protected, not for display or decoration."

Roishin nodded. "All right. Thank you."

"But," Elsie said, not removing her hand and looking deeply into Roishin's eyes. "Know this, Roishin."

Stunned, as she'd never heard her name spoken by Elsie before, she gave the young woman her full attention.

"Once you put this on, you have accepted this bond." She paused, almost as if wanting to make sure the princess understood. "It cannot be broken," she added, shaking her head. "Until and unless whomever gave this to you breaks it."

The hand was removed and Roishin looked at the gold object in her hand. "What does that mean?"

"It means your soul is connected. It can be a wonderful thing, because you always feel that person." Elsie's smile was beautiful, but sad. "I can always feel my Mam. But," she added, warning in her tone. "If it's a bad person, they can influence you, affect you."

Roishin nodded in understanding. "Can I influence or affect them, too?"

An amused expression quirked Elsie's lips. "I suppose." She met Roishin's eyes. "Just be sure."

Roishin turned the object round and round in her fingers as she chewed on her bottom lip. Finally, she nodded, looking to the young woman. "I'm sure."

Elsie nodded. "Then I shall work on your garments on the morrow."

❧❧❧❧

The next morning, Roishin awoke from a deep sleep. Eyes opening and her body curled up on its right side, she was pretty sure she hadn't moved all night, as that was the position she remembered last. And, from the ache in her hip and back, she assumed that her body wasn't thrilled at not moving.

Letting out a little groan as she rolled to her back, she noticed that, as usual, Elsie was already there, but this morning she was seated at Roishin's desk, needle and thread in hand and one of Roishin's chemises in her lap. Saying nothing, Roishin watched her for a long moment. The moments from the previous night came back to her, after the gala.

Again, she saw Elsie's kindness and understanding. Roishin liked the young woman just because of what she knew of her, and certainly thought she was so beautiful, but until last night she didn't feel she'd ever truly seen the true heart of the person inside the dutiful, efficient servant.

"Elsie?"

The blonde's head popped up, surprise on her face. Clearly, she hadn't realized Roishin had awakened. "Good morrow, milady," she said quickly, about to set her task aside. "My apologies. I was trying to get this finished before you awoke—"

"It's okay." Roishin smiled and held up a hand in supplication. "Truly. Please," she added. "Continue. I'm fine."

Seeming a bit relieved, Elsie nodded and turned back to her sewing. Roishin watched her for a bit, noting her hands as they worked. They looked to be strong hands, no doubt as Elsie worked very hard in her day, but there was a delicate beauty to them, too. She wondered if they were soft. She knew they were warm, from the very brief touch the night before on her own hands as she'd held the broach.

"Elsie?"

"Yes, milady?"

"Can I ask you a question?"

"Aye, milady." Elsie glanced over at her before returning her visual attention back to her task.

"If you were born in Scotland, how did you end up in Sursha?"

Taking a long breath, Elsie shrugged a shoulder and then said, "Long ago, me Athair fought alongside His Highness, your Athair." She spared a glance to Roishin, who still sat in bed. "Me mam had begun to get sick, so he asked His Highness to make sure I was taken care of, should anything happen." Her smile was small. "Imagine my surprise when four years ago, after Mam died, the Prince of Sursha shows up."

Tears gathered in Roishin's eyes. "Daidí went and got you?" she asked softly.

Elsie nodded, glancing at her. "He did." Her smile grew a bit. "I was so confused. Mam had died and I honestly thought it was the streets for me." She paused her ministrations on Roishin's chemise. She looked up, her gaze four years lost in the past. "I was so scared," she almost whispered. "Then, this *aingeal*"—she shook her head, looking back to her sewing—"brought me here, and Her Highness was so kind to me." She glanced over at Roishin, an amused smile on her beautiful lips. "Apologized to me before she assigned me to you."

A bark of laughter escaped Roishin's lips. "Rightly so." She grinned, watching her for a moment, admiring her skill. "Do you think you'll stay here?" she asked, pushing the covers off her legs as she figured she should actually get up. "Once your mandatory time is over?"

Elsie didn't respond to the question, seeming to think about her answer. Finally, she looked over at Roishin, who was stepping into her slippers. "I'll do anythin' for your family, milady," she said softly. "They took me in when I had nothing." She smiled sadly. "Not even me mam."

Again, almost moved to tears, Roishin headed to the garderobe as she tried to get her emotions under control before she could speak. Opening the door to the small chamber, she looked over at the servant. "Even put up with me," she murmured. She smiled when she heard a soft chuckle at that.

Chapter Eleven

"Nothing?" Cateline asked, extra cloth draped over her shoulder in case of spit-up. She gently swayed as she patted the back of the baby she held against her shoulder who had just been fed by the wet nurse.

"Nay," Eoin said, standing before his princess with military stiffness and respect. "We've been asking around for weeks, milady. Traveled all over this country."

Cateline nodded. "Do you feel it's futile to continue the search for family for this little one?" she asked, eyeing the longtime soldier and friend to Fallon.

For just a moment, he broke rank and smiled at the infant before that guarded, stoic mask returned. "Aye, milady. I am of the belief the parents weren't Surshan."

"Very well," Cateline said, continuing to burp the baby. "You may suspend your search. Fallon and I shall speak to the king."

With a deep bow, Eoin clicked the heels of his boots together and, when word of his leave was given, he turned on his heel and left the family chamber. Cateline sighed. She was of two minds: profoundly sad that this little one had been orphaned at such a young age, but also profoundly happy to bring in another child into the family—should that be what was decided, of course.

Never in her wildest dreams had she imagined she'd be the mother of one child, let alone four. As she cradled that precious life to her, she couldn't imagine herself doing anything else. If not loving and caring for her wife, her children, those in her employ or those of her country, there was no reason to even be.

Smiling when she got the little burp she was waiting for, Cateline began to rub the warm back with soothing circles, still swaying. She walked over to the fireplace, looking into the flames as she considered what was next for this little one. She didn't even have a name. They hadn't discussed this as a family, because Cateline wanted to make absolutely sure that this child didn't have family out there somewhere.

Anyone, aunts, uncles, cousins, grandparents, whatever. Someone to give this baby the best chance from her own blood. It wasn't to be. She glanced over when she saw Fallon entering the room. She looked tired, out training with the Elite Guard all day.

"My goodness," she said. "I'd hate to see the other guy." She'd had to learn long ago that, unless something was hanging off or had been cut off, the bloodied nose with blood smear across her cheek was just an average day.

Fallon grinned. "Are you going to kiss it and make it better?" she teased. When she only received a quirked eyebrow, she burst into laughter. "Aw, come on baby," she whined.

A saucy little look upon her face, Cateline sauntered over to her and reached up to murmur in Fallon's ear. In French, she made Fallon promises that would never reach the ears of their children, but certainly turned Fallon's a deep shade of blush.

"*Oui*," Fallon murmured, moving behind her to wrap her arms around her waist, thrusting her crotch suggestively against Cateline's behind.

"Get away." Cateline giggled, playfully pushing her wife away from her. She smiled when Fallon moved back up behind her, clearly being careful not to get blood in her hair.

"What's the verdict?" she asked softly.

"No family." Cateline kissed the baby's head as she had fallen asleep resting against Cateline's shoulder. "We have a decision to make."

Fallon nodded. "Let me get cleaned up and we'll talk." Fallon pinched her behind, grinning at Cateline's shocked look. "Hey, can't kiss you right now," she said, indicating her face.

Amused, Cateline gave her a sexy little side-eye before turning away, raising her chin as if uninterested. She smiled at the chuckle she heard as the warrior left the room. Cateline took a seat in one of the chairs by the fire and brought the baby down to cradle in her arms, fully asleep.

Looking at the sleeping face, she used gentle fingertips to touch the impossibly soft skin of the baby's cheek and chin. She was so little. She wondered what the destiny was for this little one. What would the kids say? They knew of her, yes, but there hadn't been any family discussion of any kind.

She knew that, ultimately it was up to her and Fallon, but their children would surely have at least an opinion. "What's your name, little one?" she whispered. She smiled when the baby made a little noise in her sleep, tiny pink tongue poking out for a moment before it was sucked back into her mouth. She wondered if dreams of nursing were afoot.

It had been the strangest thing, starting with Roishin and now with this one. Cateline's own breasts tingled as though in sympathy of a nursing mother. Obviously, she'd not nursed Roishin and wouldn't this one, but her body seemed to not quite realize that at times. Fallon had told her stories over the years of men who had lost a limb or hand or foot in battle and how, even years later, they'd get ghost pains of that missing appendage.

She wondered if that was similar for a mother of an infant, even if not breastfeeding. She glanced up when she saw a freshly washed and changed Fallon enter the chamber. She was devoid of her armor and even her bracers. It was so rare she was without those and it pleased Cateline. She completely understood that her love was a warrior, but at times it was nice to see her relaxed and just...Fallon.

"So," Fallon said, leaning down and giving Cateline a soft belated kiss hello before she plopped down in the matching chair. "What is on your mind, my love?"

"Did you see Eoin?" she asked.

Nodding, Fallon said, "Aye." She studied the sleeping babe for a moment, elbow planted in the arm of the chair and chin resting on a closed palm. "What are your thoughts on finding a local couple, or even within the castle, who'd like to have children but cannot?"

Surprised, Cateline stared at her. It wasn't that it wasn't kind or a bad idea, but it was certainly not what she'd expected her to say. "Well, yes," she stuttered. "We certainly could."

Fallon looked away, her hand opening and fingers stroking her chin. She stared into the flames,

Cateline unable to see her eyes.

"What is it?"

Fallon took a deep breath and spoke but didn't look at her. "I can't lose another one," she murmured, almost as if to herself and not to Cateline's question.

"What do you mean, 'you can't lose another one'?" she asked. "Who have we lost, Fallon?"

Not answering, the warrior glanced over at her, the usual gorgeous violet color darker, almost by an entire shade. "Don't you find it odd?" she asked, voice quiet, hushed tones.

Cateline looked at her. "Find what odd?"

"That this child suddenly appears?"

Cateline studied her wife, confused. "No, why would I?" She looked into those darkened eyes, feeling a bit unsettled. "Fallon, it was a horrible accident. Unfortunately, they do happen."

"Do they?"

"Yes, they do." Not even fully realizing it, she cuddled the baby a bit closer to her chest. "What is wrong?"

"Wrong?" Fallon asked absently. "Nothing is wrong, just simply pointing out a fact of the situation. You see," she said, eyeing Cateline as she sat forward. Knees spread wide, she rested her elbows on them. Pointing a finger at Cateline, she continued. "Who's to say that they didn't make this happen?" She indicated the baby in Cateline's arms. "Make us fall in love with her, too, only to take her." With a crazed look in her eyes, she tapped the side of her head with a finger. "I'm onto them, Cateline."

She could only stare at her, "Have you lost your mind?" she asked, eyebrows furrowed. "Did you get hit hard today, love?"

Fallon popped up from the seat like she was on springs. "I'm serious, Cateline!" She threw her hands up as if frustrated. "Why will nobody listen to me with this?"

"Fallon," Cateline hissed. "The baby is asleep. Lower your voice."

The two were interrupted by the arrival of Mary, an elderly servant woman who had been the main one assigned to the infant. "Milady," she said with a bow and a curtsey. "Milord. Shall I take the baby for a changing and a nap?"

"*Oui.*" Relieved, Cateline walked over to her. "*Merci*, Mary."

The two women carefully exchanged the baby from one set of arms to the other. With another bow, the older woman hurried away. Cateline watched her go, waiting until she knew she was well on her way to the stairs to the second floor before turning back to Fallon.

Walking over to her, she took one of her hands. "What is all this about, Fallon?"

Fallon looked at her with tortured eyes, a bit more of the woman she knew and loved returning to them. "They want to take her away from us, Cateline."

"Who? And, who is this 'they' you speak of?"

Running a hand through her hair, Fallon finally turned to her. "I didn't tell you what happened in Brittany because I didn't want to upset you."

"Upset me?" Cateline said, eyes wide. "And your behavior now is not upsetting?"

Fallon's entire countenance softened. She nodded. "I am sorry." She cupped Cateline's face and left a soft kiss on her lips. "Let's sit."

The couple returned to their seats. Cateline felt

a bit better, but she could still see that Fallon was anxious, though was trying to keep it under control. "When I got there," she began, "I met with Enori."

"The woman who married us," Cateline clarified. "And, who told you of your birthright?"

"Aye."

Nodding, Cateline considered this for a moment, then asked, "She is but one woman. You keep saying 'they.' Who is that? And, who is the 'she' they want back?"

"I believe it's her order, the one she's the priestess of," Fallon explained. "And the 'she' is Roishin."

Cateline felt the blood drain from her face. "So," she whispered, emotion edging her tone. "I was right." She popped up from the chair, hand going to her mouth. "I was right!" She turned on Fallon, who remained seated but had turned to watch her. "The day she was found, I told you, Fallon. I told you somewhere out there was a heartbroken mother missing her—"

"No," Fallon said, also getting to her feet. "That is not what happened, Cateline."

"Then what?" Tears were now welling in her eyes, Cateline feeling her heart begin to race. There was no way she'd lose her child, no way! "It's been twelve, nearly thirteen years, now. She's *our* daughter, Fallon. I don't care if another woman gave birth to her, even if *Enori* gave birth her, she's ours!"

"Aye," Fallon agreed with a nod. "She is." She looked deeply into Cateline's eyes, something unsaid in their violet depths.

This made the princess stop. "What are you not telling me? Is Enori her birth mother?" she asked, voice a whisper. From what Fallon had said over the years regarding the mysterious priestess, it would almost make sense, considering what they were learning about their youngest child.

Fallon shook her head. "No." She took Cateline by the arms, her touch not unkind, but firm. "Look at her, Cateline," she said. "Look at that child and tell me what you see."

The princess met her wife's eyes, her own filled with the anguish she felt at the fear growing in her heart. "I know every hair on her head, every feature on her face," she whispered. "Her every freckle, her every expression."

"Like you know your own face?" Fallon asked quietly, eyebrow raised. "Or," she added. "Like I know mine?"

Cateline's lips were open to say something else, but at those cryptic words, her mouth shut with an audible click of her teeth. Fallon's words and the meaning, so much more than simply their face value, hung in the air, heavy and pregnant with meaning.

"Are you saying that she is made of us?" At Fallon's nod, Cateline shook her head. "That is not possible, Fallon."

"Any more possible than what Roishin did with that child?" Fallon asked, nodding in the direction Mary had taken the infant moments before.

Hands clasped in front of her mouth prayer-style and eyes wide, Cateline stared at the warrior for a long time. She had no idea what to say, couldn't even wrap her mind around what was being intimated.

"And," she finally managed. "They want her back."

Fallon nodded. "Aye."

"And, you believe that baby, the very one that Roishin...*saved*," she said, not entirely sure what word to even use. "Was also sent by them?"

Fallon looked at her strangely. "What?" She shook her head. "Perhaps, I don't know."

Confused, Cateline stared at her. "That's what you said, what you were ranting about."

Fallon shook her head, turning away as she ran her hand through long, dark hair again. "I don't know, my love," she muttered.

"Who are 'they,' Fallon?" she asked, deciding to let Fallon's reaction go. "Enori, but who else?"

Fallon looked at her. "Roishin's father."

"And, who is that? Another member of Enori's order?"

Fallon shook her head, hands on hips as she turned to face the princess. "No. Well..." She smirked. "In a way, I suppose. According to Enori, Roishin's father is Ankou."

"Wait," Cateline said, trying to pull from her memory banks where she knew that name. "Your mother." She took a few steps closer to Fallon, who remained standing by the chairs they'd abandoned. "You said Enori told you that your mother was of the Order of Ankou."

"Aye."

"And, what is that? What is Ankou?"

Fallon smirked. "Not a what, but a who. Ankou is their God of Death and the Underworld."

Cateline looked to the fire, letting the words mull in her mind, fermenting into the understanding of an idea. "So," she finally said. "If her father, creator, whatever or however, is the God of Death..." She glanced over at Fallon, who was already watching her. "Then, doesn't it stand to reason that she'd have the gift of life?"

Fallon gaped at her, looking as though she'd been struck. "You're all right with this?" she said. "You're all right with them taking *our* daughter? The very gift they bestowed upon us?"

"Of course not," Cateline said gently, walking over to her. She placed her hands on Fallon's upper chest. "I'll never let Roishin go anywhere, Fallon. She *is* our daughter and always will be."

"But…"

Cateline shook her head. "No. It's not a matter of either/or. Our daughter clearly has a gift, Fallon. She's blessed with something you and I can never understand."

Able to see just how upset by all this Fallon was, Cateline's voice softened. She cupped her tanned face.

"You and I are good parents," she continued with absolute conviction. "We love our children, we give them all the things you and I never received, both our mothers dying so young and our fathers far too preoccupied with politics or running a country to be there."

"You think we should give her up, then?" Fallon whispered.

Cateline shook her head. "But I do wonder if she needs time with those who understand her gift. Those who can teach her." She smiled. "Perhaps, those who *gave* her that gift."

Fallon rested her hands on Cateline's hips as she rested their foreheads together. "I've lost so many in my life," she whispered. "My mamaí, Ailfred, Burke." She pulled back just enough to look into Cateline's face. "I almost lost you."

"I know, *ma chérie*," Cateline responded softly. "But I am still here, your wife, the other mother of your children, and your champion." She met and held Fallon's gaze. "I don't want to lose our daughter, my love." She left a soft kiss to even softer lips to emphasize her point. "But I worry we may lose her if we do not let her figure out who she is."

"Do you think she's in danger?" Fallon asked, her hands on shapely hips, urging Cateline closer.

"Right now?" Cateline asked, moving until their bodies were flush. "No. But is it possible, as she gets older and maybe even stronger in her gift?" She nodded her head. "*Oui.* You are the greatest warrior that the Surshans have ever known, Fallon." She snaked her arms up until her hands rested at the back of Fallon's neck. "However, this is something you are not prepared to fight. You do not have the understanding or weapons."

Fallon stiffened. "Enori said something similar to me," she said, voice low and hard.

"No," Cateline said when Fallon tried to move away from her. "No." She held tight. She looked deeply into Fallon's penetrating gaze. "You and I, Fallon," she said. "We *will* fight for Roishin, but," she added. "What we will fight for is her happiness." She smiled. "You of anyone understand what I'm about to say. She deserves to be *whole*." She studied Fallon's face to make sure she was listening and wasn't beginning to get stubborn and tune her out. "Whatever that takes, we will help her."

Chapter Twelve

Cateline started, eyes opening. She was lying on her back, the underside of the elaborate canopy meeting her gaze. Turning her head, she saw Fallon asleep next to her, her breathing deep and even. Smiling, the princess wasn't entirely surprised at her deep slumber. They'd had quite the active night, and in fact, as she took inventory of her body, she was sore.

Looking back to the underside of the canopy again, she wondered why on earth she was awake. She was tired, but yet, there she lay. She didn't need to use the privy. About to turn to her side to try to go back to sleep, she stopped. Raising her head, she listened. She swore she heard a baby crying.

Glancing over to Fallon again and seeing she was still asleep, she decided to slip out of bed. Perhaps Mary was bringing the baby to their bedchamber. It wouldn't do for her to answer the door naked for certain, and certainly not for Fallon to be seen. So, she climbed out of bed as quietly as she could and pulled on a night dress and robe, which she belted as she slipped her feet into slippers.

She glanced to the door, waiting for the knock that never came. Confused, she walked over to the chamber door and inched it open to peek out into the passageway. Empty, from what she could see. Her head whipped to the right, looking down that way. She heard it again. Opening the door just enough to slip through, she clicked it quietly closed behind her and headed in that direction.

The long hallway was quiet, lit sconces showing the way down past the family chamber door, the door to Fiona's room as lady-in-waiting, and finally to the stairs. At the top of the stone staircase, she stopped and listened. She was pretty sure she'd likely dreamt it when she heard it again. Very faint, but she heard it.

Worried that maybe Mary hadn't awoken from the baby's cries, Cateline lifted the skirts of both robe and sleep dress as she hurried down the stairs to the second floor. One direction would take her to the bedrooms of her children, the other toward the servants' quarters and the area Eoin's men inhabited.

She headed toward the servants' wing, as that was where Mary and the wet nurse were currently settled with the baby. A final decision still hadn't been made on that, as they were waiting for Garratt to return to the country to sit for a family discussion. As she got closer to the servants' quarters, she listened.

Nothing. She heard absolutely nothing. Well, certainly not a baby crying, anyway. Walking to the small bedroom Mary was sharing with the baby, she listened. Quiet. Deciding to peek in anyway, she quietly pushed the door open and looked inside. Mary was sound asleep in the narrow bed, and it looked like the baby was fine, too, as she slept peacefully.

Not wanting to wake the elderly woman, she softly closed the door. Heading out of the servants' wing, she decided to check on Roishin and Laigen, since she was there. The king would be arriving in three days to discuss Laigen's choice after the gala. Apparently, she'd narrowed it down to three—and Cateline had no idea which three.

The plan was for whomever she chose from those three to stay at Caisleán Thíar for a fortnight or two. This way, the young man and Laigen could get to know each other—and Fallon and the king would, no doubt, grill him endlessly. Yes, they absolutely wanted a good match for Laigen, but they needed him to be a good match for Sursha, as well.

Sadly, politics always had to be part of any match for a royal child. Cateline just flat refused to sell her daughter's soul for the sake of politics. She'd never, ever do to Laigen or Roishin—or Garratt, for that matter—what had been done to her and her sisters. Granted, her marriage to Fergus had been a ruse, unbeknownst to the prince and herself at the time, but it had still been horrible and a nightmare.

Her nightmare was able to end as she truly did get her knight in shining armor, but for most women that was not the case. She'd lock Laigen in the tower before she'd force her into a marriage of abuse and endless unhappiness and loneliness. And then, she thought with an amused smile, there was Roishin. She stopped at the bedchamber door of her youngest.

All was quiet. She turned the knob and quietly pushed the door open. Instantly she smiled, as the girl was sound asleep. Cateline stepped inside the room, closing the door behind her. She rolled her eyes in quiet exasperation at the trail of clothing around the room. She considered picking it up and at least putting it into a pile but didn't want to awaken Roishin. She would, however, speak to her about it tomorrow.

Instead, she walked over to the bed and leaned over to place a kiss on her sleeping daughter's forehead as she brushed some dark hair behind an ear. After what Fallon had told her the previous day, she'd had a tremendous amount of information to absorb and consider. Now, looking into that precious face, the face of a soon-to-be woman, she absolutely saw that Fallon's words were true.

She didn't understand it, and a huge part of her still wanted to deny such a crazy notion, but looking into that beautiful young face, it was so obvious. She saw Fallon in her expressions, the shape of her beautiful lips. She saw her own eyes, just the deep green of Fallon's mother. They were the same shape, as well as Cateline's smattering of freckles and her more petit frame.

She wondered if that would stay as she continued to develop womanly curves, of which Cateline noted her breasts were beginning to grow. She'd been noticing over the last few months many subtle changes in the girl, all adding up to what was to come. She'd be thirteen in a short time, and no doubt her bleed would follow, if not start before. Cateline had been twelve, Laigen not quite twelve.

She was also amazed that Roishin's hair was the same, deep, rich color as Fallon's. How was this possible? She wanted to close her eyes and plug her ears and ignore Fallon's words, but she could not. What did all this mean for them? For Roishin? Leaving one more kiss, she left the room, closing the door softly behind her.

Moving on to Laigen's door, she stopped. Again, she heard the baby's cry. Looking over her shoulder, she heard nothing. It was the strangest thing. It was like an elusive sound when she wasn't looking, but as soon as she was, it stopped. Like a shy bird, singing upon its branch unless looked upon.

Her hand on Laigen's doorknob, she suddenly

felt an intense need to check on the baby again. Her hand fell away from the knob and, as if in a dream, she slowly made her way back down the passage toward the servants' quarters. She heard it again. Quickening her steps, she felt almost panicked as though she had to reach the baby or something bad would happen.

Heart racing, Cateline was nearly in tears as the mother in her felt desperate. Her robe and gown floated behind her in her haste. Her chest was heaving, breasts aching. Her baby needed her. She needed her!

She reached Mary's room and her head whipped to the right. No, her baby wasn't crying inside that room. She was crying from down that hall. Moving away from the closed door, she hurried down the adjacent hall where more closed doors stood like soldiers at attention to line her way.

I'm coming! She reached the end of the hall, only to be presented with two options: keep going straight or turn left. She listened, straining to hear her baby. Which way? *Which way!*

Crying out in surprise, Cateline whipped around when she was touched. Hand clutching her robe tighter together, she was stunned to come face-to-face with Elsie. The beautiful young woman was also in her sleep gown and robe. Her long, blond hair was loose around her shoulders and down her back.

"Milady," she said softly. Her touch on Cateline's arm was so gentle, as was this lovely young woman's very soul, it seemed. Honestly, why had she assigned her to Roishin? Very little seemed to rattle the ever-present calm Elsie seemed to possess. Apparently, not even her precocious second daughter.

"Elsie," Cateline gasped out, her head aching even as she felt lightheaded. Almost as though she were in a fog, or coming out of one, she didn't feel herself at all.

"May I escort you back to your chambers, Your Highness?" Elsie asked softly.

No, that's unnecessary, she wanted to respond. But the words wouldn't come. In fact, it was almost like she couldn't form the words in her head, let alone on her tongue and lips. She looked into the pools of infinite patience that were Elsie's blue eyes.

"Come." She took Cateline's arm in her warm hands.

Saying nothing, the princess allowed herself to be led back to the stairs and up them. Elsie also said nothing, but her calm, quiet presence made Cateline feel better. The farther they got from the second floor, the clearer her head was becoming, though the horrible headache persisted.

At one point, Cateline had to stop. She leaned back against the cold, stone wall. Her eyes closed and her hand went to her chest.

"Are you all right, milady?" Elsie asked. "Shall I get His Highness?"

"No," Cateline said, waving off the offer with a small smile, shaking her head. She opened her eyes and studied the young woman who stood before her.

As she looked on, Elsie's nightdress and robe began to fade away, replaced by a wedding gown. The golden waves that hung over one shoulder were suddenly in an intricate updo, a bridal veil covering her face. She looked older, perhaps in her twenties. Though she looked absolutely beautiful, the sapphire-blue eyes were filled with sadness, almost an air of grief hovering around her. Moments later, the young woman dissolved into tears.

Gasping, Cateline's eyes widened and her mouth fell open. As quickly as it had come, it all disappeared, leaving the sixteen-year-old standing there before her, concern in her eyes.

"What is it, milady?" Elsie asked, looking behind her only to look back to the princess in confusion.

Cateline couldn't speak. She tried, her mouth opening and closing several times, but she was too stunned. Elsie gathered Cateline's hands in her own and looked at the princess. The air between them changed, no longer that of beloved servant and princess, but more of a frightened child and wise, comforting mother.

"There are times," Elsie said softly, looking deeply into Cateline's eyes. "Times when things do not make sense. Then," she added, "there are times when you see them with such clarity, it's beyond your understanding in the moment." She smiled, lightly squeezing Cateline's fingers. "Understanding will come."

Cateline felt herself calming, Elsie's soft words and her very presence almost like a warm hug. Nodding, she whispered, "Thank you, Elsie."

The young woman nodded. "Are you ready to go back to bed now, milady?"

At Cateline's nod, the two continued on their way once more.

꙲꙲꙲꙲

Stepping out of her boudoir after picking out the dress Fiona would be helping her with in just a bit, Cateline saw that Fallon was about to don her false torso. Before she did, she wanted one more hug from the woman.

Stepping over to her, she touched her hand, which had just reached out for the leather armor, moved from the locked trunk to the bed. Fallon glanced over at her, standing there in nothing more than her brown leather trousers, which fit her entirely too well. She grazed her fingers along a shapely behind before moving to stand in front of the warrior.

"Good morrow, milady," Fallon murmured. Cateline grinned up at her. "Good morrow, milord," she responded, a teasing emphasis on the masculine, considering their previous evening's activities.

Fallon chuckled, her hands going to Cateline's hips and pulling them into her own. "I think perhaps one of these days soon I should dress 'prepared' and surprise the fair Princess Cateline with a little unexpected afternoon delight."

Cateline's eyebrows shot up, her entire body suffused with warmth at the idea. "I believe you should," she nearly purred, sparing a glance up into Fallon's eyes as her fingers lightly trailed around the gorgeous bare breasts before her. "We'll just have to make sure the Prince of Sursha doesn't find out."

Fallon's eyes became hooded as Cateline lightly brushed her fingernails over the tips of hard nipples. "I can take him," she murmured, making Cateline chuckle.

"The same way you took me last eve?" Cateline challenged, Fallon's bark of laughter infectious.

"Not exactly." She cupped Cateline's face in gentle hands as she left a soft kiss on her lips. "I love you," she whispered against them.

"And, I love you, my warrior," Cateline murmured back. It didn't matter how many years removed from the Elite Guard Fallon was. To the princess, she knew it would always be a huge part of who Fallon was at heart, and she respected and adored her for it.

They fell into an easy kiss, Cateline's hands snaking up into long, dark hair, yet to be braided. No matter how old she got or how many years they were married, she'd never tire of Fallon's lips and tongue. She'd never tire of her hands and the way they touched her. It amazed Cateline how those hands could soothe, comfort, and excite her in equal measure.

After many sigh-filled moments, the kiss came to a natural end. They both knew they had a day to start. Fallon rested her forehead against Cateline's as they caught their respective breaths. Using the gentlest touch of her knuckles along the princess's cheek, she spoke.

"I have meetings all day with Livia and the other advisors." She left a final kiss to Cateline's lips before moving away from her so they could get her cuirass on and her dressed before Fiona arrived.

"All right," Cateline said, waiting for Fallon to put the leather pieces in place so Cateline could skillfully tie the whole contraption in place by the leather laces.

She remembered the first time she'd asked Fallon if she could help her. They'd been married but a few months, and though by that point they'd made love a million times, Fallon had still been a bit hesitant. It seemed she was unsure of how much Cateline truly accepted the role she was forced to play outside the bedroom. Being that the princess clearly was attracted to women, was she repulsed by this "prince" that the public knew.

Fallon had been trembling the entire time Cateline helped her with the false torso, so much so they'd had to untie the laces and start over so the hardened leather fit her as it was intended to do. It had taken a lot of kisses and touches and a ton of trust on Fallon's part, but eventually she'd come to understand that her wife wanting to do that for her was her wanting to truly love and support every aspect of her.

Over time, it became something they often did together, such as currently. As Cateline worked, her night came back to her, as well as what had transpired *after* their time together. Some of it admittedly was fuzzy in her brain, but she had a general idea of what had happened. She'd boiled the strange night down to her heart finding a creative way to let her know what she truly wanted.

"Fallon?" she said softly.

"Yes, my love?"

"I want us to take in the baby," she said, sparing a shy glance up into Fallon's eyes before returning her focus back to what she was doing. "I know we discussed this, decided on talking to the children, all of that. But," she added with a small shrug. "I feel it's what we're supposed to do."

Fallon didn't say anything for a long moment, so long Cateline worried she was going to argue against this. Yes, they'd make the decision together, but Fallon had a right to her feelings as well. She was concerned that Fallon didn't want this child, or more aptly, *another* child. If she was dead set against this, Cateline had no right to push her into it.

Finally, Fallon nodded. "All right," she said quietly. "If this is what you really want, Cateline, all right."

Keeping her excitement under wraps, Cateline looked into Fallon's eyes, needing to truly read her. She saw concern in the violet depths, but not disinterest. "*Mon amour*," she said softly, cupping Fallon's strong, proud jaw. "This child will not be taken from us." She caressed the soft, tanned skin there with her thumb. "You can love her."

Fallon's smile was small. "You know me all too well, Cateline." She sighed, looking down for a moment. Eventually she nodded, meeting Cateline's hopeful gaze again. "All right." She smiled, the uncertainty in her eyes clearing just a bit. "I'll speak to my father when he arrives about drawing up papers to make it legal. I'm sure it will be a perfect complement to vetting Laigen's choice in suitors."

Cateline hugged the warrior to her, crushing their bodies together. She knew at this point that Fallon was largely doing this for her, but she also knew in her heart that soon enough, Fallon would once again be wrapped around a tiny finger.

Chapter Thirteen

Maybe they were doing the right thing, she thought. She was chewing on her bottom lip and feeling antsy, struggling to stand still. She forced herself to focus, which as a warrior was one of her biggest strengths, damn it! She quietly cleared her throat and clasped her hands behind her back.

"Hello, little Isabeau," Carthac murmured. The four-month-old was so tiny in his large hands and thick arms. The smile on his face and in his eyes made Fallon almost tear up. "You are so beautiful." He leaned down and left a soft kiss on her forehead. She looked up at him with wide, dark blue eyes.

Fallon's arm automatically draped over Cateline's shoulders when she felt her smaller wife lean against her. Admittedly, Fallon was touched as she saw tears in her father's eyes.

"You know," he said, never taking his eyes off the little miracle in his arms. "You were taken away from everything you knew." His gaze flicked over to Cateline. "Not only your country, but your blood. You were ripped away from it all and brought here." He looked back down to the baby. "So, to have little Isabeau in my arms, so named after your own mother." His smile to her was broad and loving. "It makes me so happy."

"I feel the same," Fallon said, resting her head against that which rested against her shoulder.

King Carthac left another kiss on the child's forehead, then looked at the couple. "I could not be more proud than if she'd been born of either of you."

Fallon heard the words, but she searched her father's eyes, searched his expression and body language. She needed to make sure this was the case. Her gaze fell to his hands, his arms. Was he holding her safely? Was he being gentle?

"*Merci*, Daidí," Cateline said, moving away from Fallon and stepping over to Carthac and the baby, now legally theirs.

Fallon watched as she kissed her father's cheek. The two exchanged a look of the genuine affection that had been there since nearly day one. Looking at the two of them, now both looking down at the baby, talking amongst themselves, it could almost be *their* baby. They were talking quietly. Why? What were they saying?

Feeling incredibly uncomfortable, Fallon cleared her throat. She was feeling antsy again, needing to move. She almost felt like she could go one-on-one with the best warrior in the military right now. She had that much energy running through her that she was desperately trying to contain.

Bringing up a hand, she ran it along the back of her neck, noting how hot the skin was. She took several deep breaths, trying to ease her nerves. She gave a side glance to the two, noting they were laughing about something. Big laughs, all smiles as they looked at the baby, then at each other.

Hand flopped down from her neck to her side, Fallon began to rock on her heels. Like a fever, heat radiated from her neck and flowed down through her body like a little slow-moving wave. The restlessness was turning to irritation as she watched the two with the baby. Cateline had moved in closer to Carthac so they could look down at the baby together. They were still smiling. Why were they smiling?

Blowing out a breath, she turned away and wandered off toward the huge stone fireplace. Her gaze moved to the door, knowing that just beyond was a long hallway that she could run down, then down three flights of stairs and out into the warm day. Toirneach wasn't far. They could ride, they could be free. They could—

"Fallon!"

"What?" she growled, whirling around.

A very startled-looking Cateline looked back at her as she cradled little Isabeau to her chest and an irritated-looking Carthac stared at her, and Fallon suddenly felt very stupid. Looking away for a moment, she swallowed and ran a hand through her hair. Turning back, she gave them both an apologetic smile.

"Sorry. What, Daidí?"

"Not me," he growled. "Your *wife*."

Fallon looked to Cateline, who was staring at her with wide eyes. She rubbed her neck again, but this time it was because she knew she'd upset Cateline, and nothing made her feel more nervous and antsy than that.

"Sorry, my love," she muttered. "What is it?"

☙ ☙ ❧ ❧

Back propped against stacked pillows on the bed, Fallon held Isabeau cradled in her left arm while her right hand held the small, clay bottle with an infant-sized opening as the baby suckled her fill of goat's milk for dinner.

"Fallon?"

"Hmm?" the warrior murmured as she watched in wonder as the baby looked back up at her.

"I want you to see the castle physician."

Fallon glanced up at Cateline, who was sitting in a chair by the fire in her sleep dress as she fixed a small tear in one of Fallon's tunics with needle and thread. "What? Why?"

"I'm concerned that you were possibly hit on the head harder than you realized that day while sparring with Eoin's men."

"My love," Fallon said with a small smile. "I'm fine."

"I disagree." She met and held Fallon's gaze, the depths of those gorgeous gray-blue eyes stormy.

Isabeau coughed, Fallon's gaze falling to see what was wrong. The baby turned her head, denoting she was finished, Fallon eased the clay jar up and away from tiny lips to set aside. She raised the infant to rest against her shoulder as she began to gently burp her.

"How did she do?" Cateline asked.

"She did well," Fallon said, nodding over to the bottle. "Almost finished it." She hoped happy baby news would detour Cateline's line of thinking, but Fallon should have known better.

"You've not been yourself," the princess said. "Not all the time, but there have been times that you've been moody at best and downright frightening at worst." She grabbed a small pair of scissors to snip the end of the thread as she finished her mending. "I've never seen you as disrespectful to your father as you were today, Fallon." Her hard gaze caught

Fallon's again. "Frankly, there were times I felt Fergus was standing in that chamber with us, not you."

Fallon instantly felt anger slither through her but knew in that particular moment she had to absolutely tamp it down. For one, she was holding a very small human, and she knew her princess would rip Fallon limb from limb if she dare hurt her, even if accidentally. And for two, that very same hot-blooded princess was calling her out on this exact behavior.

Looking down at what she was doing for a moment, Fallon took several deep breaths, trying to tame this tiger inside that kept poking its head up. She had no idea why, and if she was honest with herself, which she didn't want to be, it was concerning her as well.

Far too often she'd looked at Cateline only to see a stunned expression on her face, or a look of disapproval at something Fallon had done or said. She knew Cateline probably better than anyone, and her loving and accepting nature was hard to truly rile up. So, for her to be saying this now, or reacting in the way she had been, something must be wrong.

What was beginning to worry Fallon the most, however, was that so often she had no memory of what she'd done or said that was upsetting her wife.

"Fallon?"

Gaze sweeping up to meet the penetrating one of the princess, finally Fallon nodded. "Aye. I'll go."

Cateline set aside the tunic and her mending materials before pushing up from the chair. She walked over to the bed and climbed on. She continued until she was straddling Fallon's thighs, leaving room for the baby between them, whom Fallon was still burping. A soft smile on her beautiful lips, Cateline ran her fingers over the baby's head, brown hair coming in.

"She's so beautiful," she said softly.

Fallon nodded, though her gaze was on Cateline. "Yes," she agreed. "She is."

Cateline met her gaze, a slow smile growing on her lips. "Flirt."

Fallon chuckled. "I have been accused of this, yes."

The smile fell from Cateline's lips, her expression filled more with sadness. "Are you happy?"

Completely taken aback by the question, Fallon stared at her. "Of course I am. Why would you ask such a thing?"

"Because," Cateline murmured, her fingers leaving the baby's head to lightly trace down Fallon's cheek. "I've sensed discontentment in you of late, or perhaps a restlessness is more accurate." She looked down at Fallon's shirt, her fingers playing with the material as she continued, her voice soft. "It's not all the time, as I said earlier. But it's there." She shrugged a shoulder, her gaze shyly meeting Fallon's again. "Even with Isabeau. Your reticence, almost blatant disinterest."

Fallon's heart was absolutely broken by the pain she saw in her wife's face and heard in her voice. She said nothing, as she sensed there was more to be said.

"Before we even knew we were to marry, when Fergus was still alive and my husband," Cateline continued, that same soft, haunting tone to her voice. "We were blessed with Laigen and Garratt coming into our lives. Even Livia." The smile that graced her lips was so beautiful. "Then Roishin came along." She looked at Fallon. "You were so present, the woman that I fell in love with almost instantly upon seeing you at my father's estate back in France."

Fallon nodded, letting her know she was listening and fully focused on every word.

"I know being a warrior is your soul, Fallon," Cateline continued. "It's who you've always been, always will be. But for obvious reasons, you've had to cut back more and more over the last ten years as your duties have grown for the country, sitting as her prince and heir to the throne. I need to know," she said, voice growing a bit in strength. "Now that military service is over, that part of your life, is our family, our children"—she placed her hand on Isabeau's back—"still where your heart is? I cannot deal with feeling unloved or unwanted ever again."

Tears instantly stung at Fallon's eyes, to know that, even unwittingly, she'd made the woman who held her very soul feel anywhere even in the neighborhood of unwanted or unloved. Nothing could be further from the truth, and she hated herself for it. Still burping the baby, there wasn't a ton she could do in that moment, but as soon as the baby was down, she intended to make it clear just how deeply she both loved *and* wanted the princess.

"Come here," she whispered.

Cateline leaned in tentatively, but Fallon used her lips to bring her in closer, to show her, as much as she could without use of her hands, just how she felt. Cateline responded after a moment, her fingers just moving to Fallon's hair when they were interrupted by a little burp from Isabeau. They both smiled into the kiss before parting.

"Good girl, sweet Isabeau," Fallon murmured to the infant. She looked to Cateline. "What say you we get her changed and in bed?" The look she gave

Cateline let the princess know she had plans for them after.

Looking deeply into Fallon's eyes, Cateline seemed uncertain for a moment before she simply nodded. They worked together to get the baby's diaper changed and the soiled one removed by a servant before she was lovingly tucked into the beautiful and ornate cradle Carthac had commissioned for Roishin upon her birth. It was canopied with filmy curtains that could be released on all four sides, as they did this night.

Isabeau asleep and kissed good night, Fallon looked to Cateline. She said nothing as she took her by the hand and walked across the space to the bed. It was a very similar bed to the one Cateline had first slept in upon her arrival at Carthac's castle in Sursha all those years ago, the one in which Fallon had taken her virginity in order to appease the nobles that the marriage with Fergus had, in fact, been consummated.

It was that very act which had lost the warrior's heart, stolen by a princess who had yet to give it back. As she undressed her princess, someday to be her queen, she needed Cateline to know this. Naked, Cateline climbed back under the covers while Fallon headed to her personal trunk that she kept near the foot of their marriage bed. She dug until she found what she was looking for. Closing the trunk, she set the apparatus atop its lid before undressing and then buckling herself into the contraption.

It amused her that once upon a time this had been part of her daily wardrobe to one point or another. Even the flaccid phallus she no longer wore with regularity. For one, she no longer needed to be out in the field with her men for days, weeks, or months at a time, and for two, she now wore a tunic that covered her crotch, so it mattered not how "filled out" her trousers were.

Walking back over to the bed, she saw that Cateline was watching her progress. The gorgeous woman was lying on her back, looking for all the world like the Goddess of Sensuality come to life. Her long, auburn hair was splayed out around her head like a halo of fire while the pale creaminess of her skin beckoned to Fallon like a siren's song.

Climbing onto the bed, she scooted over to lie on her side next to the most beautiful woman she'd ever seen in all her travels across the globe. She kissed her again as her hand caressed the softness of Cateline's side, down over her hip before moving back up along her side and finally to cup her breast.

Cateline sighed into their kiss, her back arching just a bit in silent invitation, one which Fallon gladly accepted. She ran a callused palm in a slow circle over the very tip of that rigid nipple, eliciting a sensual sigh into their kiss. Fallon made love to Cateline's mouth just as her fingers began to make love to her breast, loving how responsive she was to her touch. Fallon may not fully understand what was happening with herself lately, but she was determined to nip it in the bud now to salve Cateline's hurt or worried feelings. She'd fall on her own sword before intentionally hurting her.

Never breaking the kiss, she moved to lie atop Cateline, who accepted her with open arms and spreading thighs. Fallon rested the phallus against Cateline's wetness but didn't enter her. She had other plans, first. She reluctantly left the soft mouth and moved to explore an equally soft neck with tongue, lips, and teeth. She growled quietly into the flesh when she felt fingers in her hair and the wetness between Cateline's legs already pressed against her stomach.

Absolutely loving the taste of her wife's skin, she hummed softly as she made her way down to gorgeous breasts. She lavished a goodly amount of attention to both before she was on the move again. Her mouth watered as she smelled the wet heat of Cateline's need. Kissing a trail down along her belly, she eased herself lower down the bed until she was where she knew she was needed most. Frankly, she could spend all night there.

They both knew they had to keep it down as a sleeping baby was just across the bedchamber closer to the fireplace to keep her warm. The loud gasp from the woman beneath her would have to suffice for the usual long, languid groan Cateline would have released as Fallon's tongue slowly sliced through her wetness and swollen folds.

She loved her taste, the sounds she made, the way Cateline's body moved of its own accord like the slowly undulating waves of the sea. It drove Fallon crazy, and simply watching Cateline's hips as she walked across a room could arouse her. But this, to have her arms wrapped around her spread thighs as she teased her hard clit with the tip of her tongue, Fallon felt she could nearly orgasm just from her little whimpers.

Right now, however, was not meant to make Cateline come, as much as she'd love to. She eased her tongue away from a sensitive clit and licked her way down to her opening, gently easing her tongue inside and teasing her to foreshadow what was to come.

"Fallon," Cateline breathed. "I want you inside

of me."

She did not have to be asked twice. Fallon left a kiss in volcanic wetness before moving back up to lie upon the smaller woman again. Their kiss was deep and passionate, yet controlled as Fallon moved her hips into place between spread thighs. Cateline was so wet and so ready, she easily slid inside of her.

They both sighed into the kiss as Fallon's hips nestled flush against Cateline, her length fully inside her. Pulling out of the kiss, she looked down into the face of the precious woman beneath her. Resting on her forearms, she used a hand to gently brush auburn strands away from the beautiful face.

"I love you so much," Fallon whispered in French, looking deeply into hooded gray-blue eyes. Though Cateline had long ago become fluent in Gaelic, she wanted to use Cateline's mother tongue to show her reverence and deep respect for her princess. "Never, ever doubt that, Cateline." She smiled when she saw tears begin to well in those eyes. "I am so in love with you and so in love with our family that we've built." She left a soft kiss on softer lips. "Together."

Cateline said nothing, simply buried her fingers in Fallon's hair, urging her down for a soft, slow sensuous kiss. Any response she may have to Fallon's words were conveyed in that kiss. Fallon responded as her hips began to move, their slow, lazy rhythm with long strokes inside Cateline mimicking their kisses.

It didn't take long before they were breathing too hard to continue kissing, but Fallon remained in Cateline's personal space. She met that hooded gaze, and in it she saw all the love Fallon felt reflected back at her. As she had many times before, she found their connection so strong that it was nearly painful, and certainly overwhelming.

Cateline's nails trailed down Fallon's back, sending delicious little shivers through her as she continued her slow thrusts. It brought her back to their first night together. How badly Fallon had wanted to do this very thing: to lay the princess down and make love to her until the sun came up.

Now, so many years later as they moved together, she wondered yet again just what she'd done so very right to have this woman not only in her bed, but in her heart, her soul, in her *life*. Other than the love for her children, she'd never known anything so primal, so absolutely complete as the love and need she had for her princess and queen of her heart.

Cateline's breathing was growing heavier, her breasts pressing into Fallon's as her pleasure grew. Fallon was amazed she'd held on as long as she had, considering how close she'd been with Fallon's mouth on her.

Pushing up to her hands, Fallon groaned as instantly Cateline's hands found her breasts. She used the power of her hips to shorten and quicken her thrusts. Fallon's eyes fell closed as her own flower of pleasure was burning low in her belly, beginning the slow bloom with each push against her clit as she slammed into Cateline's hips.

With a strangled cry, she came moments later, Cateline's own cry muted as she bit her lip, coming nearly simultaneously. She clung to Fallon, wrapping her arms and legs around her. Fallon buried her face in her warm neck, panting as she desperately tried to come back to earth.

"I love you," Cateline whispered as she held her.

Chapter Fourteen

*O*h, come on!" Fallon exclaimed, angry. She reached out to the soldier, the newest in the Elite Guard. She never bothered to learn their names until they were there at least eight weeks. That was the period of time they were given to bow out of the Guard, unable to handle the strenuous, unending training. "You can do better than that!" She shoved him away, the soldier nearly falling back on his rear end in the dirt of the training field. "Now, square up, soldier."

The man shrugged his shoulders, hitching his leather armor better back into place after being pulled like a rag doll by Fallon. She may no longer be his superior officer, but everyone knew who she was, and they were all terrified of her prowess.

Eyeing her opponent, Fallon had both short swords in hand, absently twirling the one in her left hand as she watched this young man's every move, every breath, every eyelash twitch. She watched his eyes, was focused on them. The tiniest, almost imperceptible look to the left.

The blade in Fallon's right hand struck the soldier's sword to the ground while her left leg cut him off at the knee, sending the warrior down to the ground on his back, hard. Like a lion pouncing, Fallon was on top of him, straddling his stomach with the V of both blades at his throat.

She met his stunned gaze. "You just lost your

head," she murmured.

With a slap to his armored chest, she pushed off him and to her feet. Sliding her blades into their sheaths upon her back, she reached down and grabbed him by the bracer-covered forearm, he doing the same as she pulled him to his feet.

She could tell he was deeply disappointed in himself, but there was no time for a pep talk. He had to learn. Clearly, Eoin had brought him into the Elite Guard for a reason, so she needed to see that spark in him in order for him to stay in the Guard.

"Again," she ordered.

He nodded, the determination in his deep brown eyes apparent. The two squared off when something caught Fallon's eye. It was sudden movement, so fast it startled her. Off to the left, just beyond the training field and by the stables for the military horses... There, peeking out at her, was a shadow. It was in the shape of a man, but she could just see his shoulders and head. Full light of day, a shadow. How could that—

Fallon grunted, pain exploding in her nose and into her eyes, then the back of her head as it slammed back into the ground.

"Milord!"

Two hands grabbed Fallon's, one from the young soldier she was battling and the other from another recruit who had run over when she'd gone down. She was pulled to her feet, and immediately cloth was held against her nose, which was gushing blood.

Normally, she—or any other soldier—would have just had to deal with it. They'd have to pop up and try not to get killed or clobbered, unable to see as blood dripped into their eyes as the attack—or training—continued.

But Fallon was not the average soldier anymore, leader or not. She was heir to the throne, so if she got hurt, gods help the man who hurt her! She saw the fear in the young soldier's eyes from her one good eye. With a smile, she placed a hand on his shoulder.

"At ease, soldier," she said. "Well done." She glanced back over toward the stables. There was nothing there.

❧❧❧❧❧

"Ahhhhhh," Fallon muttered as asked by Cerdic, the castle physician. His examination had been going on for a full twenty minutes, and she was about ready to pop him. He was one of the few in the kingdom who knew her true identity, considering he'd delivered her thirty-seven years before. He'd examined her top to bottom—literally.

Finally, the examination of her mouth complete, he sat back on his stool. "You may dress, Your Highness." With a grunt of pain from ancient knees, hips, and old bones in general, he stood. Walking over to his desk, he sat down upon that stool to scribble a few notes in his ever-present open book.

Fallon suspected this was for him to write down his findings, but also his way of giving her privacy to dress. "Will I live, Cerdic?" she asked, amusement in her tone.

"Aye," the old man grumbled as he dipped his quill into ink before continuing to scratch out his notes on the parchment pages. "You're an extremely healthy individual," he said slowly, as if stating each word as he wrote it down. "From what you have said and what Her Highness said of your symptoms…" He turned on the stool and glanced at her. "I believe you've perhaps suffered some brain commotion."

Fallon groaned inwardly. She'd dealt with that more than once in her life and wasn't keen on telling Cateline. She could hear it now: *I told you! I was worried you'd been hit in the head too hard. No more training fields for you, Fallon of Sursha!*

Even so, as she listened to him drone on about how she needed to rest and allow her brain to heal, that very brain went back to the dream she'd had that morning. No, more like her brain was *remembering* what she'd forgotten.

She wondered if perhaps she'd actually blacked out for a moment that day when the soldier had landed a solid blow with the pommel of his sword into the bridge of her nose, fully expecting her to knock it away. It was a technique of distraction that she herself had begun teaching the men years before, and it continued to be taught today.

None of them, certainly not Fallon, had expected her to be so completely distracted. She'd forgotten what she'd seen just before he struck her. Now, sitting on that examination cot in the healer's rooms, she wondered what that had been, if anything. Perhaps she'd imagined it? Returning her focus to the old healer, she decided to consider that another time.

❧❧❧❧

Fallon was in full dress regalia, as was Cateline. They sat upon their matching thrones—Fallon's larger, of course, as prince—in the throne room. They both wore their crowns, which made Fallon feel like an idiot, but this was a pretty important meeting, so there they sat, ready for reception.

Though wanting to take another look at her

absolutely stunning wife, she knew she had to stay focused. Cateline wore her title and all that went with it like the most beautiful dress tailor-made for its wearer. Her beauty, her bearing, and the intelligence in those gorgeous eyes...she was heart stopping. Today was Laigen's day, but Fallon worried all eyes would be upon her mother instead.

The Prince's Court was also in the throne room, including Livia, who looked just as beautiful and stately as Cateline. While at her father's castle, it had been decided that the king would have private meetings with the chosen young man. This initial round was for Laigen's parents and Court.

Fallon almost felt sorry for him. Almost. He and his entourage had arrived and it was time. The double doors to the throne room were opened by castle guard, specifically chosen by Fallon and Eoin for this duty. This was her little girl, and this man would sure as hell know who he was dealing with in Laigen's "father."

That little four-year-old had stolen Fallon's heart pretty much just as Cateline had. She'd been wrapped around both their fingers ever since. Laigen was determined to see this through, and the truth was, Fallon had endless respect for the young woman.

Absolutely, she wished she'd wait a few years, but the look in the blue eyes of her eldest daughter showed her that Laigen was planning for far more than just nuptials. She knew that Laigen idolized Cateline and wanted to be just like her. She had watched her over the years and saw how she wielded her power and influence for the greater good.

One thing she fervently hoped was that whomever Laigen married, be it this man or another, the couple would wait to have children. She wanted Laigen to find her footing as the woman in the marriage, the wife and not just a broodmare.

The quiet grew as everyone focused their attention on the young man who was striding his way to the foot of the throne dais. He was a man of twenty-two with dark good looks, a squared jaw, and fine physique. He strode with purpose and confidence, his dark, intense gaze surreptitiously scanning those around him.

Fallon studied him as he advanced. She'd met him, of course, at the gala and had found out every single thing she could about him and his family. He was the son of a Spanish Duque of high standing. Charles II, King of Navarre, was the current ruler of Spain, and though he was rumored to be a disaster on the throne, the country was becoming more and more powerful.

No doubt his time would soon come to an end, and Fallon thought it wise to get an in with the country before that happened. With Cateline's ties to France and her own to both Sursha and Brittany, Fallon felt it wise to bring in another power player for allied support—or simply for one less enemy.

Sursha was mighty, but it was small. Every chess move had to count; her father had taught her that long ago on the chessboard and Ailfred had taught her that well on the battlefield. She'd considered a prince for her daughter, but any prince of Europe who was in line for the throne would have a larger slice of the pie and would no doubt try to nibble on Sursha's slice as well. Sursha would be no match.

Arranging a marriage of Laigen to a high-placed man in nobility, Sursha would receive the benefit of the coupling while retaining her independence. As this "high-placed man of nobility" stepped up to the bottom step, Fallon studied him. His name and litany of titles and those of his father and his father before him was announced by his footman. She cared nothing for any of that.

What she focused on was Reinaldo the man, not Reinaldo the title. Her father would worry about the politics of it. *She* was worried about her daughter and her happiness. She looked past his fine clothes and jewelry. She looked past his confidence, which bordered on cocky. She looked past the handsome features and the mane of dark brown hair and heavy, dark eyebrows. She looked past the long eyelashes and dark, bedroom eyes and into his soul.

There was nothing wrong with confidence and even a bit of cockiness. Her beloved eldest brother had been one of the cockiest men she'd ever known, yet he possessed a heart of gold. Had he ever had a chance to settle down and marry, he would have treated his bride like the treasure she would have been to him. As their mother had been to the king. As Cateline was to her.

Was Reinaldo capable of the same thing? Those dark eyes met her own and held. Fallon was impressed by that. His confidence wasn't just skin deep. Though born a woman, Fallon understood all too well the world of the male. A constant strutting peacock showing his brightly colored feathers...not for the female, of course, but for other males.

In humans, those brightly colored feathers could certainly be fine clothing and jewels, much as Reinaldo wore, but it was mostly a measurement of durability, strength, and who would blink first. It was a world where one cock compared itself to another cock, the hen not often involved in the judgment of who would win or lose.

It was an absolutely ridiculous dance, but Fallon knew the steps. And, in that moment, Reinaldo, bowed his head and his eyes in deference to that lock of eyes. *Wise, lad. Very wise.* Next, Fallon watched how he received Cateline.

Very quickly, a glimmer of lust washed through those dark eyes, but Fallon didn't take offense to that. That visceral reaction she understood very well, as she'd had the same one on a night long ago in France, the night of her brother's wedding to the very same woman. What mattered was that Reinaldo reined it in quickly and deferred his gaze and head in deference to the Princess of Sursha, as well.

The true test was now: Reinaldo of Spain rested dark eyes on the woman he'd traveled so far to see. Laigen was present, and she looked more beautiful than Fallon had ever seen her look. She'd spoken to her daughter that morning, Laigen seeking her out for advice.

"Daidí," she had said, *breathless as she hurried into the family chamber.*

"Yes, my dove?" Fallon said, catching herself an armful of seventeen-year-old angst.

"How do I handle this today?" she asked, looking up into Fallon's face, anxiety in her own.

Fallon cupped her face and held her still as she looked deeply into her eyes. "You be yourself," she said softly. "You're intelligent, you know who you are, and you love your family and your country." She smiled, dropping her hands. "Never forget that, and you'll be fine."

Laigen was quiet for a moment, but then asked, "Am I doing the right thing, Daidí?"

Fallon wanted to scream, "No! You're too young!" But, she and Cateline had talked long and hard about this. Right now, Laigen was listening to them, allowing them to help her through this process. As her parents, they'd rather this than force her to wait a few years where she could end up going off half-cocked, submitting to emotion and pretty words rather than reason and a plan for a full future.

"You must believe it in your heart, Laigen," she responded. "If you do not, back out now. If you do, hold your head high and see what this time with Reinaldo will bring." She smiled and leaned forward to leave a lingering kiss on Laigen's forehead. "We're with you. Go with your heart, Laigen," she said again, looking into the young woman's eyes. "We already know he's right for the country, but he must be right for you." She lightly tapped the end of her daughter's nose.

As she'd done since she was a child, Laigen curled her arms into herself as she snuggled into Fallon, who instantly wrapped her arms around the smaller woman.

"I love you, Daidí."

Fallon smiled. "I love you, my sweet."

The young woman who now sat upon the dais, though on a lower level than the prince and princess, sat with a straight spine and will of iron. She looked beautiful, yes, but it was clear she was not there to flirt, and she was not there to find a man to rule her. She was there to find a partner, and to see if there was a love match.

Fallon had never been more proud. She wanted to reach over and take Cateline's hand to experience the moment with her, but it was not appropriate now. So, Fallon's gaze remained on Reinaldo, who was looking at Laigen.

The way he looked at the lovely young woman was amusing in that clearly Laigen had made an impact on him during their last meeting at the gala. Fallon would call it outright puppy dog eyes, though he was obviously trying to hide it.

After Laigen was introduced and Reinaldo had given her the deepest bow of respect of the three, it was Fallon's responsibility to take over as the Prince of Sursha and Laigen's father. She eyed the young man who stood stock-still, almost at attention. From some of his behaviors, she wondered if the young nobleman had seen military service.

"Welcome, Marqués Reinaldo," she said, voice friendly yet formal. "My wife, the Princess of Sursha, and I are honored you've accepted our invitation."

The Marqués bowed again. "'Tis my honor, milord," the Spaniard said, his voice low and deferential. "I very much look forward to my time in your kingdom, milord."

Fallon had to admit, she was impressed the young man spoke a decent amount of Gaelic. It wasn't exactly a language Western Europeans saw as worth the effort. Many looked at the Gaels much as Cateline had in the beginning: an ignorant, barbaric people. Surshans in particular prided themselves on educating everyone as best as they could, including the girls.

"I have brought gifts for you," Reinaldo said. He turned to his entourage and snapped his fingers. Two men hurried over to him carrying a trunk. The lid was opened and the gifts were brought out.

There were fabrics, spices, a sword for Fallon

with their family crest etched into the blade, and then, to Fallon's delight, oranges! Other than perhaps Livia, having been born in Italy, none of her family had ever had the delicious fruit. The climate in Sursha was not at all conducive to growing citrus fruits, and she wasn't sure the area of France where Cateline had been born grew them either.

The only reason she'd enjoyed them was from a mercenary campaign she'd been part of in Spain many years before. She'd never forgotten about the sweet, juicy treat.

"And for you," he said, looking up at Laigen, who remained in her seat, though Fallon could tell she was mighty impressed and intrigued. He looked to Fallon. "May I?"

Reinaldo indicated the dais with a glance of his head. When Fallon waved him on, the Spaniard climbed the steps to Laigen's chair. He produced a lavish gold ring with a sapphire that nearly matched the color of Laigen's eyes.

"A trinket," he said. He said it primarily for her ears but still loud enough for Fallon and Cateline to hear, no doubt wanting to impress the would-be in-laws. "Of my affections."

Laigen took the ring from him, examining it this way and that. The look she gave him told Fallon that she was most definitely considering the situation.

"Thank you, Marqués," Laigen said softly, sliding the ring onto the forefinger of her right hand. She looked down at it, giving him a smile.

"*De nada,*" he said softly, taking her hand and bringing it to his lips.

Fallon finally glanced over to Cateline, who was already looking at her, eyebrows raised in question.

Chapter Fifteen

The banquet tables were all set up, seemingly miles of food. Probably not, but it was a lot. Roishin hadn't been in the throne room for the arrival of the Spanish guy, and she certainly didn't lament the lack of invitation. Honestly, it had been nice to have some time to herself while the family got all gussied up.

She had spent that time outside and practiced with her bow. She'd gotten pretty darn good at that. She wanted to show her Daidí what she could do. Now, in a stupid dress—it was an event, after all— Roishin made her way along the tables of food. She picked this and that off a platter, dropping it to the plate she carried.

She came to a platter that had some strange sort of fruit that was orange and sliced into wedges. Never seeing that before, she set her plate down on the table and picked up one of the slices. It looked like it once had been a round orange thing, the wedges little half-moon shaped. She brought it to her nose to sniff, wincing at the strange smell that was both sweet and tangy at the same time. Very strong, but not unpleasant.

Looking around, she saw that nobody was paying the smallest bit of mind to her, so she returned her focus back to the strange food. She held it by the edges of the rough, orange peel, eyeing the soft innards, which was covered by a strange white material.

"What on earth?" she muttered. Glancing across the way, she saw Fallon place one of the wedges into her mouth, peel side out. "Okay..." she murmured, looking back down to the fruit in her hand.

Bringing it up to her mouth, she tentatively touched the tip of her tongue to it, curious. Looking around surreptitiously to make sure nobody was watching her, she did as the warrior had done. If *she* could handle it, Roishin could. She tucked the slice into her mouth, peel side out. She bit her teeth into the soft flesh of the fruit and her eyes popped open wide.

Her mouth was filled with the same sweet-tangy flavors she'd smelled, but far more concentrated as it was a lot of juice. She tried to swallow it all while keeping the fruit wedge in place with her teeth.

Sensing somebody moving up behind her, she turned to see Elsie, who was about to place a fresh platter of food down on the table. She looked over at Roishin and quite clearly was trying not to smile, though was failing. She finally had to resort to placing her hand in front of her mouth.

Roishin's *What?* came out more like a grunt around the wedge. Then, to her horror, she began to drool, the tangy juice sending her saliva reflexes into overdrive.

Elsie's smile got a bit away from her as she removed her hand to grab the edge of her tunic that covered her simple dress. She gently wiped away the tiny stream making its way down Roishin's chin.

Not sure whether to laugh or cry, Roishin did neither as she eased the fruit wedge out of her mouth. She squeezed her eyes shut as a little shiver ran through her at the aftertaste. "I honestly don't know if I love this or hate it," she managed.

"What is that?" Elsie asked, looking down at what essentially looked like a deflated wedge of... something.

"Is an orange."

Head whipping up, Roishin found herself looking into amused dark eyes. Elsie bowed and quickly excused herself to get back to work. Though a little disappointed that she left, Roishin understood. She grabbed the plate she'd been loading and placed the remains of the fruit on it.

"What is an orange?" she asked.

"It's a wonderful fruit that grows on trees back in Spain," he said. He gave her a winning smile. "You are Princess Roishin, yes?"

"Aye," she said slowly. "Roishin will do. And you're the maybe, could be, wants to be, potential brother-in-law?"

His laughter was deep and rich. Nodding, he grinned, looking delighted. "*Si*." He reached past her and picked a few cubes of cheese from a platter on the table. "Tell me about you, younger sister of Laigen." He looked her in the eyes as he bit one of the cubes in half.

She considered, eating a little bit of finger food from her own plate. "Well," she said finally. "No longer the youngest, so that will be something new. But I love to read, play chess, and practice with my bow.'

Heavy eyebrows shot up. "You use a bow?" He pantomimed the nocking of an arrow and shooting with a bow. At her nod, he looked impressed. "I never met a female archer before."

She smirked. "I'm not sure archer is entirely accurate. I haven't received my invitation to join the Elite Guard's archery guard quite yet."

He chuckled. "Perhaps we should go out, you and I. Practice our bows together."

"You like archery?"

He nodded. "*Sí.*" He wrinkled his nose. "Never was good with a sword."

Warming up to this strange man—a little— Roishin smiled and nodded. "Me, either. I honestly have no idea how Daidí uses *two* at the same time."

"I've heard of this," he said. He looked down at her, a wide smile upon his handsome face. "I like you, Roishin."

"I like me, too. And, what exactly is your name?" she asked. "There were far too many of you at the gala for me to bother learning the names of."

He smirked. Giving her a deep bow of respect, he said, "I am Reinaldo, Marqués de Velencia."

Roishin nodded, not terribly impressed by titles. "So, Reinaldo," she said, ignoring his. "What do you think of my sister?"

She nodded in the direction of the lovely young woman who was standing with Livia, the two laughing at something they were talking about. Though she didn't know the whole story, she knew that Livia held a very special place in Laigen's heart. In many ways, she looked up to her as a second mother figure.

Reinaldo followed her nod, his features softening a bit. "I think she is the most beautiful woman I've ever seen," he said, meeting Roishin's gaze again.

Roishin nodded. She had opinions on that, but admittedly her sister was very beautiful. "What do you think of her mind?" she challenged.

He looked surprised by the question and nibbled on another cube of cheese as he seemed to be considering his response. Roishin watched him. She knew that Laigen wasn't the obsessively curious person that Roishin was, but she was not stupid, nor a fool. Sure, she could, and often did, use her feminine wiles to get her way, but Laigen was a thinker, and this man needed to understand that.

"Well," he finally said. "I've not yet gotten to spend time with her mind." He gave the teen a charming smile.

Roishin quirked an eyebrow. "I strongly advise that you do, Marqués."

He bowed again. "Duly noted, Princess."

⚜⚜⚜⚜

Later that night, Roishin lay in bed. She was absently stroking the broach pinned to her sleeping gown, Elsie making adjustments in all her chemises and sleeping gowns so the gold bauble had something to attach to. She was thinking back over the night's events. As normal, she'd tried to be a fly on the wall as much as possible, just observing, learning.

She'd watched Laigen with her suitor. It had been kind of nice, honestly. She liked the young Spaniard, from what she'd seen of him, anyway. He'd be in Sursha for at least a fortnight, possibly longer if things went well. She was curious about him, wouldn't mind getting to know him better, and certainly was thrilled to perhaps have an archery buddy.

It would be over Laigen's dead body to learn such a thing and her mother was just entirely too busy. Garratt didn't take her interest all that seriously and preferred swordplay, anyway. Fallon had worked with her often and supported her pursuits, but like Cateline, she was very busy. So, she'd basically been on her own to practice or even just to enjoy a day out in the woods with her bow and quiver.

Maybe she could ask Elsie. She snorted at the very thought. First of all, her mother would kick her behind for taking the servant away from her duties. Plus, as they'd all gotten older, the royal children and servants didn't maintain the same friendships and freedom to play together as they'd had as children.

Part of that was that both parties were busier with very different pursuits as they got older, but she also had a sneaking suspicion that it was no longer as encouraged, as feelings could begin to blossom in a garden where weeds and flowers could cohabitate but served very different purposes.

The crazy—and confusing—part for Roishin was that out of all the kids she used to play with when she was younger, most of them had been boys. They'd been the boys who worked in the stables, or the blacksmith's son, cobbler's son, whatever. She'd always had a very strange relationship with girls. She felt so shy around them, sometimes paralyzingly so. She also felt so awkward around them and didn't enjoy many of the same things they did.

Never had she been interested in dolls as Laigen was. Heck, Laigen had the very first doll that had been given to her. It was an old rag doll that one of the servants still had from her daughter way back when. It was one of her most prized possessions. Granted, she no longer played with it, but it had meant something to her throughout her entire life at the castle.

For Roishin, her prized possessions were her

books and her bow. For all her lack of interest in the servant girls as playmates, something had steadily been changing inside of her. No, she didn't want to find a girl to go skipping through the castle halls with her and giggle like Laigen and her friends used to do. She found herself watching the girls...well, certainly the older teenagers and women.

She was utterly fascinated by them. She didn't feel any less awkward around them; she was more so, in fact. If only she had the ease and grace that Laigen did. She'd never envied her older sister in any other way, but that was one thing she definitely wished she possessed that her beautiful, self-assured older sibling had.

Roishin was changing, and she could feel it daily. Her body certainly was. She was growing like a weed, becoming taller and outgrowing everything. Her boobs, beginning to make an appearance, were sore and tender all the time. She just felt...*awkward*. She wasn't a little girl anymore, but she certainly wasn't an adult. She was in no way adequate for Elsie.

Her eyes popped way open at that unbidden thought. Where the heck had that come from, and what did it even mean? The young woman's face came to mind as it so often did. She knew she had a crush on her personal servant for sure, but didn't that happen with someone who was a little bit older than you? You admire them or want to be more like them? Respect them. Right?

Her mind's eye was *so* helpful by reproducing an image of full lips, long hair the color of honey. Most helpful of all was the recall of the little bit of cleavage Roishin had seen that night that Elsie had removed her tunic and unbuttoned her dress just enough to reveal the triskelion attached to her chemise.

And then tonight at the banquet dinner for Laigen and Reinaldo, when Elsie had used her own tunic to wipe the mess Roishin was making with the juice from the orange. Her eyes closed as her hands came up to cover her face. Her groan of embarrassment was muffled behind her palms. Of course Elsie had done that, like cleaning up a child.

No doubt to her, Roishin *was* a child because, well…she *was*. Kind of. She'd be thirteen very soon, and she knew of girls in the village who had been married by that time.

"Stop it," she muttered. She smirked. "Even if Elsie saw you as anything more than the pesky obligation in duty you are to her, you wouldn't know what to do with her, anyway."

☙ ☙ ❧ ❧

It was pitch-black, but she was moving, though with the darkness, it was hard to tell in which direction. Suddenly, down a long, inky-black tunnel was the tiniest bit of light. She was soaring toward it. The bit of light got larger and larger until she realized it was the baby blue of the sky.

Exploding out of darkness, she realized she was soaring up into the sky. Never slowing, she turned away from it and saw the vastness of the ocean beneath her, as well as what looked like a massive mountain with no core that jutted up from the deep blue water. Soaring back down, the water getting closer and closer, she leveled off, now parallel with the ocean as she continued at unimaginable speeds.

As she flew above the waves, she thought maybe

she was a bird, but then looking down at the water that sped by, she saw a huge, dark mass that was the shadow. Looking up from it, she saw a ship just ahead, sails puffed out from the tall mast. As she got closer to the ship, she saw sailors coming and going, doing this and that to keep the vessel moving.

As the mass soared closer to the vessel, the waves began to pick up, at first lapping at the curved sides of the ship but then sending the ship bobbing through the water like a toy in a wash tub. As she moved above the ship, a wall of water followed, crashing over the deck and knocking the mast over like a mere twig from a branch. Sailors cried out in fear as they held on for dear life, many washed overboard.

She heard one look up and meet her gaze "Bāhūthā!" he called out, terror in his eyes.

And still she continued on. The sun overhead reflected on the ocean below, a companion glittering like gold upon the waves. Just up ahead, a large island. A castle at the highest point stood strong, a flat waving proudly from its tower. But before the castle was reached, a harbor came into view below. The ships docked bobbed violently as she passed overhead, one careening into the other.

Beyond that, a market, alive with people who looked up into the heavens, yet none met her eye. The massive shadow that was she eased over the island, slowing. Below she saw a wagon pulled by a single horse with a man at the reins. A woman sat beside him, packed wares in the wagon. A large, round basket was just behind the woman, a sleeping babe inside its protective design.

She flew over the wagon, slowing for just a moment as the horse suddenly bucked, whinnying violently and running in terror. The wagon and its occupants were at its mercy. And still, she continued. Slower still, another castle, more inland and crowded by wooded land. A large, open space, men upon it. The glint of steel as blades crossed and clashed.

One figure, ready to strike. She moved to fly over that figure. As she moved overhead, the figure's head looked off. In that moment, the figure was brought down by a hit to the head. She looked away as she eased over to the castle, looking down upon the aged stone towers and parapets.

Another flag waved, like a finger waggling at the massive shadow that moved to cover the entire structure. She slowed and finally stopped. Looking down, she saw a glow, blue and dim, deep within the castle itself. The gaping maw of a chimney came into view. Down she went, back into darkness.

Speeding down, she emerged out of the mouth of a large fireplace in a huge room, dim and empty. She floated toward the stairs and up, the steps passing by at a dizzying pace. Leveling out low, she was soaring again just a bit above the stone floor. She slowed then stopped at a closed door, wooden, and ribbed with iron.

Slowly, she eased under it, emerging in another room. The glow. It was blue and pulsed. Still a bit dim, but she knew it would get brighter. She moved off to the right toward the bed and the source of the light. Like smoke, creeping its way up the covers, some fallen to the floor. Easing up and over the top of the bed, she saw that a single figure lay asleep.

Slowly, slowly she moved down toward that light. Almost there, almost there. The face could be seen through the glow. A girl, not yet a woman. Not yet...

"No!" Roishin cried, eyes exploding open as she launched herself up and out of the bed. She landed on the stone floor on her hands and knees, ignoring the pain as she turned over to her behind and crab-crawled away from the bed.

She was gasping for air, terrified as she looked back at the large piece of furniture she'd just been sleeping on. Her gaze swept over the bed and to the door, looking desperate for...what?

"Roishin?"

She cried out again at the voice and then the sudden hand on her shoulder. Trying to scramble away from it, she looked to see a frightened Elsie kneeling next to her. The tears were hot as they streamed down Roishin's cheeks, her chest heaving as the terror still gripped her.

"No," she said weakly.

"It's okay," Elsie whispered, holding her hands up in supplication. "It's okay."

Her heart still beating wildly, Roishin nodded, taking in gulps of air to try to calm down. She allowed herself to be taken into the warm, strong embrace of the servant. Their comfort helped to lull her heart rate to a cadence not quite as dangerous.

She allowed herself to fully fall against the young woman. She rested her head against her shoulder and took a long, deep breath as gentle fingers combed through her hair, brushing the mass back from Roishin's face.

Nothing was said, nothing needed to be said. Roishin could hear Elsie's own heart racing; no doubt her outburst had scared the living daylights out of her as she'd begun her morning duties. At length, though not moving away from Elsie, Roishin spoke.

"I'm sorry,"

"You don't need to be," Elsie murmured, continuing to stroke her hair and her back. "Want to talk about it?"

Roishin shook her head, still far too easily able to see it. "No."

Chapter Sixteen

Uncharacteristically quiet, Roishin sat at the table. She picked at her food, her mind quite far from family chitchat. Luckily, with Reinaldo there, the focus was on him and Laigen. It was easy for the young princess to remain quiet. She felt a gaze on her and glanced over to see Fallon watching her.

A question in her eyes, Roishin gave her the biggest smile she could, which she knew was nearly imperceptible. She was still very shaken from her rude awakening hours before. But, as she met her daidí's gaze, her own drifted to the bruise that was fading at the bridge of her nose and around her left eye—the remnants of a nasty shiner.

They'd been told it was just an accident on the training field, and it wasn't at all uncommon for her to have bumps and bruises. But, as she looked at that one, something niggled at her, and she felt very uncomfortable. Looking away, she returned her gaze to her breakfast plate.

As surreptitiously as she could, she glanced over to the tapestry that covered the door to the secret passageway and ultimately, to the trunk. She wondered if her parents knew about that. Did her siblings? Looking away when she felt a presence move in next to her, she glanced up to see Elsie, who was helping to gather empty platters and plates.

The young woman spared a glance at her, the

concern in her beautiful blue eyes apparent. Roishin gave her a ghost of a smile, just enough to let her know she was okay. With a subtle nod of understanding, the servant moved on to another part of the table to continue her task.

"So, Roishin," Reinaldo said from where he sat at the other end of the table, seated between Garratt and Laigen.

She met his gaze. "Yes?"

"Laigen and I will be heading to stay with King Carthac in a few days," he explained. "But when I return, would you care to join me with your bow?"

She was able to give him a smile, the first real one of the day. "Aye." Mary entered the family chamber, baby Isabeau in hand. For reasons she didn't understand, Roishin said, "May I?"

Mary looked to her and then to Cateline, as if for permission. At the nod she received, Mary walked over to Roishin. "Get her head, now," she said softly.

Roishin allowed the baby to be eased into her arms. Once she was stable, she looked up into the older woman's face. "Thank you, Mary," she said softly.

She'd spent no time with the baby since the day of the accident that had claimed the lives of her parents. In that moment however, she felt an intense need to hold the baby, to look into her eyes. She knew Isabeau had just been fed and changed. She cradled the infant, looking down at her beautiful little face.

Her eyes were such a deep, dark blue rimmed by a ring of even darker blue. She wondered if they'd stay that color, as she knew a baby's eyes could change. But, looking into those eyes, which looked back up at her, she saw...she saw...

Dark blue eyes squinting in fierce concentration, long brown hair flew out behind her as she ran. Powerful thighs propelled her across the landscape. Leather armor covered the torso of a grown woman of perhaps twenty. Her forearms were covered in brown leather bracers, darkened from blood, which also stained her hands.

Her mouth opened as a raging cry escaped her lips. Her hands held a large sword, the blade still covered in blood and gore, raising over her head from powerful arms. Following was another young woman, roughly the same age, perhaps a few years younger. Her mane of golden hair framed a tanned, beautiful face. Dark green eyes penetrated the soul as she, too, carried a large blade. In fact, looking at her eyes, she saw they were her own *eyes. The second young woman was just as intent as the first was on their target. They got closer and closer, and closer...*

Gasping, Roishin stared down at the babe in arms. It took her several moments to catch her breath. She felt somebody behind her, stabilizing the baby as she nearly dumped her in shock.

"I'm sorry," she gasped. "I'm sorry."

"Shhh," Fallon murmured, gently taking Isabeau from her arms. She left a kiss to Roishin's head as she lifted the baby up and away, over her head.

≈≈≈≈

After breakfast, Roishin had been released to go do her lessons for the day. Her parents, particularly her mother, had been absolutely insistent that the children were educated. As much as she loved to learn, she hated the strict, structured schooling from Master Waverly. He annoyed her, this man from England.

Luckily, this guy also spoke French, which she was already fluent in. So, the only language she had to learn from him was Latin. Not fun. Today in particular, she wasn't of the right mind to really focus.

Finally, in frustration, Master Waverly threw his hands up and left her for the day. She was not sad to see him go. Her afternoon free, she stood in her bedchamber, looking around. Everything was neat and tidy, her bed made to perfection. It was clean, as clean as a bedchamber could be in a drafty castle, anyway.

Her gaze swept back to the bed and that horrible...*dream* she'd had. It had been so vivid, so incredibly real. She'd never been so terrified in her entire life as she'd been when she'd awoken. Her knees were terribly bruised from landing on them on the floor from such a distance.

Walking over to it, she ran her hand over the heavy quilt, made for her by her mother. It amazed her how it could be May outside but it was November inside. The stone held in so much of the cold. Pushing that random thought out of her mind, she remembered Elsie being there for her. The way she'd held her, so incredibly kind and giving.

Pushing aside her crush on the servant, she considered who she was as a person. Yes, she'd gotten to know more about her of late, her story, how she'd arrived in their home, but Elsie was such a quiet young woman. Not just in that she didn't often speak, she just had a quiet nature about her, a quiet way.

It was so calming for Roishin. Honestly, she could just be lying in bed while Elsie did her morning duties, neither saying a word, and just the young woman's presence was enough. She was just so darn *nice*. She truly wanted to get to know her. What did she like to do? What did she think about? What was her favorite color?

One thing she did know was she wanted to do something nice for her. She was so good at her job, so utterly efficient and thorough. It hit her like a blacksmith's hammer that she rarely to never thanked her. Yes, it was her job, and yes, she was being paid a wage, but still. She wanted to find out something she liked or liked to do and gift her with it.

Nodding at her decision, she decided to locate her daidí to find out how to go about such a thing. She hurried out of her bedchamber and down the hall to the stairs to the third floor. She headed to the bedchamber farthest to the left, clear at the end of the hall, which belonged to her parents. The door was open, which usually meant that the children were welcome.

"Daidí?" she said, heading inside. "Mamaí?"

Like her own, their bed was made to perfection and the huge room was also neat and tidy. Personally, she thought cynically, she felt hers looked better, but perhaps she was biased. She saw nobody in the chamber but noticed the trunk that was near their bed had something hanging out of it.

Glancing over her shoulder to make sure nobody was coming, she walked over to it, curious. She'd seen that trunk a million times and had even sat upon it while chatting with one or both of her folks. It was always locked—not that she'd tried to open it or anything. This time, however, it was not.

She wondered if perhaps somebody had left the chamber quickly for some reason, leaving whatever they had been doing halfway stuck under the lid. She looked down at the trunk, a finger playing with her bottom lip as she considered. She knew she should just turn back around and leave the bedchamber and go read or something.

After another glance at the open bedchamber door, she decided a little peek wouldn't hurt. She lifted the lid, glancing to the door every so often, to see there were several items in the trunk. Many pairs of trousers folded neatly, as well as several daggers. She was careful not to lose a finger, as not all of them were sheathed.

She pushed those items out of the way, finding something that truly stumped her. Initially, she thought it was an intricate sword belt for her daidí's double blades that she'd never seen before—that is, until she realized that all the leather straps were connected to a centralized object.

Her mind went back to a visitor they'd had a few years back from a far-flung kingdom who had brought some truly bizarre gifts for the king, prince, and princess. One had been an erect penis carved out of ivory. The leather object she held in her hands looked an awful lot like that.

"Oh my gods!" she exclaimed, the item falling back to the trunk.

She looked down at it, no idea what it was used for or why it was in Fallon's trunk—a trunk that seemed to be filled with such personal things. Suddenly, something caught her eye. She spared a glance at the leather penis-shaped thing again before digging under it a bit. Just the barest bit of bright blue was sticking out.

Easing it out, she saw that it was a folded cloth

the exact same color blue as Enori's cloak had been, and it also had the gold stitching around it. Unfolding it, it wasn't a cloak but a blanket, perhaps? It wasn't large, more like a lap blanket at best.

Gasping, she looked to the door when she heard voices coming from the hall headed toward the bedchamber. Cursing under her breath, she eased the trunk lid closed after making sure the clothing was back in place. She had no time to refold the blanket, so she took it with her when she ducked into the garderobe.

She heard her mother's voice chatting with a servant as they entered the room, voices somewhat muffled behind the thick wood of the door. Roishin began to hum obnoxiously while sitting on the plank seat, though her trousers were still in place. She wanted her mother to know she was there so it wouldn't seem like she was hiding.

While in there, she folded the blanket as small as she could and stuffed it down baggy trousers, nowhere else to put it. Finally, feeling like she could pass the mamaí test, she headed to the door at the bottom of the stone steps. Pushing it open with a flourish, she stepped into the bedchamber.

"I feel *so* much better!"

Cateline glanced over at her with a mixture of amusement and disapproval in her eyes. She quirked an eyebrow. "What are you doing in here?"

"I came in here to talk to you, you weren't here and," she added dramatically, "I had to go." She pointed to the closed garderobe door as she plopped herself down in one of the chairs near the fireplace.

Shaking her head, Cateline smiled. "All right. We'll be done in a moment."

Popping up, Roishin saw this as her perfect opportunity to ditch the contraband and come back. "I shall return. "

Heading out, she rolled her eyes in relief when she hit the hallway beyond the bedchamber door. She felt bad, guilty for snooping, and she really, really hoped the blanket wasn't something they used or looked at often. If so, she'd be sunk. She had no idea how she was going to get it back in that trunk.

She was going to head to her own bedchamber, but as she passed the family chamber, her eyes landed upon the tapestry that hid the secret door. Her pace slowing, she glanced back toward her parents' room to see nobody in sight. She quickly ducked inside the large room and headed to that tapestry.

She pushed it aside and let herself in through the unlocked door. Once it closed behind her, she was in pitch darkness. She stood there, her heart beating rapidly. She could leave, she thought. She could simply open the door again and continue downstairs. But then Enori's face popped before her mind's eye.

That sight had a strange effect on her. It made her smile and made her want to cry in grief. Suddenly, she craved her presence. Chewing on her bottom lip, she turned her head to look into the deep darkness of the passage, knowing on the other end were three stone stairs and the lid of yet another trunk.

Of course she associated that trunk with the night Enori had sent her on a goose chase that ended up in the very chamber she'd just left. But, somehow, she knew it represented something more. Pushing away from the thick wood of the door, she trailed her fingertips along the smooth stone on either side as she made her way.

Though she had no candle and the darkness was complete, she felt like she was being drawn forward. It was as though an invisible rope were tied around her waist and somebody was standing at the other end of its length slowly tugging. Dutifully, she followed.

She'd been walking a while, and something told her to slow down and kick her feet forward with each step until her toe tapped lightly against the first step. Her heart was racing as she took that first step, then the second. Her hands went up until they felt the smooth underside of the trunk lid.

Taking a deep breath, she lightly pushed, heart lurching when it gave. Pushing farther, she took the next step and the third, and the lid pushed up fully with her advance. She did not see what she expected to see. Her eyes were huge as she slowly climbed out of the trunk.

She stepped into what looked like a dimly lit tunnel of a cave with rough-hewn walls of stone. It was larger than the passageway she'd just traversed but wasn't as large as the main hallways of the castle. Looking to the left, she saw that the tunnel disappeared into thick blackness, as did the tunnel off to the right.

She felt extremely exposed standing there. She had no idea where she was and no idea what to do. Chewing on her bottom lip again, she was about to make a decision when she heard distant voices. Her heart skipped a beat when she realized they were getting louder, seemingly headed her way.

She looked around, trying to find the source of the bit of light that shone in the tunnel. There was no torch anywhere. Then, she realized the light wasn't firelight at all. No, it had a blue tint to it. Confused, she looked to see if perhaps the tunnel wasn't as deep as it seemed, or if there was an exit close by, or even an opening of some sort.

Nothing. The walls, floor, and ceiling were solid stone. It was then that she realized the glow was coming from *her*. She looked down at herself. It wasn't a reflection of anything; she wasn't wearing any jewelry or metal. It was just...her. She gasped when the voices got even closer, now close enough to hear footfalls, too.

Looking behind her, she was horrified to see there was no trunk to climb back into. She stood in front of a solid stone wall. Looking around in every direction, she turned in a full circle before instinct had her reaching inside her trousers and pulling out the blanket.

Though it wasn't all that large, certainly not large enough to cover a bed, she sank to the ground, pulling her legs in as tightly to her body as she could and pulled the blanket over herself, trying to cover as much as possible. She made sure the toes of her shoes weren't sticking out and all but held her breath.

Heart racing and blood pounding in her ears and throbbing in her throat, she waited for the worst. The voices were upon her now. They sounded like two men, though they spoke in a language she didn't understand. Their voices were calm, conversational and, to her horror, their steps stopped not far from her.

She squeezed her eyes shut, silently pleading with them to please move on. The craziest part was, they seemed to be in the same conversation they had been in the entire time. Voice tone hadn't changed, no impassioned emotion of stumbling upon an interloper. Just...chitchat.

Please, oh please, oh please! One of them burst into laughter at something the other one said. Then, with a slap of masculine affection to a shoulder or back, the two continued on. By this point, Roishin felt downright nauseous and like she was going to pass out from holding her breath.

When their footfalls grew distant, she was about to push the blanket off her head but stopped. More footfalls. She silently growled, hoping she hadn't stumbled upon some sort of major thoroughfare wherever she was.

This time there was no talking, and the noises sounded like a single person. The footfalls weren't as heavy as those of the two men who had just wandered through. These were softer, lighter. And, they stopped directly in front of her.

Squeezing her eyes shut again, Roishin waited. One heartbeat, two, ten, fifty, four thousand... *Leave!* No such luck. Not only did the person not leave, but she heard garments shifting as they squatted down. One heartbeat, two, ten, fifty, four thousand all over again.

The blanket was lifted and peeled back until Roishin's head was fully exposed. She looked up through her hair to see Enori looking back at her.

Chapter Seventeen

*M*erci, Tessa," Cateline said with a smile as she excused the servant who had been helping her. With a curtsey and a bow, the seamstress hurried from the bedchamber.

Quite good with needle and thread, the princess very much enjoyed fixing the nonstop mending needs from her wife. Like a child, Fallon somehow managed to get a hole in or tear her clothing on a regular basis. And, this was with her essentially retiring from the military. My goodness, she thought. How bad was this when Fallon was at the height of her career in the Elite Guard?

The trousers that needed fixing this time were a heavier leather than normal, and she didn't have the correct thread, so had gone in search of the castle seamstress to see what she had. She set the spool of thread down atop the table before walking to the trunk, which she'd left unlocked in order to find Tessa.

The pair of trousers she'd been asked to work on were partially flopped down over the side of the trunk, trapped beneath the lid. She opened the trunk just enough to bring out the heavy leather trousers. These were more the type Fallon wore during the colder months, allowing good protection for her in the elements back during her days in the field or on missions.

The trunk lid fell back into place as she carried the

heavy garment to one of the chairs near the fireplace. Seeing the chair, she remembered Roishin had been sitting in it twenty minutes before when she'd said she needed to talk to Cateline. Needing to get Tessa's advice on working with a heavier thread and larger needle, she'd forgotten about her daughter's request.

Not sure how long the mending would take, she decided to leave the trousers and mending implements on the chair and go find Roishin to see what she'd needed. Humming to herself, she headed out of the bedchamber to go in search. In twenty minutes, the gods only knew what the girl had gotten herself interested in.

She headed to the second floor, anticipating that Roishin was probably in her own bedchamber. She smiled at a couple servants she passed on the way to the second floor and down the hall to her daughter's bedroom door. It was closed, as expected. She knocked firmly to be heard through the thick wood and waited.

After a few moments there was no answer, so she knocked again, harder. When there was still nothing, she pushed the door open. To her surprise, Roishin wasn't curled up in front of the fire reading. In fact, there was no fire in the fireplace at all. The room was clean and neat—thank you very much, Elsie—but was empty.

She noted that Roishin's bow was still hung on the wall, as was her quiver of arrows, so she figured she had to be inside the castle somewhere. Closing the door, she chewed on her lower lip for a moment as she considered where the precocious young woman had gone. Deciding to check the kitchen, she'd see if Millie had seen her.

No luck there, Cateline headed back up to the third

floor. She decided to head back to her own bedchamber to get Fallon's trousers fixed. If Roishin still wanted to talk, she'd know where to find her. Reaching the second landing, she continued on to the final flight of stone stairs that would take her to the third floor. Just reaching the top, she noticed something.

Glancing down the hall that led to the family chamber and her bedchamber with Fallon, she saw what almost looked like smoke. It was low to the ground, hovering just a foot or so above the floor. Instantly, her stomach roiled and she began to sniff the air. A fire in a castle was a huge fear, as it could easily get out of hand.

There was no telltale stench of flame nor acrid scent of smoke. Plus, she realized, there was no source. It wasn't as if the "smoke" was coming from her bedchamber, or from beneath a door. It was just... *there*. She followed its progress with her eyes, this smoke moving of its own accord. It took a right into the wide doors of the family chamber.

"What on earth?" she whispered.

Following yet keeping her distance, she reached the double chamber doors, one side closed, only to see the floating dark cloud heading to a door she knew well but hadn't used in many, many years. She gasped when she realized the tapestry that usually covered it was hung up on the iron handle to the door. It looked as though that door had been opened, the tapestry getting caught upon closing.

Instantly, she knew where Roishin had gone. She hurried over to it, the smoke seeming to dissipate as she moved through it. She looked down to see it returning, swirling around her skirted legs, moving up her body, weaving and waving around her. It reminded her of a snake, never forgetting when one had scared her nearly to death in the gardens in France back when she'd been a girl.

She gasped as the rising levels of smoke—which had no scent and seemingly no temperature to it—rose to her face. It felt like she was being watched or closely observed by the hazy, darkened air. Pulling herself out of her stupor, she waved her hands through it, the smoke billowing away from her and dissipating completely.

All she could do was stand there for a moment, struck dumb by what had just happened. Suddenly, she was filled with a horrible feeling of impending doom. "Roishin," she whispered, panic settling in.

She grabbed the iron handle of the door and yanked it open. Running as quickly as her skirts and space would allow, she hurried through the passageway, which was dark for much of its length until a bit of light began to break through the darkness. She saw that the trunk lid was open and light from the room beyond was seeping down into the tunnel.

Her heart was racing as she hurried up the stairs, holding her skirts up so she wouldn't trip. Hands braced on the edge of the wooden trunk, she looked around the room beyond. It was Fallon's old room and exactly as she'd expect it to be. No mattress on the bed frame. If she hadn't been so worried, she would have taken a moment to remember that bed. But right now, she needed to find her daughter.

Climbing up the final stair, Cateline carefully made her way out of the trunk. Standing in the room, she went to the door up the other set of stairs. Finding it locked, she was relieved. Roishin couldn't be up on the parapets as the door needed a key to unlock. Next, she went to the closed door to the small circular tower room.

Pulling it open, she peeked out into the rotunda beyond. No movement, and quiet. However, Roishin had left her bedchamber nearly half an hour before. The chances were slim that she would still be anywhere near the passageway and trunk if she'd decided to go explore. She'd have to follow.

The smell off to the left made it quite clear it was the communal garderobe for the Elite Guard, which was bunked in the castle. The opening to the staircase straight ahead was her only other option. She'd never been in this part of the castle, Fallon making it very clear to her and the children to stay clear,

Standing at the top of those stairs and looking down into the darkness beyond, she considered. Would Roishin go this way? Would she defy Fallon's warnings? The image of her second daughter's mischievous and somewhat cocky grin came to mind. Rolling her eyes, Cateline stepped into the winding staircase. Much like the passageway she'd passed through to get to the trunk, it was very dark, though she didn't know this landscape like she had that passageway. She used her fingers to trail along the curving stone walls on either side of her, taking each step slowly. Her own footfalls echoed, setting a disquieting ambiance, as she could never tell if anyone was coming up or not.

Her heart was racing, something niggling at the back of her neck making the hair stand on end. She felt that same unease she had before entering the passageway to the trunk and Fallon's old room. Something was wrong—it was very wrong. She couldn't get her mind to stop telling her this. It was nearly yelling the warning at her.

Something is wrong. Something is wrong. Something is wrong.

She hurried her steps, breathing coming in quick, panicked bursts as she was nearly in tears. She hurried as quickly as she dared until finally she was expelled from the suffocating staircase and into a hallway. Looking around, she saw that it was long and seemingly unending. The floor, walls, and ceiling were all made of large gray stone bricks.

It was dim, mounted torches lit sporadically with deep pockets of shadow in between. The hallway was lined with closed doors. These, she surmised, must be the rooms held by the soldiers. She felt uneasy and certainly unwelcome.

She tried to orient herself to figure out where she was on the second floor. Or, had she gone past the second floor altogether? How far down did the stairs take her? Hearing a distant squeak of hinges, she glanced over her shoulder quickly before turning back around to hurry in the opposite direction.

Finally, she reached the end of the hallway, certain she was going to end up at the stairs that would take her down to the first floor. Instead, she found herself at a junction with two more hallways, both looking exactly like the one she'd just come from. This made no sense. Turning, she looked back the way she'd come, only to see that she was looking at a stone wall.

She stared at it, utterly confused. She *knew* she'd just come from that direction. Again, she heard a noise. This time it was in the tunnel off to the left. It sounded like shuffled steps, as if somebody wasn't quite picking up their feet as they walked. She stared down that hallway, trying to peer through the darkness past the last lit torch she could see.

As she watched, one by one the torches extinguished, as if a huge invisible hand snuffed out the flame. She could hardly move, her feet frozen to the spot as her eyes were trying to convince her brain this was what they were seeing. More shuffling.

Move! Run! Finally, she forced herself to do exactly what the screaming voice inside her head was telling her and took off. Her flowing skirts swam around her legs as she sprinted down the hall to her right. She screamed and skidded to a halt so quickly that she fell to the stone floor. Lying there, she looked on in horror at the man who had stepped into the mouth of the hallway.

The large man stood there, booted feet wide in an aggressive stance. Her gaze flew up over leather trousers, tight due to his girth, and his rotund belly covered by the tunic over his short-sleeved shirt beneath. Meaty hands with sausage-like fingers poked out from the leather bracers he wore.

His heavy, dark beard covered his entire lower face. His long, equally dark hair was swept back in a thick braid. Dark, deep-set eyes were focused on her. His sword was belted at his side, which one meaty hand gripped and slowly began to pull from its scabbard.

"How do you still live?" she whispered, eyes wide and chest heaving with her terrified breaths.

He said nothing as he began to advance on her. Backpedaling, Cateline managed to scramble to her feet and turned only to run right into the arms of a startled Elsie. Crying out, Cateline pushed her away.

"Get away from me! No!"

"Milady!"

Taking fistfuls of the young woman's tunic,

again she tried to push her away, only to be shaken a bit by hands on her shoulders. The movement was just hard enough to get her to take a much-needed breath. Focusing for a moment on the blue eyes of the servant, the princess released the tunic and whipped around, nearly in tears with fear at what she'd seen.

The tapestry. She was staring at the tapestry that covered the door to the secret passageway. "I don't understand," she said, her hand coming up to press against her own chest. Her breathing was heavy and erratic. She started when there was a touch on her arm.

Elsie gently turned Cateline back around to face her. "Milady?" she asked softly. "What happened?"

Cateline took a moment, not entirely sure. "Roishin," she finally said, meeting the young woman's eyes. "I must find her. I...I couldn't find her." Her panic began to rise with her emotional confusion. She shook her head, tears welling. "I couldn't find her."

Elsie took her in a comforting embrace. "Shh, milady," she whispered, cupping the back of Cateline's bead.

Cateline held on to her. "I feel as if I'm losing my mind, Elsie."

"I assure you, you are not."

The young woman's presence was so comforting to Cateline. She allowed herself to be hugged as though she were a babe and the servant a motherly caretaker—and not for the first time. She squeezed her eyes shut.

"I feel faint," she said, blinking her eyes rapidly as she tried to snap herself out of it.

"Come, milady," Elsie said, pulling out of the hug. She looked into Cateline's eyes for just a moment before taking her by the arm and leading her out of the family chamber and toward the bedchamber she shared with Fallon.

"Have you seen Roishin?" Cateline asked, holding on to one of the bedposts for support as Elsie quickly moved the decorative pillows and set them atop Fallon's trunk.

"Nay, milady," Elsie said, moving back over to lead her to her side of the bed and urging her to sit. Once Cateline did, quickly removed the princess's shoes. "Not since breakfast. I can go look for her while you rest, if you like."

Cateline nodded as she scooted farther onto the bed before leaning back to rest against the pillows Elsie had stacked for her comfort. The young servant was about to leave but Cateline reached out, taking her hand to stop her. When Elsie turned to look at her, she asked, "Do you believe in ghosts, Elsie?"

Elsie turned back to the bed, Cateline releasing her hand. "Milady?" she asked.

"Ghosts," Cateline said again. "The dead." Cateline felt so silly asking, but she was deeply shaken by whatever had happened, even if it had only been in her mind. If that were the case, it was even more terrifying to her. "Even if they were a bad person, they can come back and haunt us?"

Elsie looked down at her hands for a moment, which were clasped in front of her. Finally, she looked up to meet Cateline's gaze. "Milady," she said softly. "I do believe there can be restless souls, yes. But," she continued, shaking her head. "I do not believe that is what ails this house."

Surprised, Cateline stared up at her. "Then, what?" When Elsie looked away, her eyebrows knitting and lips pursing, Cateline begged. "I must know."

Looking down at her hands again, finally those soulful blue eyes met those of her mistress once more. "There are things, milady," she whispered. "That wish nothing more than to cause confusion and chaos wherever it goes. There is no cost too high nor too low."

Cateline looked on, mesmerized. The intensity of Elsie's eyes in that moment was almost frightening. The softness of her words were as deep as that of her gaze. "Like what?"

"I dare not mention his name," she said. "For to do so is to whisper invitation."

"I saw something today, Elsie," Cateline said. "I know I did."

"What did you see, milady?"

"A mist, dark like smoke. It seemed to have a mind of its own." She looked away. "I am not crazy, I assure you."

"No, milady," Elsie said, her warm hand covering one of Cateline's, which rested upon her own leg. "You are not."

Cateline looked back to her. "You know what I saw. Don't you." It was a statement, no question in her mind.

Elsie's nod was slow. "Aye." She looked as though she were about to say something else but stopped herself. "I must go, milady."

The words were simply that of a servant who knew she needed to get back to work, but the tone was anything but. It also brooked no argument from the princess. Cateline simply nodded. "Will you send somebody to fetch Fallon, please?"

Elsie nodded. "Aye, milady." With a squeeze,

Elsie released Cateline's hand. She turned to leave but stopped, turning back to the woman reclined on the bed. "Cateline?" The princess started at the sound of her name from the normally docile servant's lips, giving her her full attention. "You must protect Roishin," Elsie said softly. "At any cost."

With those cryptic words, she turned and left.

Chapter Eighteen

Taking the stairs two at a time, Fallon plowed through the castle like a storm. Gods help anyone who got in her way. She thundered her way to the third floor and their bedchamber, out of breath by the time she reached it. Tessa, the castle seamstress, looked up, eyes wide in startled surprise from where she sat by the fire. She was knitting.

Fallon's gaze went from her to the bed, where Cateline was tucked in, curled up with her hands tucked under her chin like a little girl. Taking a moment to calm herself once she saw her wife was okay, the warrior looked to the seamstress.

"Is she all right?"

"Aye, milord," the older woman said. "She didn't want to be alone, so Elsie had me come up here after you were sent for." Nodding, Fallon walked over to the bed. "Shall I send up some food, milord?" she asked, gathering her belongings to prepare to leave. "Her Highness slept right through the midday meal."

Fallon nodded. "Aye." She glanced over to her. "Send Millie up personally, if you would. And, did they find her?"

Tessa shook her head. "Not to my knowledge, milord. I know the castle guard has been searching these past few hours." With a nod and bow, Tessa hurried from the bedchamber.

Climbing onto the bed, Fallon spooned up

behind her wife, knowing she had a few moments before Millie would be up. This was a family situation, and Millie was the only one she trusted to be around it.

"Baby," she murmured, gently pushing long, auburn curls behind an ear. She smiled when she saw the beautiful profile of the woman she loved. She kissed the side of her head. "Baby."

Cateline started, her body jerking as she came into wakefulness. Her eyes blinked open and she took in a deep breath. Head turning, she glanced at Fallon. "Where were you?" she murmured, turning her body so she lay on her other side, facing Fallon. "I've been so scared."

"I'm sorry, love," Fallon murmured, leaving a soft kiss to softer lips. "I was down at the harbor dealing with that labor dispute," she explained softly. "I told you about that this morning." She left another kiss. "What happened? Where's Roishin?"

Cateline's head lifted suddenly and she looked around the bedchamber, then back to Fallon. "She's not back?" she asked, eyes wide. "They haven't found her?" She pushed to a sitting position, as did Fallon.

"No, according to Tessa. What happened?" Fallon asked again. She knew the girl could be a handful at times, but she'd never done anything to intentionally scare her mother, nor would she. That fact made Fallon very nervous.

"She came in this morning to speak to me about something," Cateline explained, bringing up a hand to push the mane of hair away from her face. Clearly it had come loose while she'd been sleeping. "I was busy with Tessa, so she left, said she'd come back." She looked at Fallon, her eyes welling with tears. "She never did, so I went looking."

"And?" Fallon asked softly when there was nothing more forthcoming. She used a fingertip to wipe away a tear that managed to fall.

"I..." She looked away from her, a hand coming up to cover her mouth. Shaking her head as she looked off into a moment that clearly upset her, she whispered, "Something is wrong in this place, Fallon." She met the warrior's gaze. "Very wrong. I ended up in a nightmare that culminated in Fergus coming after me."

"What? Fergus? Did you fall asleep—"

"No!" She climbed off the bed, running her hand through her mass of hair as she began to pace. "I was wide-awake, Fallon. I saw this, this..." She shrugged dramatically. "I don't know. It was like this, this smoke or mist." She looked to Fallon, eyes wide. "It crept along the ground. I followed it and ended up at the door to our secret passage in the family chamber."

Fallon was immediately off the bed like a spring. "Did she go to the trunk?"

"I thought so. It was open, and I went into your old room. She wasn't there, so I kept going. I went down to the barracks."

"Were you hurt? Are you okay? Did they—"

"No." Cateline gave her a comforting smile, walking over to her and taking her larger hand in a smaller, soft one. "Nobody bothered me."

Blowing out a relieved breath, Fallon nodded. It had been instilled in the men for decades, but after what had happened to Livia so many years ago— beaten and left for dead by one of her men—she never, ever wanted her family put in that potential danger again. She'd made it an absolute hand-in-fist law that the women and girls stay out of that part of the castle, no matter what.

"But," Cateline added. "That was where things took a nightmarish turn. I was awake, Fallon. I know I was. But then, suddenly, there he was." A violent shiver ran through Cateline's body as she hugged herself.

Fallon pulled her into her arms, able to feel how much she was trembling. "Was he spirit?" she asked carefully, not sure what to think or say.

"I thought so perhaps, but then," Cateline continued, her voice quiet. "Next thing I knew, Elsie had me by the arms and was looking at me like I'd lost my mind." Fresh tears began. "I had never gone anywhere, Fallon. I was still at the door to the passage."

Stunned, Fallon was about to speak but felt a presence. Turning, she saw an extremely contrite-looking Roishin standing just inside the open door of their bedchamber. Instantly, she felt anger flow through her like lava.

"Where have you been?" she demanded, releasing Cateline and hurrying over to the girl. "Where?" She grabbed her by the shoulders, her grip like iron. "Do you have any idea how much you've scared the hell out of your mother?" She shook her. "Do you!"

"Fallon!"

Nearly seeing red, Fallon stumbled back a few steps as Cateline's voice cut through her rage. She literally had to brace herself with a hand on a table for stability to not fall. She felt like she was watching the other two through the fog of a dream. As if in slow motion, she saw Cateline's hands go to Roishin's shoulders—the firm touch of a frantic mother, not the grip of a seasoned warrior.

She saw tears slowly falling from Roishin's eyes, turned an incredibly vivid green in her upset. She saw the slow movement of Cateline's hand as it reached up and brushed hair out of Roishin's face. She heard their voices, though they were slow and slurred in the haze Fallon was in.

Lifting her own hand, she felt like she was moving it through water. Looking up, she saw Enori standing just outside of the bedchamber door. She was dressed in her ever-present white gown, though this time she wore her blue cloak as well.

The anger returning, Fallon pushed through her dense reality, moving around her wife and daughter, who didn't even seem to notice her. As soon as she stepped over the threshold of the bedchamber, she was in Enori's stone chamber in the cave.

Taken totally off guard, she stopped, looking around in shock. When her eyes landed on Enori again, who stood a few feet away, the warrior's rage returned in spades. Reality sped up again, and she was over to the priestess in a heartbeat. Hand around her throat, she had her pressed against the hard stone of the wall.

"I warned you," she growled. "Stay away from my daughter!"

The blonde stared up at her, cerulean eyes calm. "Remove your hand from me."

In response, Fallon tightened her grip. "I will kill you for taking my—"

Suddenly, an immense pressure began to build in Fallon until finally it seemed to explode, and she flew through the air. Landing against the wall clear across the chamber, she hit hard, then slid down to the stone floor to her rear end. She sat there, dazed.

"I highly recommend you never put your hands on me again," Enori said calmly. She walked over to Fallon and extended a hand down to her. She waited patiently until Fallon took it, the smaller woman surprisingly strong as she helped pull Fallon to her feet. "Now, sit down and listen."

Fallon's head was killing her. She smirked as she couldn't help but think that the damn healer would be mad at her for yet another brain commotion. She would have absolutely defied the woman and tore her to shreds if this wasn't about Roishin. She made her way over to one of the stone stools at the table and sat.

Enori untied her cloak, shrugging the heavy garment from her shoulders and walking over to a spike pounded into the stone, which she hung it on. "I did not take Roishin," she began, walking over to a shelf where there were several little leather pouches. She fingered through them before grabbing what she was looking for. "We have a very significant problem, Fallon."

"What?" Fallon asked, watching as the priestess pulled one of the pouches away from the others and set it aside as she poured some clear liquid from a clay jug into a wooden cup. She then reached her fingers into the pouch and took a pinch of powder, dropping it into the liquid.

There was a quiet sizzling sound as Enori walked over to Fallon. "Drink this," she said. "It will help with the pain in your head."

Fallon stared at her. She wanted to ask how she knew that but wasn't about to give her the satisfaction. Instead, she looked down into the liquid. She sniffed, smelling nothing except the water that was the liquid. Taking a careful sip, she also tasted nothing out of the ordinary, so she drained the cup.

"Roishin has grown stronger and more powerful much earlier than I expected," Enori said, sitting on the stool across the stone table from Fallon. "Obviously, we knew it was coming for her to mature in her gifts, but thought we'd have a little more time." She met Fallon's gaze and held it. "Not only did she find a door, she managed to open it."

Fallon cocked her head to the side. "I do that every single day." That retort was met with a very unamused quirk of a delicately arched eyebrow. Fallon, a woman who had been self-assured her entire life, felt absolutely stupid around this being, and it drove her crazy! Clearing her throat, she set the emptied cup back on the table. "What does that mean?" She was, however, quite stunned to realize the blacksmith's hammer that had been pounding inside her skull was fading, and quickly.

"It means she found her way here." Enori indicated the cave around them. "You see," she said, gaze boring into Fallon's. "There are doors all over the world, Fallon. Some are created naturally and exist in nature." A little smile spread across her lips. "One you found as a small girl."

Fallon stared at her. She had no idea why, but unbidden came her waterfall to her mind's eye. Enori nodded.

"Yes. You've always known it was something special, Fallon." Reverence was in Enori's soft voice. "You've always marveled that it looks nothing like Sursha."

Fallon could only stare at her. "How did you know that?" she whispered.

Enori said nothing, just gave her a sweet smile.

"You've just never been able to figure out how to open it," she said softly. Her tone grew a bit stronger as she continued. "Some doors are put there on purpose. The door Roishin found was put there nearly four hundred years ago."

"How do you know?" Fallon asked, her voice quiet. Her mind was racing all over the place, and it had nothing to do with the bonk to her head. She was stunned.

"Because I was there when it was built."

"The trunk," Fallon whispered.

"The trunk." At Enori's nod, Fallon ran a hand through her hair. Her mind was filled with so many questions, many of which she felt like she already had the answers to, but she didn't know why—or how to access them.

"Fallon."

The warrior spared a glance to the other woman.

"Roishin's father is not the only one who passed gifts on to her." Her gaze bored into Fallon's again, nailing her to the spot. "So did her mothers."

"Mothers," Fallon said. "You said Cateline and I *both* are her mothers."

Enori nodded. "I did, and you are."

"So," she said slowly. "Cateline and I..." She didn't even know how to finish the sentence, not entirely sure what she was asking.

"Her light is glowing brighter, Fallon," Enori said. "And he knows she's there. He's found her."

"Who?" Recognizing that the question-and-answer period was over, Fallon shook her head. "What is happening in my house?"

"An ancient evil," she explained. "Here since the beginning of time." She pushed up from her stool and walked over to the same shelf where she'd gotten the pain powder for Fallon. She poured two wooden goblets of wine from another clay jug. She set one in front of Fallon before reclaiming her seat with her own wine. "He has no physical form, so must use that of humans, animals, weather, whatever he can."

Fallon took a sip of the sweet wine, considering the words for a moment. Suddenly, the shadow she'd seen that day on the training field came to mind, then what Cateline had just told her earlier that very day.

"This *thing* wants to take over Roishin?"

Enori shook her head. "Not exactly. He wants to manipulate her to do his bidding."

"How?"

"We do not know, yet." Enori sipped her wine. For the first time since Fallon had met this woman, she seemed concerned, truly concerned. "We don't know the extent of Roishin's power, Fallon."

"She's a child, Enori," Fallon said passionately.

"No," she said softly. "She is a demigod, and far more god than human."

Fallon stared at her, slouching where she sat as though the air had been knocked out of her. It took her several moments to wrap her mind around that one. She took a long sip from her wine. Finally, she asked, "Is that why you want her?"

Enori studied her. "Is that what you really think, Fallon?"

"I don't know what to think," Fallon murmured, setting her wine down and running her hands through her hair as she blew out a breath. "What *do* you want with her?"

"As I said last time we had this conversation: to train her," Enori said simply. "We need to find out what her powers are and how to contain them until she's old enough to have self-awareness, self-control. To keep her safe. And," she added. "To keep *you* and your family safe. He's already gotten to you and Cateline."

Fallon's heart literally began to hurt at the thought of losing her daughter. She forced back the sting of emotion as she looked away from the woman who sat across from her, compassion in her beautiful eyes.

She thought about the past nearly thirteen years with her. Roishin was her buddy; they did so much together.

A small smile touched her lips when she remembered the day she brought Roishin to her waterfall. She hadn't really understood it, but she'd felt such a need to do that. Now, as she sat in a cave so far from home, she had to wonder. Had some part of her known the whole time? Known what, though? Which part?

She thought of how Roishin had joined her so many times for business in the village. The constant chatter of the girl, the way they bantered and teased each other. Her hand came up, thumb gently easing a tear off her cheek. She looked at the moisture on the tip of the digit, which glistened in the firelight from the fireplace.

That, of course, brought her back to their very real reality. Tears. Roishin's tears, and what she could do with such a simple essence. Then she thought about something Enori had said the last time she was there: *You've seen what she can do with her tears, imagine what she could do with her blood.*

Though she still didn't exactly know what that meant, those words had much more meaning to her today. She looked up when she felt a warm hand rest upon the bracer that covered her other forearm. She looked up to see Enori looking at her. She couldn't speak, her heart was broken.

"I promise you," Enori said softly. "This is not goodbye."

"How long will she be gone?" Fallon managed.

"She must mature. As a child, she is incredibly vulnerable."

Fallon nodded. It wasn't an answer exactly, but at least a bit of an idea. "Let me speak with Cateline."

"May I?"

Fallon met her gaze and held it, immediately that protective shield coming up when it came to her princes. Ultimately, she knew Cateline deserved that right, to ask any questions she may have or express concerns. She deserved to hear it directly from Enori, woman to woman, as it were.

Nodding, she said, "Yes." She blew out a heavy breath before taking her wine and downing the rest of it. "I must go." When she pushed to her feet, Enori did as well. Glancing around the chamber, Fallon asked, "Uh, how do I leave?"

Enori smirked, nodding to the doorway of the chamber. "Through the door." She walked over to the stone slab at the center of the chamber and scooped something into her hand. Walking over to Fallon, she opened her palm. "Don't lose this again," she said softly but firmly.

Fallon looked down to see the medallion her father had given her so long ago, and which she'd childishly removed during her last visit, as contentious as it was. She walked over to her and gathered up the medallion, the gold chain dangling from her fingers.

Nodding, she closed her fingers around it.

"Thank you, Enori," she said softly.

"For what?"

Fallon looked down at the medallion again before she gripped the chain, allowing the heavy gold serpent-wrapped crystal skull to fall, straightening the chain with that action. She lifted it up and over her head, setting the chain in place at the back of her neck. She met the priestess's eyes.

"For bringing her back home," she said quietly.

Chapter Nineteen

With a grunt, Fallon landed, yet again, on her behind. Staring up, dazed, she realized she was in her old bedchamber, her legs still partially in the trunk. "That woman is going to be the death of me," she muttered, pulling her legs free.

Getting to her feet, she looked down into the trunk, half expecting to see Enori staring back up at her. Nope, just the stone stairs that headed down into the passageway. She stood there for a moment, her mind growing foggy once more. Why was she there? She looked around the old bedroom, hoping she'd see something that would spark a memory.

The bed, even without its mattress. Immediately she saw Cateline's face. The goofy smile faded as that face morphed into terror, then tears. Knocked into action, she nearly threw herself down through the trunk to the stairs and passageway below. She ran through the tunnel, heavy footfalls echoing all around her against the stone until she exploded into the family chamber.

Running through that room, she reached the one she shared with her wife. It was empty. Panic setting in, Fallon stormed out and pounded down the stairs to the second floor and down the hall until she reached Roishin's bedchamber. Her forehead rested against the closed door as relief so great reached her that she nearly burst into tears.

Just on the other side of the thick door she heard loud exclamations through tears and a quieter, soothing voice. Nothing could be understood, but she knew it was the voices of Cateline and Roishin. Forcing herself to take a deep, centering breath, she opened the door and stepped inside the room, closing the door behind her.

Sitting on the bed was a sobbing Roishin, Cateline holding her, trying to calm her. Fallon stood there, feeling so utterly out of place when her daughter just stared at her. Normally, she would have flown off that bed and into her arms or would have shot some teasing remark at her with the accuracy of her best bullseye.

In that moment, looking into those deeply hurt green eyes, she knew Enori was right. She couldn't even keep her daughter safe from *her* and these paralyzing rages that were erupting with more and more frequency, let alone some unseen evil. Maybe, she thought, absolutely hating herself, maybe the "unseen evil" was her.

Forcing herself to push that particular thought out of her mind, she walked over to the bed. Cateline was eyeing her the entire way, even as she continued to stroke Roishin's hair with a comforting hand. It wasn't exactly anger she saw in their stormy depths, but uncertainty and a bit of fear.

"Where have you been?" Cateline asked quietly. "You vanished."

Fallon nodded, walking over to the bed. Clearing her throat, she indicated the piece of furniture. "May I sit?"

Both parents looked to Roishin, as it was her bedroom and her bed. Finally, she nodded, though she cuddled closer to her mother. Never feeling more like a horrible person in her entire life, Fallon sat down, hands in her lap as she tried to gather her emotions and words. She looked down at her hands, feeling ever the chided child. Finally, she garnered the courage to face her wife and daughter.

"I was with Enori."

Roishin studied her, eyes hard. "How?" There seemed to be a test in that one, simple word.

Fallon met her gaze and held it. "Through the door."

Roishin dissolved into tears, sounding relieved this time. Fallon's maternal need to comfort her child overrode her sheepish guilt. She scooted over to two of the most important people in her world and wrapped her arms around them both. Roishin clung to her, but Cateline was a bit tepid in her response.

Leaving a kiss to her daughter's forehead, Fallon looked to her wife, who moved away from her yet kept a protective arm around Roishin. Fallon stayed sitting where she was but gave her wife the space she clearly needed from her. She knew she needed to explain everything in order to fix this. *I'm sorry* wasn't going to cut it anymore, regardless of just how sorry she was, and just how out of her hands it had become.

"Roishin didn't mean to scare us today," she began softly, meeting Cateline's guarded gaze. "You and I discussed how incredibly special she is." She didn't want to go further, as she wasn't sure what Enori had told Roishin. Strangely, she didn't feel it was for her or Cateline to explain her lineage. "But, as her gifts are growing, something very dark has noticed." Her gaze bored into Cateline, needing her to really hear her. "And, it's here."

She saw understanding begin to bloom in the stormy depths, and she was so grateful. Never looking away from them, Fallon reached over and took one of Cateline's hands. It took a moment, but finally soft, warm fingers wrapped around her own. Something passed between them, that pledge of everlasting love and understanding, and Fallon felt her world right itself, if just for a moment. The situation was far from over.

Turning her attention to Roishin, she said, "Sweetheart, I am so sorry about earlier. I'm so sorry I was so rough with you." She looked away, almost holding her breath as emotion pricked at the backs of her eyes. She swallowed, trying desperately to keep centered, when she felt a small hand take her own.

Tears in her eyes, she turned her head and saw Roishin looking at her. In that moment, she wasn't looking at a thirteen-year-old girl, she was looking at eternity itself. If she hadn't believed Enori before, she would have been convinced right then and there.

Something passed through mother and daughter, no words necessary. Fallon saw the light return to those beautiful green eyes, so much like her own mother's, she was told. In their depths she saw understanding, she saw forgiveness, and she saw love. Smiling, Fallon leaned over and left a kiss to her daughter's forehead again, filled with gratitude.

Releasing the girl, she took a deep breath and looked to both. "We need to come up with a plan to get rid of this bastard before something truly catastrophic happens."

"We'll never get rid of him as long as I'm here, Daidí."

Fallon could only stare at her for a moment.

"Did Enori tell you that today?"

Roishin shook her head. "She didn't have to." She looked from one to the other. "I just realized, just now," she began. "He's been using your strengths against you." She focused on Fallon. "You're a protector, Daidí, a warrior. He's turned that into aggression. And, Mamaí," she added, looking over at Cateline. "Your love and natural concern for your children, he's warping into fear and paranoia."

Fallon could only stare at her, mouth hanging open. Looking to Cateline, she saw similar surprise in her eyes. Their gazes met, then returned to Roishin. "Roishin," she said gently. "Do you want to go with Enori?"

Roishin didn't respond for a long time, her eyes falling to look at her hands, which fidgeted in her lap. Finally, she said. "I do and I don't." She met Fallon's gaze. "I mean, lately I've felt this intense need to be with her. Almost as if to be with her will help me understand me." She glanced over to Cateline. "I don't want to leave you, though." She looked back to Fallon. "Either of you. Or Laigen and Garratt. Livia. Isabeau."

She tucked her bottom lip in as if to try to hold in her own emotions over the situation. Regardless of the aged soul that resided in that body, Roishin was still only a thirteen-year-old girl at the surface.

"Can Enori come here?" Cateline asked softly, looking to Fallon as she gently ran her fingers through Roishin's long hair, which trailed down her back. "She's a human. Right?" There was so much uncertainty in her voice.

Fallon certainly couldn't answer to the second part of Cateline's question, no idea what to think of the priestess. "She can come," she said, as she understood it. "But I think the problem is that none of us can keep Roishin safe here." Fallon indicated the bedchamber and castle and world beyond that. "I think Enori and the Order of Ankou has special…ways, to keep her safe there." She smirked. "Wherever *there* is."

"In the caves," Roishin said, a note of awe in her voice. "It's unlike anything I've ever felt, this connection. Princess Enori. Keeper of the Doors Andrev. Even Warrior Donan, who I think is a little odd—they all understand me." Eyes bright, she looked from Fallon to Cateline and back. "They know what I'm talking about when I mention the dreams, and Enori understood when I told her how I felt about Elsie, and—" Eyes wide, her hand came up to clap over her mouth.

Fallon looked past the girl who looked like she wanted to hide beneath the quilt to Cateline, who met her gaze. *Elsie? Do you know about this?* With the subtle shake of Cateline's head in response, Fallon turned back to their daughter. It was extremely hard not to feel defensive or like a complete failure as a parent, though Fallon knew they weren't, nor was that what was Roishin was saying.

It still hurt, and she still hated the situation.

⚶⚶⚶⚶

Fallon deepened her voice a bit as she sang all the different parts of the song she was singing to Isabeau. Her eyebrows shot up as her voice rose to sing for the mother swan before deepening again for the father swan. A tale as old as time—love. The baby smiled and blew spit bubbles in reaction to the performance.

Grinning, Fallon lowered her face to a pale, rounded belly and blew loud, obnoxious raspberries against the skin, making the infant squeal and giggle loudly. She finished the song as she finished changing the little one. Picking her up in strong arms once the nearly five-month-old was dressed again, she placed a soft kiss on the baby's head.

"We're no longer stinky, are we?" she asked, shaking her head. "No, we are not." She glanced over when Cateline entered the room, a small clay baby bottle in hand. She walked over to the pair and handed it to Fallon.

"*Bonjour*, Isabeau," she murmured, leaving noisy kisses to the baby's neck, earning more squeals. Cateline's smile was beautiful. "Happy girl this evening."

Fallon nodded. "*Oui.*" She grinned over at Cateline.

Cateline rolled her eyes, smacking Fallon playfully on the behind. "If you want to feed her, I can finally get your trousers fixed."

"I can do that." Fallon nodded down toward the diaper change on the bed with a raised eyebrow, as her arms were quite full.

Chuckling, Cateline nodded. "I'll take care of it." She grabbed it and carried the mess to the garderobe to allow what could to fall down into the moat. The rest would need to be washed out.

Fallon carried the baby and bottle of goat's milk to one of the chairs near the fireplace and sat down. Getting settled, she cradled Isabeau in her left arm and held the bottle in her right. Now that it was settled that the baby was theirs, they were moving her out of Mary's room and to their own, just as they had

Roishin as an infant.

Despite their own upbringings, or perhaps because of it, neither believed in having somebody else raise their children. With both of their mothers dying so young in their lives, both had been raised by servants as their only mother figure. Fallon had essentially been raised by house servant Collette and Cateline by Marie, who had remained her lady-in-waiting until after Cateline had married Fergus. Once Marie had left to marry Henri, Livia had stepped into the role for a time.

Certainly, servants had helped with Roishin as a baby, and Laigen and Garratt as children, and they would continue to do so with Isabeau by helping with routine tasks like dressing and cleaning. But for the actual day-to-day parenting, Fallon and Cateline believed fiercely that was *their* job.

Because of that, there was no doubt, Fallon thought sadly, why she was so bothered by the situation with Enori and the Order of Ankou. She understood, absolutely, at a fundamental level that this had to be done. Yes, for Roishin's safety, but also because Enori and the others understood what she and Cateline couldn't even fathom, let alone help their daughter with.

But oh, how it hurt! And, she had to admit, it made her feel incredibly angry. Now that she understood that her rising anger of late wasn't wholly her doing, she tried to make it work for her, even as she still felt its toxicity. She was trying desperately to keep it down, to channel it into other things. Such as, she thought with a smile, feeding the little one in her arms. Still, she knew it was only a temporary measure.

She'd have to do something later to get the

aggression out—perhaps training the tar out of an unsuspecting soldier on the practice fields, or, more hopefully, maybe Cateline would be up for some rather...intense private time together later. The woman of the hour and star of Fallon's endless fantasies returned after taking care of the diaper and getting it to the laundress.

She followed the stunning redhead with her eyes as she made her way to the matching chair to Fallon's, whose leather pants were already waiting there with needle and thread from earlier that day.

As she gathered up the pants, Cateline glanced over at Fallon, a knowing twinkle in her eyes. "I see," she said, voice nearly a purr.

Fallon grinned, turning her focus back down to the baby.

"You know," Cateline continued conversationally as she organized herself for her task. "It's a good thing you cannot get me pregnant." She eyed Fallon without moving her head. "We'd be on our fifteenth child by now."

Chuckling, Fallon glanced back over at her. "Do you honestly think I'd do that to you?" She laughed outright at the look she got. "Are you complaining, Princess?"

Though Cateline didn't respond verbally, the side-eye Fallon received told her that training fields would not be necessary later. The subject making her wonder out loud about what Roishin had said earlier, Fallon readjusted the bottle a bit for easier access to Isabeau.

"What do you know of the situation with Roishin and Elsie?" she asked. "Has something happened?"

Cateline shrugged a shoulder as she concentrated

on her sewing. "I think Roishin has a crush," she said. Shaking her head, she briefly met Fallon's gaze. "I don't think it's anything more. That is, I've never seen anything inappropriate from Elsie. Nothing above a truly devoted servant to her family."

Fallon nodded, thinking the same thing but wasn't sure if she'd missed something. She was, however, surprised by her wife's next words.

"That being said, I want Elsie to stay with Roishin, Fallon. Until all this is settled and Roishin is safe."

Studying the other woman, Fallon's eyebrows fell. "What do you mean? Why?"

Cateline was quiet for a moment, as if organizing her thoughts on the subject. Finally, she spoke. "Twice now, while in one of these crazy...*fogs*, I guess they can be called, Elsie has been there. She's just shown up, and I just have a feeling in my gut that she understands all this somehow. I can't explain it. It's almost like she can see into the soul." She met Fallon's gaze. "Does that make sense?"

Though Fallon had no experience with the young servant beyond her basic duties to the family, she'd certainly seen that with Enori, and with Roishin, for that matter. Nodding, she said. "Aye. Why do you want her to stay with Roishin? And, do you mean literally?"

Cateline nodded. "*Oui.* I think she'd do anything she could to protect Roishin, and I have the feeling she'd sense if something were wrong. If nothing else, she could come get one of us." She held Fallon's gaze. "I do not think Roishin should be alone until she is safe."

Fallon considered then asked, "Do you want to

bring her in here with us?"

Cateline shook her head. "No. I don't think that's necessary. She is a smart girl and now understands what is happening." She let out a long, tired sigh. "And strangely, right now I think Elsie can do more for her than we can."

"Do you think she's like Roishin?" Fallon asked slowly, not even entirely sure what that meant.

"To a point, yes."

Fallon stared at her, quite surprised at that. She'd certainly have to pay closer attention to this young woman. "All right. I'm fine with that, as long as the poor thing won't kill Roishin by time this is all over."

※ ※ ※ ※

Night had fallen and the castle was quiet. The baby slept soundly in her cradle nearer the fireplace than the bed where two figures slept just as peacefully. Soft, deep breathing could be heard, as well as the quiet crackling and popping from the fireplace, which sent a pleasant orange glow to the surrounds.

Beneath the closed, double chambers doors was a small bit of space between the bottom edge of the thick plank wood and the cold stone floor. A dark mist eased through the space, slow and purposeful. The mist swirled and meandered until it was all inside the bedchamber.

Moving low along the floor, it billowed its way to the canopied bed. It arched its way up and over until it reached the naked form of Fallon. She lay on her back, head turned away from Cateline, who lay on her stomach, arms tucked up under her pillow. Her long, curly auburn hair draped across her own pillow and Fallon's left arm.

The mist ducked and danced above Fallon's head, swirling itself round and round and round until it was all in a coil, spinning above her. It stopped, the mist thinning itself into the width of a very small twig. The point of that narrow stream eased down to the slightly opened lips of the sleeping warrior, then, inch by inch by inch, disappeared inside her mouth.

Chapter Twenty

Chewing on her bottom lip, Roishin glanced over again at the figure that lay in the small bed that had been brought into her chamber to her absolute and near-paralyzing shock. She lifted her head to get yet another look at her unexpected guest. Elsie lay on her side, her back to Roishin. She wore a simple sleeping gown, something Roishin had never seen her in. And, as a bonus, her hair was down, a golden wave across her pillow.

"Are you okay, milady?" came the quiet voice from the resting body.

Roishin's head fell quickly back to her own pillow, eyes squeezing shut. "Yup. Just sleepin'." *Crap.*

Elsie lifted her head and glanced at her over her shoulder before turning her body so she was facing Roishin's side of the large bedchamber. From the glow of the fireplace, Roishin could see her face.

"Are you okay?" she asked again, her voice soft in the night.

Roishin faced Elsie, the expanse of her bedchamber between them. Her desk had been moved to make room for the small bed, which had been taken directly from Elsie's room in the servant's quarters. No doubt, many a confused look had followed that bed on its journey down the hall.

"I am." She studied the young woman's face, noting she looked tired. "I'm so sorry you ended up in here." She snorted. "No doubt the last place you wanted to be sleeping right now. Well," she added with a smirk. "Trying to sleep while a pesky princess prattles."

Some amusement crossed Elsie's lips, but she shook her head. "No, it's all right, milady. I understand why Her Highness asked me to do this."

"Can you...Will you...call me Roishin, when we're alone?" Roishin asked. She scrunched up her face in distaste. "I'm not into the whole titles thing. I get why they're there, it's just not me."

Elsie studied her for a moment as if weighing the request against possible consequences, but then nodded. "Aye." She quirked an eyebrow, just a bit darker blond than the hair on her head. "If I get into trouble..."

Roishin grinned. "Honestly, do you think you'll get into trouble being around me?" She snickered at the look that received.

It looked like iron, perhaps? It was smooth, cold and black. It slowly moved farther away, slowly, slowly.

A soft voice, a female voice, lyrical, beautiful. Unable to understand what was being said—a chant. Softly, softly, softly. It was mesmerizing.

The smooth, black iron...something...moved even farther away. Now it was easy to see that it was a box of sorts. Treasure chest? The lid was open and a swoop over and down inside showed that it was empty. Farther away from it yet revealed a figure standing in the shadows. More chanting, which seemed to come from the figure.

Suddenly, with a loud CLANG, the lid slammed closed. The figure, still in shadow, held up a huge iron lock.

Sapphire-blue eyes opened, and the chanting grew louder.

Green eyes popped open, blinking a few times before they remained open. Glancing to her right, Roishin saw that Elsie, too, was just waking. She lay there on her back, staring up at the ceiling for a moment before she sat up. Her long hair fell forward like a golden curtain. Roishin was awestruck. Elsie's hands disappeared underneath that curtain for a moment, as though rubbing at her face and sleepy eyes. A moment later, that hair was pushed back from her face by her hands, a golden wave sent down her back.

Roishin wondered what it felt like. Was it as soft as it looked? The young princess's gaze darted away as Elsie turned her head to glance over at her. Trying to focus on herself and getting her brain working, Roishin took a deep breath.

"Milady," Elsie said quietly. "I mean, Roishin. What do you wish to do with your day so I know how I can best be of service to you?"

Chewing on her lip, Roishin considered. All sorts of fun things popped into mind, including wandering the grounds of the castle, taking a stroll through the massive rose garden. She could teach Elsie how to shoot—

Okay, she needed to stop. No, this wasn't a vacation day for either of them, regardless of how drastic a change it was for both of them. Yes, this was a serious situation, serious enough for poor Elsie to be put on constant guard duty, but there were still things that had to be done. Pushing her own mass of hair back from her face, she sat up.

"You know, Elsie," she said, meeting the servant's gaze. "What you do here is a whole lot more important than any meanderings I may have in mind." She gave her what she hoped was a sweet smile. "How about instead of you stuck hanging out with me today, I hang out with you? I can help you with whatever you'd normally do."

Elsie looked surprised, and honestly, touched. "Um," she said softly. "Only if you're sure, Roishin. I don't mind."

Roishin gave her a winning smile. "See that? And neither do I. It's settled. You lead, I'll follow."

༄ ༄ ༄ ༄

The two young women got ready for their day in Roishin's bedchamber, Roishin offering Elsie use of her garderobe and boudoir for privacy to get dressed and freshen up for her day. What Roishin had worried would be strained and uncomfortable had been anything but.

She'd lost her shyness—to a point—and managed to not stare at the beauty who shared her space. In return, Elsie had been sweet and surprisingly talkative.

They'd discussed favorite flowers, and yes, Roishin had finally found out her favorite color—blue. Somehow, that didn't surprise Roishin. It was such a calming, tranquil color, and Elsie didn't look all that surprised at Roishin's favorite color of red. As fiery as the young princess was, it no doubt made sense to her.

The truth was, Roishin was seeing Elsie in a very different way this day. Of course she was stunning; that went without saying. But now she was seeing her as a regular person, one with feelings and thoughts and memories and opinions. One who thought roses were the most beautiful flower and wished to one day spend time in the gardens just to wander and enjoy unbidden.

She was a woman of soft voice but huge heart, Roishin sensed. She wondered what it would have been like had they met in another lifetime where they were closer in age and either both servants or simply average villagers who could become friends. Though they'd chatted, understandably Elsie had her guard up still.

What was she like when the guard was down? What was she like when she felt comfortable to fully be herself? Roishin knew she'd been through a lot, and at a very young age. Even still she hadn't lost her heart, hadn't lost what Roishin suspected was a true sense of wonder beneath that incredibly mature top layer.

"You know where I want to take you?" Roishin said, the two leaving her rooms and heading for the stairs and the kitchens.

"Where's that, milady?" Elsie asked, her manner stiffening a bit once they were away from the privacy of the princess's bedchamber.

Roishin hated hearing her titles upon those beautiful lips again but certainly understood. "To the waterfall," she said. She smiled over at her companion as they walked. "Near Daideó's castle," she explained. "There's this incredible waterfall that Daidí took me to." Her smile widened as she saw it again in her mind's eye. "It's secret."

Elsie glanced at her, eyebrows raised in interest. "Secret?"

"Aye." Roishin pulled open the door for Elsie that would allow them to enter the hallway that led to the kitchen. "Daidí said nobody else knows about it. He discovered it as a lad."

"Thank you," Elsie said softly, entering before Roishin. "I'd love to see it."

Suddenly, a new life goal was etched into Roishin's brain as the two headed down the hallway. She stopped their conversation as she knew she was in Elsie's world now and needed to heed how it worked and respect her place in it.

The kitchen was a largish room and, as it had every time Roishin had been in it, felt like the eternal pits of the Christian Hell. Instantly, her hair felt like it was stuck to her scalp from the constant fires burning and humidity of water always boiling for this or that. Millie, the longtime castle cook and friend of her parents, was standing at a massive pot. She used powerful forearms to mix whatever was inside with a paddle.

The blonde, who looked to be in her forties somewhere, glanced at the pair. She didn't bother to hide her surprise at seeing Roishin following the servant after she glanced at Elsie.

"What's this?" she asked. "Take your princess to work day?"

Roishin cackled. "Oh, Millie, Millie, Millie," she murmured. "No, this fine young woman was saddled with me, so I'm helping her," she explained, nodding toward Elsie, who was already gathering filled platters to be placed on a tray that would be brought up to the family chamber.

She wanted to make it very evident to anyone who overheard the conversation that this was not

Elsie's fault nor choice. From what she'd learned over the years, the servant class could be a gripey bunch. Though Fallon and Cateline treated them very well, there was still always an underlying sense of vying for position or privilege.

Those who were perceived as having any sort of favoritism, even if it wasn't truly the case, could find themselves shunned or gossiped about. Roishin absolutely did not want that for Elsie. In fact, she wouldn't stand for it. She knew they'd be talked about, so Roishin wanted to set the terms of *what* would be talked about.

"Oh?" Millie questioned, hand on rounded hip.

"Aye," Roishin said, walking over to Elsie to watch her load the tray, waiting to help. "Seems I've got some evil following me now," Roishin continued conversationally as she glanced over to the cook. "Mamaí wanted to ensure that nothing crazy would happen to me."

Millie chuckled, nodding. "Finally started your bleed, did'ja?" She spared a glance to the teen. "That bloody wench certainly does make you feel mad at times." She sent a loving look to the princess. "Congratulations on becoming a woman, milady."

Roishin gave her a winning smile before turning back to Elsie, who she saw was trying to hide her grin. "What would you like me to do?" she asked her.

"Um," Elsie said, meeting her gaze for a moment before looking to the large table which Millie used to knead the dough for her incredible bread. "If you could grab that bowl of bread slices, milady?"

Roishin gave her a little curtsey. "I can."

"Grab that fruit, too," Millie said, hitching a thumb to a bowl filled with berries. "Fallon is feeling a bit rough this morning and asked only for that."

Instantly, Roishin felt a stab of worry. "Is Daidí all right?"

Millie shrugged, glancing over at the two young women. "Cateline came in this morning to get milk for Isabeau and said His Highness woke up feeling just awful."

Chewing on the inside of her lip, Roishin walked over to the indicated bowl, absently grabbing it and bringing it back to the tray. It was possible—even probable—that Fallon could have snagged herself a late spring cold. But, with everything else happening, Roishin worried about everyone in the castle.

❧ ❧ ❧ ❧

The two had opted to divide and conquer. Once they reached the family chamber, Roishin intended to take the fruit directly to her parents' rooms, as she knew Cateline would stay with Fallon if she was ill. She headed to their bedchamber while Elsie readied the breakfast table for the other family members, who would be drifting in soon.

A small tray in hand with food for her parents as well as a pitcher of wine, Roishin lightly tapped the closed bedchamber door with the toe of her boot. A moment later, Cateline opened the door, baby Isabeau in her arms. Her eyes widened when she saw a smiling Roishin standing on the other side.

"Do I even want to know?" Cateline chuckled.

"I'm helping Elsie today," the young princess explained easily as she breezed by her mother after sticking her tongue out to make her new little sister smile.

She walked over to the small table between the matching chairs by the fireplace and set her tray down. A glance to her daidí had her concerned. Fallon was reclined back against stacked pillows. She wore a sleeping gown and her long, dark hair was unbraided. She looked pale and tired.

Looking to her mother, she asked softly, "What's wrong?"

"She woke up this way," Cateline responded, swaying with the baby as it looked like she was trying to get her to settle into sleep. "Nauseous, chills."

Roishin walked over to the bed on Fallon's side. Hooded violet eyes opened as Fallon glanced over at her. She smiled. "Good morrow," she said, voice weak.

"Not so sure about that," Roishin murmured. She took one of Fallon's hands, noting it was clammy. "Millie sent me up with the fruit you asked for. Want some?"

Fallon glanced over to the table where the food had been left. Closing her eyes again, she nodded. "Aye. I'll try and get something down."

Roishin smiled, squeezing the fingers wrapped around her own before she released the hand and hurried to the fruit. She grabbed a slice of Millie's famous bread, too. She hoped maybe it could help soak up some of that nausea.

"I will not do it, Fallon," Cateline said. "I will not leave you like this, and I will not leave Roishin while this...this...*thing* is hunting her and our family."

Roishin glanced over to her parents as Cateline joined Fallon on the bed, rubbing Isabeau's back as the infant was becoming drowsy. Clearly, they had been mid-conversation when Roishin had arrived. For her mother to continue it in her presence obviously meant it was serious enough that it couldn't wait and they didn't mind her hearing. Far too often she'd wandered into a room and her parents had grown quiet, their discussion hovering midair waiting for her to leave.

"My love," Fallon said, grunting as she tried to push herself up into more of a sitting position against the pillows and large backboard. "I'm fine. I get sick about once every twenty years, and I think my time has caught up with me. But," she added, pinning Cateline to the spot with her gaze. "I cannot get well and worry about you and Isabeau, too."

Cateline was about to climb off the bed as finally little Isabeau gave in and closed her eyes. Roishin hurried around to her side of the bed. "I'll take her, Mamaí," she said softly, reaching for the baby after she'd set down the sturdy wooden tray on the bed between the two adults. "You two eat."

"*Merci*, my sweet," Cateline said, the two gently passing the sleeping infant from one set of arms to the other.

Baby in her arms, Roishin walked over to the ornate cradle, which she, too, had apparently been reared in. As much as she didn't want to purposefully listen to her parents, she perked her ears as she lovingly lay Isabeau down for her nap.

"Fallon, I—"

"It is not safe for you here, Cateline!"

Roishin made soft cooing noises to the baby, who had awoken at those loud, harsh words. "It's okay, little one," she murmured. Instinctually, she rubbed her hand over the baby's rounded belly to try and soothe her back into slumber.

"Please, Cateline," Fallon said, voice much quieter and filled with pleading.

"How am I any safer with the king, Fallon?" Cateline argued.

Roishin squeezed her eyes closed for a moment before she turned around, facing the bed and the arguing couple. "Because that's not where the danger is, Mamaí." Though Roishin's words weren't much more than a whisper, she may as well have screamed them. Cateline's head whipped around to look at her, eyes wide. "Forgive me," she murmured.

She'd been told a million times over her life it was impolite to intrude upon a conversation that didn't involve her. But this one did.

"Cateline," Fallon said, reaching a hand out to take one of her wife's. "Laigen will be leaving with Reinaldo this afternoon, their own trip upped several days to get them out of here until this is over. You and the baby will go with them."

"And, if I refuse?"

Fallon sighed. "Cateline," she murmured.

Roishin gasped as something occurred to her. Eyes wide, she looked to her mother. "Mamaí, please come with me for a moment. I need to talk to you."

She waited near the double doors of the bedchamber until Cateline climbed off the bed and walked over to her. Opening one of the doors, Roishin allowed her mother to exit the room first before she followed, closing the door behind her.

"I had a dream last night," she said softly, for some reason her gut telling her this was for her mother's ears only. "I think it was trying to tell me how to get rid of this. But," she added, her eyes pleading and hands resting on her mother's arms. "I must get it to focus on me. The less people here in the castle, the less divided attention." She lightly squeezed the arms she held. "Please, please take Isabeau and go."

Pain filled Cateline's beautiful eyes. She cupped Roishin's face. "My child," she whispered, so much love in those two words. "I cannot leave you to the slaughter."

"You won't." Roishin shook her head, as sure of this as she was the sun would rise soon. "There was a reason you wanted Elsie to stay with me. You knew it instinctively, didn't you?"

"Roishin." Cateline tried to pull away from her, but the teen held her.

"Didn't you?" Roishin insisted. "You knew she was like me." She smirked. "On some level."

Cateline didn't look at her for a moment, but when she did, she nodded. "*Oui.*"

"How did you know this?"

Cateline gave her a small smile. "My gut."

Roishin smiled. "You trusted *your* gut on that, please trust *my* gut on this. Go with Laigen."

Chapter Twenty-one

They stood by the bed, Fallon insisting on getting to her feet to hug her wife goodbye. Cateline hung on, her face buried in her neck. She was concerned, as the skin was cooler to the touch, but she knew she had to do this.

"I love you so much," she whispered, her hand resting against the side of Fallon's jaw. "Please," she begged. "Please promise me that if you're not feeling better by tomorrow, you'll call for Cerdic?" Pulling out of the hug, she looked up into Fallon's pale face. "Promise me."

Nodding, Fallon gave her a ghost of a smile. "I promise." She left a lingering kiss on Cateline's lips. "I love you."

Fallon pulled out of the hug only to take a step back and plop down onto the bed. She looked exhausted just from that short time on her feet. She was breathing heavily, as though she couldn't catch her breath, and her hand came up to her forehead.

"That's it," Cateline said, about to remove her cloak. "I'm not going."

Fallon looked up at her, eyes dull. "Cateline," she said. "Do not make me order you to go," she said softly. "Roishin is not our only child, my love."

"Damn it, Fallon!" Cateline turned away from her, hands on hips. "Horrible thing to do, to guilt me like this."

"I'm not trying to make you feel guilty," Fallon said. "It's a fact."

Cateline's head fell. She squeezed her eyes shut before opening them and looking back at the woman who watched her from the bed where she perched. "Fine, yes, you are right." She walked back over to her. "Come, let me tuck you in before I go."

Dutifully, Fallon swung her legs back onto the bed and pulled them up so she could push them beneath the covers. Cateline pulled them up to just above her breasts once Fallon was settled. She looked down at her as she brushed dark strands off her forehead before she left a kiss there.

"See you soon," she murmured.

Leaving that bedchamber was probably the hardest thing Cateline had ever had to do. She knew she was absolutely leaving part of her heart and soul with the woman lying in that bed. She knew she had to go, knew she had to protect Isabeau, who was by far the most vulnerable of them all. There was absolutely nobody else she'd trust to care for the baby, especially under these circumstances.

And besides, though she was only five months old, hadn't she already lost one set of parents? She knew what they faced was far bigger than herself, and she had to trust that Fallon and Roishin and Elsie would stop it all.

Quickly making her way out of the castle, she saw the party that would be heading to the king's castle, two carriages loaded down with luggage, their horse teams already in place. Laigen was saying her goodbyes, Reinaldo standing by. Celine would accompany her as her personal servant and Fiona would accompany Cateline.

Now, it was the second-hardest goodbye of her life. Roishin was just being released from a hug with her older sister, who was totally unaware of what was happening. None of them fully understanding, there was no real way to explain it to Laigen. So, for her it was just an excited goodbye as she was another step closer to possibly becoming engaged to the young and handsome Reinaldo, Marqués de Velencia.

As Cateline stepped up to the group, Roishin turned and looked at her. The moment their eyes met, the princess took her young daughter into her arms. They clung to each other. Cateline was terrified this would be the last time she ever saw her, no matter how things went.

"You're growing so much," she murmured into the hug, noting she could no longer tuck her daughter's head beneath her chin. "Overnight," she said softly. Pulling out of the embrace, she did not release Roishin. She smiled at her, cupping her face as her hungry gaze swept over every feature, every freckle, and every dark shadow in the deep green depths of her eyes.

"Maybe I'll be as tall as you are by time you get home," Roishin teased.

Cateline smiled at that. "I think you'll be tall," she said quietly, for Roishin's ears only. "Like your daidí." She placed her hands on both sides of Roishin's head and closed her eyes as she kissed her forehead. "I love you, my Roishin."

Tears welling in Roishin's eyes, she gave her a brave smile. "I love you too, Mamaí." She quickly hugged her tightly again. "This is not goodbye," she whispered into it before releasing her mother and hurrying away, the soft sounds of her sob following her. Cateline watched her go, yet another piece of her soul left behind.

☙☙☙☙

"Good night, little princess," Cateline murmured softly against the head of Isabeau. She stood at the cradle for a long moment and watched her sleep. It amazed her how quickly the little one had become part of their family. It was as though she'd always been.

With a heavy sigh and even heavier heart, she closed the filmy curtain so the baby could sleep. It had been a very long couple days on their way to the castle and bedchamber where it had all begun for her—again. She felt so utterly alone as she hugged herself. She looked around and took in everything.

The queen's chambers. Fallon's own mother had once lived in these rooms, she thought. She'd been gone so many years, thirty-five, to be exact. She'd died when Fallon had been but two. For not the first time, she wondered what Queen Roishin would have thought of her, Cateline, who would one day wear the same crown.

This made her look at the only other ring she wore besides her wedding ring. It was the ring Fallon had given her, which had belonged to Fallon's mother. She smiled as she looked down at it.

"Her favorite ring."

Gasping, Cateline whirled around to see a woman leaning against the closed bedchamber door. Her hand was still upon the handle, as though she'd just let herself in. It took a moment, but then she remembered her.

"Enori."

The woman with short blond hair looked exactly as she had the day she'd married her and Fallon. How was that possible? She was absolutely stunning, probably the most beautiful woman Cateline had ever seen. It went beyond her physical appearance and was an ethereal quality that the princess hadn't noticed the day of her wedding.

She was so otherworldly, dressed in a flowing white gown that caressed her every womanly curve like a lover's touch. Her eyes, such a strange and beautiful color of light blue, watched Cateline very closely.

"How long have you been standing there?" Cateline asked, feeling very uncomfortable at just how startled she was and how easily this woman had gotten in.

"Long enough to know we need to talk," Enori said softly. She pushed away from the door and walked over to one of the chairs by the fireplace. Her feet were bare, the skirt of her gown fluttering around her legs with each step. It almost reminded Cateline of water. "Join me?"

Forcing herself out of her stupor, Cateline did as asked and took the other chair.

"It was her favorite next to her wedding ring," Enori said, her eyes flicking down to the ring upon Cateline's finger. "But then, you know that."

"Yes," Cateline said. "Fallon told me."

"Yes, but she hadn't needed to," Enori said, her gaze looking into Cateline's, head slightly cocked to the side. "Had she?"

"Of course she had to tell me that," Cateline said, absently twisting the ring this way and that. "I would have had no way of knowing."

"No?" Enori challenged. "Do you know how

Fallon's mother died?"

"I do not. Fallon has never been told, and I've never asked Carthac."

Enori crossed one shapely leg over the other. "Roishin was born in Brittany, born of the Order."

"The Order of Ankou," Cateline said, a statement more than a question.

"Yes." Her gaze met and held Cateline's. "You see, Cateline, those of us who are born of the Order, we are Ankou for life. It is who we are, and we pass down the gifts Ankou has given to us to our children and their children's children and so on. Fallon was born of Ankou through her mother and a normal man, in Carthac."

Cateline stared at her, confused. "Are you saying that Fallon is like Roishin, that Ankou is her... parent?"

Enori smiled and shook her head. "No. Ankou was not father to the elder Roishin, nor Fallon. But Roishin, Fallon's mother, was born of a woman endowed with Ankou's gifts of her family line." She shrugged. "Born of the Order."

Understanding, Cateline nodded. "I see, yes. So, Fallon has these gifts?"

Enori nodded. "She does." She gave the princess a sweet smile. "Her gifts as the warrior, her speed, the way she can almost *smell* what an opponent will do next. Can hear his heartbeat, the very blood flowing through his veins before he strikes. She can sense it all."

Cateline was unable to hide the smile of pride that graced her lips. "*Oui*," she said softly.

"And, it is because of who you are that you saw through her ability to hide herself, Cateline."

Smile falling from her lips, the princess looked back to the woman who studied her from just a few feet away. "Meaning?"

"Meaning, how do you think Fallon has survived all these years as a man in this kingdom?" She leaned slightly forward in her chair, her gaze boring into Cateline's. "She is clever, I agree. Her disguises, changing the shape of her body." A slow little smile quirked her lips. "In various ways."

Cateline looked away, blushing.

"Nothing to be ashamed or embarrassed by, Princess," Enori said softly. "But you see the woman inside. You always did." She paused until Cateline looked at her again. "You called her beautiful."

Cateline nodded. "Yes," she whispered. "From the moment I first saw her."

"Yes, because you truly *saw* her. You saw through her innate ability to change herself, her mask."

"What do you mean?" Cateline asked, eyebrows drawn. Somewhere deep inside, she knew Enori spoke the truth, she just didn't have the full picture. "What does everyone else see?"

"Fallon, Prince of Sursha," Enori said easily.

"So, how do I see through it, then?"

"Two reasons," Enori said, sitting back in the chair again, arms resting along the arms of the chair and her hands dangling off the rounded ends at the wrists. "One, though the body is long dead, the soul retains the gifts of its mother. And, two," she added. "Though the body is long dead, the soul retains the love and recognition that it already has for another soul."

A wave of anxiety washed through Cateline at those words, forcing her to pop up from her chair like a spring. "What are you saying?" She gasped, her hand clutching the robe that covered her sleep dress.

"You know what I am saying," Enori said, eyeing the standing woman.

"That I am Fallon's mother?" Cateline said. "That's absurd!"

"Of course you're not." Enori gave her a little grin that bordered on saucy. "Fallon's mother is dead and buried. But," she said, holding up a finger. "Her soul lives on, as do they all. The earthbound existence," she said, indicating the bedchamber around them and castle beyond that, "dictates the relationship. Mother and daughter, wife and husband, sister and brother. But the love between souls is never destroyed, and is always recognized. Love at first sight." She smiled. "Even for a newborn child found in the woods," she nearly whispered. "Or," she added, gaze intense. "A princess for her servant."

No words, Cateline fell back into the chair she'd just abandoned, a trembling hand running through her hair.

"You see, Cateline, Fallon's mother Roishin was to take the throne in Brittany, the crown of the Order. She was taken from our shores as a very young girl so this would never happen. She was dropped into an Irish house of nobility and left none the wiser."

"By whom?" Cateline asked.

"By the very same evil that stalks your family now. Once we found her, she was already married to Carthac and had the two boys. They were unhelpful to us, but when we found out she was pregnant with her third child, we thought maybe this would be the one." Her smile was beautiful. "It was. It was Fallon. Roishin's job was complete. Her soul was needed elsewhere in Fallon's life, not as her mother."

"Then how?" Cateline asked, her voice barely above a whisper.

"As her queen."

Feeling absolutely nauseous, Cateline closed her eyes, taking several slow breaths as she tried to ease her rattled nerves and stomach. Finally, she felt she could speak without throwing up. "You murdered Fallon's mother?"

"Ankou is about order," Enori said gently. "The ultimate order is death. The Order of Ankou rights wrongs, Cateline. We put things back when man or evil takes it away."

Tears were in Cateline's eyes now, her brain and heart overwhelmed. "Roishin," she whispered, swallowing. "My daughter. Are you going to…"

Enori's smile was so lovely. She reached across the table that separated their chairs and took Cateline's hand in her own. "No. Roishin will be taught how to handle her gifts, how to develop them."

Swallowing again, Cateline asked, "Will she be part of the Order?"

"Cateline, Roishin *is* the Order."

Chapter Twenty-two

Y ou know what's happening, don't you?"
"What?"

"They're trying to get around you. They're trying to take away your position, usurp your place, not only in your own country but your own household!"

"That's not true."

"No? Then why are you left here alone? Why, they've left the big, bad warrior to suffer by herself while they all head on to the important business of the kingdom. In short, Fallon? They left you behind. Again." A chuckle punctuated the statement of the strange voice, one moment seeming female, the next male, and at times, a mixture of both. "I don't know, Fallon, I'm certainly no expert, but I'd say yet again you're not good enough to join Court."

"That's not true. That's not what happened."

"Are you sure?"

"Yes..."

"Daidí?"

"See? Roishin is here to check on me. She's still here."

"Yes, the child. She left you with a child!" The tsking of a tongue. "Such a caring wife, wouldn't you say? All you've done for her, got her away from that monster, and she leaves you with a child?"

"Please stop. Please..."

"You know, I have to wonder about that handsome Spaniard. Maybe, just maybe—"

"Stop—"

"Cateline left you here because she wanted to see what a real *man was like—"*

"Stop!"

"I don't know, Fallon." A heavy sigh. "Just my observations, of course."

"Daidí? Please wake up. Please." Sniffles. "You're scaring me."

"She's lying to you!"

"Shut up!"

Her eyes blinked open. Fallon took a moment, trying to get her bearings. She felt wetness on her cheeks and realized she'd been crying. Bringing up a hand, she felt the tears on her fingertips, rubbing thumb and forefinger together until the liquid was gone.

Sensing she wasn't alone, she turned her head and saw an extremely worried-looking Roishin sitting on the side of the bed. In fact, the girl looked like she was about to burst into tears. She studied her face. Big, dark green eyes, such an unusual color. Her mother's eyes, she'd been told so many times. She wished she could remember them.

Her gaze saw the freckles sprinkled across Roishin's cheeks and the bridge of her nose. Just like Cateline's. She smiled at that thought. Then she wondered who else was looking at Cateline's freckles, admiring how they made the gorgeous woman even more gorgeous, somehow.

Who?

"Daidí?" Roishin said softly, reaching out and taking one of Fallon's hands. "Are you okay?" She sniffled. "You were crying and whimpering in your sleep."

"I'm okay."

"Are you?"

Fallon's eyes squeezed shut for a moment. When she opened them again, she looked back to Roishin. She was smirking. *Smirking!* Studying her, she could tell the little brat was about to start laughing. Laughing at what...Fallon's misery? At the fact that she was laid up like some pathetic invalid? That she was left behind? That her wife—

Eyes squeezing shut, Fallon took several deep breaths. "No," she murmured.

"No, what?"

With a roar, Fallon's hand snaked out and found the flesh of a soft throat. Gripping, she used inhuman strength and slammed Roishin's smaller body to the bed. Rolling over from her back to hover over the girl, Fallon sneered down at her, her upper lip pulled up to reveal her teeth like a wild animal.

She relished the fear she saw in those very eyes she'd just been marveling at. Now, they were wide and filled with terror, the terror of the warrior's power. Pale fingers grabbed at the tanned hand that tightened its grip around Roishin's throat. In response, Fallon tightened her grip even more.

It wasn't enough. No, she wanted more. Never

taking her eyes off that terrified verdant gaze, Fallon used her free hand to reach under her own pillow. Her fingers found the leather sheath first before they felt the hard, cold steel of the grip. With a tug, the blade came loose from its protective case and was brought into view.

The morning sun coming through the windows glinted off the blade and the rose etched upon it. Roishin's gaze widened even more as the blade came into view. Tears began to gather, her lips moving even as her vocal cords were paralyzed by the iron grip around her throat. Little squeaks and gags were the only thing that managed to escape as her fingers clawed more desperately, and uselessly, at Fallon's hand.

With the adept movements of a lifelong warrior, Fallon twirled the dagger so the grip now rested in her palm blade down rather than up. She raised her hand—

Gasping, Fallon flung herself across the bed, away from her daughter, who still sat next to her, a hand in her own. She couldn't catch herself in time before she tumbled right off Cateline's side of the bed. With a grunt of pain, she landed on her shoulder on the hard stone floor. The huge rug spread beneath the bed did little to protect or cushion her body from the hard fall.

"Daidí!" Roishin screeched, jumping off the bed and running around it to kneel next to Fallon, who lay there, dazed. Tears streamed down her cheeks as she brushed long, sweaty strands of hair that partially covered Fallon's face as she'd rolled over to her back.

Trying desperately to work through the pain in pretty much every part of her body, Fallon looked over at an openly crying Roishin. "Under my pillow," she managed. "Get it."

Nodding, Roishin jumped up and pretty much dove atop the bed, just her feet hanging in view before she scrambled her body back down again onto the floor next to Fallon. Roishin helped her sit up. She knelt next to the warrior again, the sheathed dagger in hand. The girl looked from it to Fallon, clearly waiting for further instructions.

"Take this," Fallon said, wrapping her hand around the leather sheath as she looked into Roishin's eyes. "Take it away from here." Realizing she was scaring her daughter even worse with her cryptic request, Fallon forced a smile. "Go to Livia. Tell her I need something to help me feel better." She squeezed the hand that held the dagger. "Use this to cut herbs or whatever she needs."

Roishin looked down at the dagger she held again, then to Fallon's eyes. There was clear uncertainty in her expression, but she nodded. "Aye."

Fallon grabbed her and pulled her into a painfully tight hug, eyes squeezing shut as she inhaled the scent of her hair, her skin, and her very essence. Finally, after leaving a kiss on her forehead, she whispered, "Go now."

Roishin met her gaze, the tears continuing to slide down her cheeks. Nodding, she tucked the sheathed dagger against her chest and pushed to her feet. With one final look down at Fallon, she turned and hurried from the bedchamber, closing the door softly behind her.

Chapter Twenty-three

Terrified by what had just happened, and what she'd seen in Fallon's eyes, Roishin sprinted from the bedchamber once the door was closed behind her. She cradled the dagger against her chest as she ran, almost afraid that if she didn't hold it tightly, it would magically escape her hands and fly back to her parents' room.

She ran blindly until she reached Livia's quarters, which were in a different part of the castle near where the servants bathed, but it was the only place in the castle where an entire suite could be created for her. Inside her chambers, Livia had a bedroom, living space, and her own garderobe and bathing facilities. She also had space to hold meetings as a trusted advisor for the prince.

Out of breath, she raised her fist and pounded on the closed door.

"Roishin?"

Turning, she saw Elsie step out of a room farther down the hall where laundry was done. She stepped out into the hall, clear concern on her face. The tears came harder at the sight of the servant. Roishin ran over to her, immediately taken into a warm hug.

"What happened?" Elsie murmured into it. "Is it your daidí?"

Roishin held on and nodded but then shook her head. Laughing at herself as she realized she'd probably confused the poor thing, she pulled out of the hug, looking down at the dagger she carried.

"Roishin?"

Glancing over her shoulder, the princess saw Livia step out into the hall. She looked from Elsie to Roishin. Walking over to them, she brought up a hand and gently cupped Roishin's face.

"What's wrong?"

"It's Daidí," she said. "Something really wrong with her, Livia. She gave me this and asked me to ask you to help me find something to make her feel better, but she—" Cutting herself off, Roishin's eyes opened wide at realization of what she'd said and whom she'd said it in front of. She saw the widening of Livia's dark eyes, too.

Oh boy.

Looking to Elsie, who was listening, she met her gaze. The sweetest, most understanding smile brushed full lips. In that moment, somehow Roishin didn't feel that she'd revealed anything that wasn't already known, or at least suspected. But how? Swallowing hard, as she still felt she had just betrayed her family in the most horrible way, she turned back to Livia.

If nothing else, that little oops at least forced her to calm down. "I was given this," she said, holding out the dagger. "For you to cut herbs or whatever." She met the dark gaze, hoping the older woman saw her fear and worry. "Something is very wrong."

"Is it?" Elsie asked softly.

Turning to look at her, Roishin nodded. "I think so. I know Daidí's sick, but—" Though that giant secret was out in the open, she didn't want to add to her folly. "Behavior is weird."

"Roishin," Livia said. "I need you to be honest

with me. What is happening?"

"Perhaps we should go in there?" Elsie suggested, nodding toward Livia's chamber door as some servants were headed their way, carrying large laundry baskets.

The three women entered the space, Livia closing the door. Arms crossed over her chest, she looked expectantly from one to the other. "Elsie, are you aware of all this?"

The servant nodded. "Aye."

Nodding, Livia looked to Roishin. "What's happening? And, why did Cateline leave with Isabeau? She would never have left Fallon while so ill."

Roishin's mouth opened and closed a few times as she desperately tried to think of how to answer that question. She wasn't quite sure that, *Well, you see I have these crazy super powers and some dark, evil thing is trying to kill my entire family so it can have its way with me,* would suffice. Running her hand through her hair, she tried again.

"There is something dark that comes here, Livia, and I believe it's attacking Daidí. Mamaí left with Isabeau to protect the baby. She didn't want to," she said, shaking her head. "But Daidí made her go."

"What is it?" Livia asked. "Dark?" she shook her head. "What does that mean?"

"Well," Roishin said. "You know, it's kinda like—"

"No," Elsie said, lightly touching Roishin's arm to stop her. She met the surprised gaze of the princess with her usual calm. Turning back to Livia, "What is here is ancient, always looking for a way to harm, cause trouble, hurt." She shrugged. "Shake everything up."

Livia nodded. "All right," she said slowly. "What

is it?"

"I can say its name because it is already here. *Bāhūthā*."

"How do you know that?" Roishin whispered, ice flooding through her veins.

"The morning you had that terrible dream," Elsie explained. "You ended up on the floor."

Roishin nodded, remembering all too well.

"You said it. As soon as I heard his name from your lips, I knew we were in terrible trouble." She looked to Livia, who was watching the two carefully. "God of Chaos."

Livia swallowed and looked away, as if absorbing all she'd been told. Finally, she looked at the two standing before her. "One night," she began softly, Roishin moving over to her as it looked as if the advisor was barely holding it together with what she had to say. "I was awakened out of a deep sleep. Standing next to the bed was a figure. He was only there for a moment, but I saw him."

Roishin rested her head against Livia's as she wrapped an arm around her waist. "It's okay," she murmured, sensing how difficult this was for the woman she saw as an aunt.

Livia leaned into the comforting embrace as she continued. "It was the man who hurt me very badly many years ago." She shrugged a shoulder. "Long dead." She gave Elsie a small smile. "I thought he was a ghost."

Roishin saw Elsie's eyes widen a bit at that and a small gasp escape her lips. She wondered why.

"Like Cateline," Elsie whispered to herself. "Have you seen the mist, too?"

Livia shook her head, but Roishin gasped. "In

my dream!" She looked from Livia to Elsie. "It came out of this tunnel thing in the ocean and it came here." She pointed down at the floor. "Sursha, then inside the castle." She eyed Elsie. "Have you seen it?"

Elsie shook her head. "No. But I felt it coming." She looked shy for a moment. "I feel it here now. Where it is."

"Where is it?" Livia asked slowly.

Elsie met her gaze. "With Fallon."

Chapter Twenty-four

*S*ighing in contentment, she rolled over from her back to face the woman she'd woken up with every single morning since they'd been married. That is, when Fallon was in the country. Reaching a hand out, Cateline's eyes opened when she felt nothing but cold sheet. She was alone in the bed, and it seemed Fallon had been gone for some time, as there wasn't even an indention in the pillow from her head.

Lifting her own head, she looked around the bed-chamber. Sometimes Fallon would get up and go to her desk and begin reading and writing correspondence with the various nobility in the country as well with those outside the Surshan walls, as it were. Carthac had wanted her to take over more and more of those tasks, to slowly start becoming the voice of the country.

Nothing there, either. As she sat up, the covers fell to reveal Cateline's naked breasts. Pushing her hair out of her face, she noticed something on the floor. The princess climbed out of bed and grabbed her robe. She shrugged into it, belting it absently as she walked over to what she'd noticed.

Blood.

Eyebrows falling, she looked around the room again. There was nothing to suggest Fallon had hurt herself, and she knew she certainly hadn't. Looking toward the double doors, she noticed more blood. Growing concerned that maybe one of the children—

Roishin came to mind—had come in after an accident and awoken Fallon for help, Cateline's heart began to pound faster.

Hurrying to the door, she pulled open one side and stopped, startled to see that it wasn't the long hallway beyond but the long, narrow passageway to Fallon's old room. She stared down into the darkness, once so very familiar and comforting to her. In that moment, it felt like a dark maw of death.

She heard something distantly and could just barely see light at the end of the tunnel. The trunk lid had been opened, it seemed. Light from Fallon's room was shining through to show the way. She stepped into the passageway and hurried, feeling a sense of impending doom in her stomach. Her bare feet slapped against the cold stone with every harried step.

Finally, she reached the three stone stairs, upon which she noticed more blood. Looking up through the trunk body, she saw the ceiling of Fallon's old room. She began to climb out of the trunk, only to see more blood, like a bloody handprint upon the wood box of the structure. The bedroom was empty, however the mattress was back on the bed frame.

All of Fallon's clothing, including her false torso and phallus, lay upon it. Her bracers rested atop her neatly folded tunic and boots were placed at the foot of the bed on the floor. Her short swords were sheathed in their back holster, also on the bed, as was the sheath for her rose dagger. It was kept in her boot during the light of day but under her pillow at night. The dagger was missing.

Glancing to her left, she saw the door that led up to the parapets was slightly open. A bloody handprint was upon the wood. "Oh, gods," she gasped, hurrying *up the short flight of stairs to the door.*

Pulling it open, she saw it was night, even as she'd awoken to the morning. The wind was blowing at a dangerous rate, already causing her hair to whip in her face before she'd even peeked her head out. Off to the left, she saw her. Fallon stood, naked on the parapet, looking out over the wooded land below.

Her back was to Cateline, her long, dark hair whipping wildly around her shoulders and head. Fallon was a magnificent creature to behold: her shoulders were wide and muscular, as were her arms and her back, which tapered down into a narrow waist only to flair in womanly hips and a firm behind. Muscular thighs and pronounced hamstrings led down to muscular calves. A goddess, Cateline thought. An absolute goddess.

Her gaze straying from the perfection of form, Cateline's eyes noticed Fallon's right hand. It was bloody, as were the fingers that were wrapped around her rose dagger, the blade deadly sharp and also streaked with blood.

"Fallon?" she called out.

"It's over," Fallon said, her voice flat and quiet. Somehow it was heard over the howls of the wind.

"What's over?" Cateline asked, almost afraid to hear the answer. She took a step out of the tower room and onto the walkway of the parapet.

"He's not a threat anymore."

"Who?"

Fallon slowly turned around, the entire front of her naked body splattered with blood. The worst of it was her face. It looked as if a bloody hand had been placed directly on her face, a perfect handprint, then smeared down over her neck and between her breasts.

"You can come back home now," she said, her

head slightly lowered so she was looking up at Cateline with her eyes through dark hair, strands caked together with more blood. "All better."

"What happened, Fallon?" Cateline asked, "Whose blood is that?"

The slow smile that spread across full lips sent a chill down Cateline's spine. "It's over," she said, almost a whisper. "I took care of the problem." She lifted her hand holding the knife, as if emphasizing her point.

"Where's Roishin?" Cateline asked, her heart beginning to race. "Fallon, where is she?"

The smile widened.

"Fallon!" Cateline hurried over to her. "Where is she?"

Fallon lowered her face to Cateline's, their lips a mere breath apart. "You want to know?" she murmured.

"Please. Please tell me."

Cateline grunted, eyes opening wide. Slowing looking down, she saw Fallon's fisted hand held against her stomach, red beginning to blossom on the material of Cateline's robe. She looked up into Fallon's face, stunned.

"No more babies for you," Fallon whispered.

꒰ ꒱ ꒰ ꒱

A loud cry erupted from Cateline's lips as she shot up in bed. Her eyes were huge and she looked around, panicked. She looked down at herself, just barely able to make anything out in the remnants of the firelight in the fireplace. Her sleeping gown was as it had been when she'd gone to bed hours before.

Her hand went to her stomach. No blood, no knife. Her chest was heaving as she tried to get a full breath. She was still in the queen's chambers at Carthac's castle. Her gaze fell to the cradle and she flew out of bed. She needed to make sure Isabeau was okay. She nearly burst into tears of relief when she saw the baby was sleeping peacefully.

As she stood there, the dream came back to her. It had been so real, so damn real! Looking to the doors of the bedchamber, she knew absolutely that she needed to get home. Fallon needed her.

Glancing back to the cradle, she chewed her bottom lip. Decision made, she turned away from the cradle, then gasped. Hand to heart, she looked at Enori, who leaned against the bedchamber door.

"My goodness!" she gasped. "You frightened me."

The look in Enori's eyes was anything but amused or playful. "Say please," she said softly.

Chapter Twenty-five

On hands and knees, Fallon managed to get herself to the trunk where she stored her clothing, weapons, and other objects of personal meaning. It was unlocked from the night before, her being far too weak to worry about relocking it. Besides, she'd been in the bedchamber the entire time, so she wasn't entirely worried about somebody stumbling upon something they shouldn't.

Flopping over to her backside, she took a breath, so exhausted. After a moment, she pushed the trunk lid open and peered inside. Lying atop her clothing were her double blades, tucked into their back harness. She looked down at them, deciding what she wanted to do. Truth was, she didn't trust herself right now.

She felt Roishin would do well to hold on to her dagger. In fact, she was considering telling her to keep it. It was something she wanted her to have, anyway. As for her short swords, Livia was probably the best one to hold them until all this was over. Garratt was in and out, and he wanted too much to please Fallon.

She knew that if she asked for them back, he'd happily do it, whereas Livia would outright tell her to find a parapet and jump. She smiled at that thought. Yes, Livia was definitely the best option. Grabbing them, she heaved the blades out and onto her lap when she froze. She'd heard something.

Where the trunk was, and because she was sitting

on the floor, she was effectively hidden from the entire chamber. She was alone, she thought. Peeking under the bed, she was stunned to see movement over by the double doors. Looking around the trunk, she saw nothing, yet from another glance under the bed, she saw lower legs and boots. Black.

She slowly slid both blades from their sheaths, nary a sound made as her gaze never left those boots. They were sauntering, as if on a random Sunday afternoon stroll through the rose garden. Blades free, Fallon left the leather sword belt and harness where it lay as she moved to her belly.

She slowly began to crawl under the bed, her stealth one of her best weapons even in her current state. The boots began to wander over toward the fireplace, stopping again as if the person were checking things out, perhaps even warming his hands by the fire. Fallon eased her way closer to the other side of the bed, her intention to ambush her unwanted guest.

Her heart was racing and her head was pounding. The closer she got, the more nauseated she felt. She had to pause, blinking her eyes several times as she was beginning to sweat profusely. Her hair was hanging in front of her face in long, sweaty strands. She shook her head a bit, trying to brush the hair aside with the move.

Focused again, she saw that the boots were on the move again. Away from the area of the fireplace, they were moving back toward the bed, which meant right toward her. She moved forward again, any noise she made disguised by that of his steps. Her gaze fell to the boots, studying them.

She didn't recognize the design, certainly nothing the military of Sursha wore, and they were pretty much the only men who wore boots. Common villagers wore leather shoes, as they were more affordable. And frankly, they had little need for boots. They weren't often slogging through swamps and rivers of distant lands on campaigns.

The boots reached the bed, just three feet away. Fallon's gaze was pinned to them, her fingers flexing and reflexing on the grips of her blades, just as she'd done a million times in her life. She took several deep, steadying breaths, trying desperately to get her heart to calm its racing.

She needed to focus, because with what they were dealing with, this was life or death. If she died today, Roishin was in imminent danger, as was Elsie and Livia. And, what would Cateline come home to? Laigen?

Even more determined to beat this, to break out of this horrible spell or cloud or *whatever* this bastard had her under, she held the grips even tighter. Two more steps... *Come on!* She watched, her gaze focused on the ankles. One quick swipe of one blade would bring him down, the second would gut him.

Her left hand slowly began to move up toward her shoulder, the blade easing its way silently over the rug she lay upon. She could smell him now. Could smell his sweat. She could hear his heartbeat as though it was beating in her own chest.

Come on, come on, you bastard!

One more step closer...

Her blade inched up a bit more, her eyes never leaving their target.

The other foot, moving...

Her jaw muscles pulsed as her teeth clenched inside her mouth, so ready.

The forward foot was about to come into range when it stopped, moving back to its previous placement next to its mate. After a heartbeat, the leather began to bunch at the ankles. He was going to kneel down.

Before a cry of surprise could even leave her lips, Fallon was grabbed by the ankles and yanked in one fluid motion out from beneath the bed backward, her blades slicing through the rug as they were dragged.

Chapter Twenty-six

Though June was upon them, it was so early in the morning that it was still a bit chilly. The three figures who hurried from the castle wore cloaks to help fend off the crisp morning air, two carrying baskets, one a dagger.

The Crown owned a large swath of land around the castle proper, wooded land. This land was designated for hunting to feed those that dwelled within the castle walls, as well as any other sort of gathering needed such as wood and vegetation. That was where Livia led her two charges now.

"What are we looking for again?" Roishin asked, eyes everywhere as they hurried into the woods.

"It's called wild valerian," Livia explained. "Lucky for us, it blooms this time of year."

"And," Elsie said, the second of the three carrying a basket. "This will help His Highness feel better?"

Roishin glanced over at the young woman who walked next to her, somehow surprised to hear the masculine referred to, considering Roishin had already made that wonderful blunder earlier that morning. She figured with just the three of them all in the know, the damage was minimal, but then she saw a small group of castle guards not far away. All three bowed, but only one spoke.

"Good morrow, milady," he said, bowing to

Roishin and nodding to the other two. "Need an escort, milady?" he asked, hand immediately going to the pommel of the sword belted at his hip in a gesture of their services to the three.

"Thank you," Roishin said with a smile. "We are fine." She indicated the baskets Livia and Elsie carried. "Off to gather herbs."

The guard bowed again. "We'll be near should you need us, milady."

She gave the trio a winning smile and kept going with her own trio. "What does this wild valerian look like?" she asked, scanning the vegetation all around them which, quite honestly, all looked alike to her unskilled eye.

"The stem is kind of thick and hairy." Livia glanced at her two companions. "Hollow. It has little flowers, white and light pink. Five petals on each."

Roishin nodded. "Aye-aye."

Livia looked past her to Elsie. "And, to answer your question, Elsie, this will make Fallon sleep. I think with our current situation, it's our best bet."

"What do we do when we find it?" Roishin asked. "Serve valerian salad? Force feed?"

Livia chuckled. "Nothing quite so violent. I'll make a tea."

"How do you know this, Livia?" Elsie asked.

Livia met the servant's gaze. "I honestly don't know, Elsie." She gave her a lovely smile. "Ever since I was a child, I've just had an idea, an instinct for plants, I guess."

Elsie's smile was so beautiful in that moment. "How wonderful!"

Roishin looked back and forth between them. For just a minute, she was able to forget about the horrible situation they were in and just enjoy being between these two women that really meant something to her. She didn't think they knew each other well, if really at all. Likely, nothing more than Elsie helping at meals in the family chamber.

It was kind of neat for the three of them to be outside of their daily roles and obligations and just be three people all on the same mission. She wondered, though, would it ever be possible to just spend time? Outside the castle walls, outside of status and position?

She sent a shy look over at Elsie, receiving a small smile in return.

Chapter Twenty-seven

King Carthac had been alerted and the baby left with Collette, the woman who was the king's closest advisor and had been a mother figure to Fallon and her brothers. Cateline now held on for dear life as Enori guided the horse they rode to pound the earth through the darkness. Cateline wasn't sure they were going to make it without running headlong into a tree, but somehow, their horse went this way, that way, over that fallen tree, and back that way.

Just up ahead, she saw Fallon's waterfall. Her eyes widened in surprise, not entirely sure why they'd gone there. She had no idea where Enori would be taking her, though she had assumed home. She ducked her head as they raced under a low-hanging branch. Finally, Enori slowed the mare.

Just a few yards from the outside wall of the cave system that the waterfall wonderland was tucked into, Enori waited for Cateline to slide off the beast before she followed. Without saying a word, Enori smacked the animal's rump to send it on its way before she grabbed Cateline's hand and tugged her after her.

They hopped over the small spring and kept going. Her hand released, Cateline stood back as Enori ducked into the crag in the wall before following suit. She gasped once she cleared it, for a moment afraid they were in danger. Three heavily armed men stood just on the other side. They were warriors, based upon their dress and weapons, though not of Sursha. Their heads were shaved, though some sported full facial hair and one had no mustache but a long goatee.

She relaxed when immediately Enori began talking to them, clearly comfortable. They were speaking in Breton, which was close enough in languages Cateline knew to pick up a word here and there, but the conversation was fast and it was hard to keep up. She was able to make out her name, as well as that of Fallon and Roishin, and they were apparently going to accompany them.

Had they gone to the waterfall simply to meet these men, then all head out together? That was answered when Enori glanced over to her.

"Come," she said.

The five of them headed around the moonlit pool that bubbled and gurgled merrily as water rushed down over the tops of the rocks and down into it. Cateline looked up, able to see the moon and stars through the open hole in the cave roof. She thought what a romantic night this would be, to make love on Fallon's flat rock next to the water.

She longed for those days, when everything was wonderful, beautiful, and so much simpler. She wondered if they'd ever have those days again. She was torn out of those thoughts when one of the men stepped up to her. As the group reached the waterfall, which roared off to their left, she looked around, confused, as there was nowhere to go. It was either walk right into the stone wall or walk into the water.

She looked at him, only then realizing it was just the two of them. Where had Enori gone? Where were the other two men? She looked back to the man who waited patiently for her to turn to him.

He pantomimed picking her up and lifting her up to the waterfall. Her eyes widened, looking at him like he was crazy. He smiled then pantomimed it again, nodding as if that was what she should do.

Glancing to the waterfall again, Cateline took a long, deep breath. Finally, she nodded, looking at him. With firm yet gentle hands, he gripped her at the waist and, as if she weighed nothing more than a sack of grain, lifted her off her feet, She looked into his eyes, searching for any bad intentions, but there was nothing in their brown depths but purpose, and clearly that purpose was getting her where he needed her to go.

Cateline squeezed her eyes shut, waiting to be submerged beneath the spray, but instead she felt hands grabbing her waist. Opening her eyes in surprise, she glanced over her shoulder to see one of the other men standing behind her, hands upon her waist merely to steady her. Immediately she heard the roar of more water.

She gasped when she saw they were standing inside a large alcove behind yet another waterfall. Gasping again, she looked to the left when she felt a gentle push against her arm. The man who had lifted her was halfway through the wall, his left leg still seemingly one with the stone, only for it to appear as he stepped fully up to her.

Eyes wide, she looked up at him, unable to speak. He gave her a kind smile before touching her arm again and nodding forward. The man who had steadied her was already several paces ahead of them, as was the third warrior and Enori.

The deep recess led to natural steps in the stone on one side of the waterfall. Cateline's eyes

were everywhere, noting this time it was an enclosed
cavern, likely what Fallon's waterfall had looked like
eons ago. It, too, had a deep pool of inviting-looking
water. She focused on where she was headed so she
didn't accidentally end up in it.

Once down the steps, the five of them hurried
down a tunnel that seemed to be part of a cave system.
Enori was at the lead, the three men placing themselves
in front of and behind Cateline, helping her when she
needed it in this unknown terrain as they turned down
this tunnel then down that one, all with the barest
light from torches mounted on the wall now and then.

Finally, in a random tunnel that looked like any
of the others, Enori stopped. She reached for Cateline,
the warriors standing out of the way as the princess
hurried over to her. They stood before a wall made of
stone.

Taking Cateline's hand, Enori looked her in the
eye. "Step very lightly," she said.

Cateline looked from the woman's intense gaze
to the wall and back to her again. Shaking her head,
she said, "I can't—"

"You can and you must."

Looking back to the wall, she looked back to
Enori. "I'll follow you—"

"No." Enori shook her head. She brought a hand
up and placed it upon Cateline's cheek. "You are
the gatekeeper here, Cateline," she said softly. "This
door was built for you a long time ago." She smiled.
"Remember what I told you last night?" At Cateline's
nod, she said. "Why are you going back?"

"For Fallon, I must save her. "

"Then you have found your key," Enori whispered. Her hand fell away, almost like a caress. "Open

the door."

Cateline turned back to the wall. She had to remember, she had just walked through a waterfall *and* a wall. She had to do this. She had to do this for Fallon.

Taking several deep breaths, Cateline stepped up to the wall, her own heavy breathing blown back at her against the stone. She saw Fallon in her mind's eye. She saw her beautiful face, saw her smile and the love for her she had in those unique violet eyes.

Taking another step forward, Cateline initially felt the hard, cold of the stone press against the toe of her shoe, but then, as though pressed against malleable clay, her foot continued. She gasped and nearly stopped from shock when she felt a hand to her shoulder squeezing encouragement.

Her breasts heaving with her quickening breaths, she pushed her foot through the denseness, expecting it to touch something else hard, such as floor, but instead she nearly stumbled. Her arms whipped out to balance herself as her foot fell, only to finally land on something hard.

Remembering what Enori had said, she knew she had to trust this so she braced on that foot and moved her other one. It, and half her body, pushed through the denseness of the wall, and as if passing through a fog, she was through.

She cried out in shock to find herself on the first step down into the trunk. She was nearly in tears, overwhelmed by everything as well as being proud of herself for doing it. Remembering why she was there, she kept going, hitting the tunnel floor at a sprint once she was down the stairs. She was relieved to hear the others were following.

Chapter Twenty-eight

Pulled fully out from under the bed, Fallon managed to flip over to her back. She just barely got a blade raised to block a blow that would have decapitated her. Snarling atop her was the living embodiment of the shadow peeking at her from around the stables that day on the training field.

She now understood why she hadn't recognized those boots—they weren't of this world. They weren't leather, just...*black*. The shadow come to life atop her now held a blade that was black as midnight. No glint of steel, no jewels or fancy etchings. The man and his sword were darkness personified.

With a grunt, Fallon pushed him off her, effectively changing their positions. Teeth bared, her hair hung around her head in a stringy curtain as she used all her strength to try to bring both of her blades down into his chest as she straddled his midsection.

The faceless opponent held her off with both hands wrapped around her wrists. It was pure muscle against muscle. As she looked into the midnight face, she saw eyes slowly begin to appear. They pinned her to the spot.

"Ailfred," she whispered. Her grip eased just enough to give her opponent a shot at her.

Crying out in pain, Fallon took a fist to the mouth, sending her head flying back and her body off balance enough to find herself sailing backward. She landed on her back, head hitting the stone floor hard. One of her blades skittered across the floor with a clang. She saw the black figure rise, face nothing more than a black mask again.

Whipping her legs up, she used the muscles of her powerful core and arms to spring to her feet. She dove over toward her fallen blade when the shadow lunged with its broadsword right where she'd just been lying, mere inches from impaling her.

Landing on her right shoulder with a grunt, she slid across the stone, grabbing her blade as she went. She used the momentum to turn to her back and arch her arm back. She was about to let her blade sail through the air when Cateline stood before her.

Confused, Fallon froze. She held on to the grip of the blade, ready to let it fly at any moment. As she watched, her wife stared down at her, long, curly auburn hair loose around her shoulders and down her back. Her hands came up to cover her mouth, looking as though she were about to cry.

"What has happened to you?" she whispered behind her hands. "You're bleeding."

It was then that Fallon realized that she tasted the coppery bitterness of blood. She used her tongue to slide over her teeth to see if she'd lost one. As she watched, Cateline's hands fell away, her eyes brimming with tears. She lowered herself to the floor and crawled over to Fallon.

"My love," she whispered. She moved over and on top of her, her hair falling around them, narrowing the world to just the two of them. "Make love to me, Fallon," she whispered.

Feeling herself relax, Fallon's eyes slid closed as she felt the softness of Cateline's lips against her own, just brushing. It was the softest touch. Unable to help herself, she responded, garnering a soft moan from the woman on top of her. Fallon sighed when a gentle hand cupped her breast.

She froze. Eyes opening, she rolled them to the side to see Cateline's other hand wrapped around the grip of the short sword Fallon had let go of. As she watched, that hand slowly pulled the blade closer.

As she lay there, she realized the delicate and petite frame that was her wife was growing heavy. She grunted as her entire body was being pushed down into the stone floor. She tried to turn her head out of the kiss but she couldn't, the body atop hers feeling as though sand had been poured inside of it, more and more added by the second.

She tried to pull in a breath, but the weight was so great upon her lungs, she couldn't. Finally, she brought her own hand up, the one still gripping the blade she'd been about to throw. She used her one free hand to try to push the dead weight off her. It felt like a horse had fallen on her.

Growling through gritted teeth, she squeezed her eyes shut as she pushed with that one hand as she brought the other up. She held the grip with the blade pointed down, ready to stab this thing until it was off her. It no longer looked like Cateline; it was just a black blob of mass.

Raising her hand as high as she could, she was about to plunge the blade down when she heard a scream and her hand was caught. Opening her eyes, she saw that the blob was gone and now a man knelt over her. His head was shaved and his long goatee was tied off an inch from the end with a short leather tie.

The man was large, brown leather armor

revealing powerful arms with bracers wrapped over thick forearms. He held Fallon's sword hand in both of his. With a growl of frustration, Fallon brought up her other hand that held her second blade. With a cry of bloodlust, she used it to slice the man's hand that was wrapped around her own, right across the knuckles.

Blood began to pour out as he cried out in pain, releasing her hand. If only she'd had a better angle, she would have amputated the damn fingers. As soon as he let her go and fell to his back cradling his hand, Fallon threw herself atop him. Snarling like a wild beast, she gripped both her blades and raised them high overhead, ready for the kill.

"No!"

Fallon fought as she was grabbed by the shoulders and yanked off her quarry to be slaughtered. Pulled back with incredible force, she was on her back again. This time there were two trying to kill her.

More warriors with shaved heads and beards. She growled as she fought against them, using every fiber of her being to not give in. One tried with gritted teeth to get her fingers to release her blades. It wasn't going to happen.

"I'll kill you!" she snarled.

One of them punched her in the crook of her arm hard, making her entire arm go numb and her fingers release. Her blade clanked to the floor, her other arm meeting the same fate. Both men were breathing hard as they seemed to be trying to get her to surrender.

It was then that she saw two figures standing near the fireplace. They were smaller. Women. One was holding the other. The one being held was Cateline and she was crying. Or, *was* it Cateline? No, she thought. No. No, no!

"You bitch!" she raged, fighting against the demon men again who were trying to hold her down. "You tried to seduce me to kill me! Succubus!" With near superhuman strength, she pushed one of the men off her and turned to her stomach, using powerful legs to kick the other man off her as she began to crawl her way over to the lying visage. "You tried to kill me," she snarled.

Yet again, her ankles were grabbed and she was yanked backward, her nails scratching across the stone as she was pulled. She was picked up and slammed back down on her back again.

"Now!" one of the warriors called out.

Exhausted, Fallon stopped fighting for a moment. She knew her time was coming, time to meet her end. She whimpered, hot and bitter tears rolling down the sides of her face and into her hair. One man was at her arms, holding them down while the other all but sat on her legs. She watched as a woman in a cloak, blue with gold stitching, moved into her line of sight. She'd been the one holding Cateline. More tears.

The woman, an angel, Fallon thought. She had to be. Her short blond hair just brushed the pale skin of her forehead. Her eyes, so beautiful in color, like the sky and the ocean had met. Full lips were moving, almost like a hum as she was speaking, but the words were so quiet. A chant.

She produced a leather pouch and opened it, dipping her forefinger and thumb inside. Fallon watched, eyes hooded as she was so ready to go. So ready for it to end. "You're going to kill me," she whispered. "Just like Fergus."

The woman never stopped her chanting as she met Fallon's gaze. She glanced up at somebody, and

Fallon saw another man move in to hover over her. It was the first demon she'd sliced his fingers. Wounded and bloody hand cradled against his chest, he used the other to grasp Fallon's face, forcing her mouth open.

Fallon squeezed her eyes shut as she felt powder sprinkled onto her tongue. Her mouth was forced shut, no choice but to swallow as saliva instantly began to gather, almost like froth. She jerked, her shoulders leaving the floor and her head falling back, leaving her neck arched. Her eyes squeezed shut and mouth opened in agony.

The grip on her legs and arms became firmer as her entire body began to convulse, her head slamming back into the stone floor before she felt hands cupping the back of it, preventing another slam. An animalistic, guttural cry escaped her lips as her entire body arched, the only parts remaining on the floor those being held down.

The soft chanting continued up by her head, making her think the angel in the cloak was likely the one cupping her head. It felt as if all of Fallon's insides were melting, turning into molten lava and trying to leave her body through any means necessary—even right out of her chest.

The pressure built and built until finally, like an explosion, she screamed until her voice cracked and gave out. It felt like her very soul exploded out of her body in that moment, leaving a very exhausted and scared shell behind. Her body went limp, breasts heaving and clothing stuck to her with the glue of sweat.

The hands upon her eased and finally released her. She felt the softest lips press against her forehead. "It is over," was whispered. "Now, we must find where he went."

Chapter Twenty-nine

"Cut right here, Roishin," Livia said, squatting down and holding the flower they'd been seeking away from the others so she could get in there with the blade and cut the stem loose.

"More over here," Elsie called out.

Livia glanced over there. "Wonderful," she said. "We'll need quite a lot. No idea how much or how long we'll need to give this to Fallon."

Roishin sawed through one stem, then a couple more that were in the general area. Livia was having her do the cutting because there were other flowers and weeds nearby that she didn't want to accidentally get mixed in.

Job once again completed, Roishin backed away to follow along dutifully as the expert did her job. Elsie had begun to carefully pull the flowers, making sure she got stem, leaves, and flowers before dropping them into her basket. The young woman was currently bent over such a task, Roishin's gaze managing to find a shapely behind, even noticeable with the added material of her skirt and tunic.

Deciding to stop being obnoxious, she turned away. Glancing back toward the castle, she saw something. Turning to face the huge structure up the hill, she realized it was just smoke coming from one of the chimneys. The sun had risen, so she saw it billow against the painted colors of the morning.

About to look away, she realized that the smoke didn't continue out a few feet from the chimney then dissipate like normal. It continued to not just stream out, but it got higher and higher. She followed its progress, noting that, like the long body of a snake, the stream ended, clearing the chimney and was now free-floating in the sky.

"What is that?" she asked softly, as if to herself.

She took a few steps, her gaze never leaving the strange anomaly. If she didn't have such a bad feeling in her gut, she would have thought it beautiful. So graceful, as it seemed to weave and swim through the air. She shielded her eyes as she followed it up higher into the sky, the brilliant light of the morning sun blinding her for a moment.

She felt somebody step up beside her. Somehow, she knew it was Elsie, her shoulder just brushing Roishin's. They stood there watching it together, Roishin entranced.

"I think we need to get you inside, milady," Elsie whispered, her tone soft yet edged with a bit of worry.

"It's so beautiful," Roishin murmured. In the sky, as if dancing just for her. She couldn't take her eyes off it.

"Roishin," Elsie said. "Let's go inside."

"No," Roishin said absently, moving away from the servant as she continued to watch it.

A slow smile spread across her lips as she watched. Suddenly, a hand was upon her face and she was forced to look into Elsie's. Irritated, she tried to push the young woman away. Damn it! She wanted to watch.

"Now," Elsie said, her voice stronger.

Roishin glared at her. "I said, *no.*"

Moving to push past her again, Roishin was grabbed once more, her face cupped in both hands and held in place as soft lips pressed against her own, lingering. She was so startled, she stopped moving, almost stopped breathing. She returned the soft touch, her entire body filling with a sensation she'd never felt before, but it certainly had her attention. After a long moment, Elsie pulled away, leaving Roishin standing there, stunned.

"What is that?" Livia breathed from where she stood by her basket.

It took Roishin a moment, but she shook herself out of her reverie and turned to the older woman who was watching with fear in her eyes. Knocked out of her trance from moments before, Roishin looked back to Elsie, who met her gaze shyly before they both hurried back over to Livia.

"We need to go in," Roishin said, grabbing Livia's basket and shoving it at her. As she watched, the snake-like figure in the sky shot straight up high into the sky before it evaporated, disappearing. "Is it gone?" she asked, looking to Elsie, who was also watching it. "Did it go?"

Elsie met her gaze and shook her head. "I know not."

"No!"

Roishin's head whipped around to the cry of a man, his voice echoing through the trees. Following that was a loud grunt and then the clash of swords. She thought to herself, wasn't that where those castle guards had been? Looking to Livia, she saw that she, too, was looking in that direction and seemed to be just as confused.

"I think we should go," Roishin said.

Before they could move, it was over. The silence was near deafening until light whistling could be heard, a happy tune. Roishin's heart was racing as she continued to look in that direction. A moment later, sure enough, one of the guards, the very one who had spoken to her upon their passing earlier, appeared through the trees.

He was alone and was casually twirling his sword, not a care in the world. As happy as his tune was and as casual as his little stroll seemed to be, there was just one little thing that hinted at the fact that not was all as it seemed. His tunic was splattered with blood and his sword literally dripped with it. As he twirled the weapon, blood flung off to land on a tree he passed.

He smiled at the three women, all seeming to be frozen where they stood. "Beautiful day," he said with a friendly smile. "Nice blue sky." He pointed heavenward. "Quiet day in the woods." His arm holding the sword was held out to indicate all that was around them.

"Where are your compatriots?" Roishin asked.

"Dead," he said simply.

"Run!" Elsie exclaimed.

Roishin turned and took off, hoping against hope they had enough space between them that they could get to the clearing of the grounds and scream for help before he could get to them, with so much foliage for him to get around or trip over to slow him down.

A loud crack rent the air, followed by a zipping sound. Livia cried out, flung forward as she'd been running. She landed face-first in the overgrowth, a crossbow bolt sticking out of her back.

"Livia!" Roishin screamed. She began to run over to her, but her hand was grabbed and she was nearly yanked off her feet.

"No!" Elsie growled, pulling her deeper into the forest.

The trees grew closer together, the woods more dense and much harder for him to follow, let alone get a good shot. Crying out, Roishin lost her balance and tripped, running headlong into a tree. She just barely caught herself with her hands before her head slammed into its thick trunk.

She crashed into a patch of…something. She cried out when little pricklies poked into every part of her where there was bare skin. Elsie was instantly by her side, trying to shush her as she worked to get the briars out of her arms and hands.

"Be quiet," she hissed.

Roishin literally bit her lip in order to not cry out as the stickers were picked out of the palm of her left hand, which was already scratched and bloody from the hard crash against the tree.

"Where is he?" she all but mouthed to Elsie.

Resting her hand on Roishin's shoulder and giving it a little squeeze, Elsie used impressive stealth to lean over Roishin's body to peek around the tree. She moved away from the princess a moment later,

"I don't see him," she whispered into Roishin's ear. "I'll be right back."

She took the knife from Roishin's hand, which had been put back in its sheath after the final flower she'd cut for Livia. She slowly slid the blade free from the leather and turned it around to place the grip in Roishin's fingers. The message was clear: *If he gets close to you while I'm gone, do what you must.*

While lying there, Roishin took inventory of the rest of her body. Her ankle hurt like crazy, no doubt badly twisted in the fall. She didn't think anything was broken, but those darn briars sure gave her a beating. Suddenly, Livia's body came back to mind. The tears were instant, though she again bit her lip to stop any sound.

She could save her, she thought. Yes, she could save her. She had to be able to. She forced the tears away. There was no time for that. Closing her eyes, she took a deep breath, slowly releasing it. Opening her eyes again, Elsie was nowhere to be seen. Getting worried, Roishin sat up as slowly as she could. In a sitting position, she listened.

Nothing.

Wincing as she forced herself to her knees, she tried to hear something, *anything* to give her an idea of where he was, where Elsie was. She slowly picked her way out of the briar patch, hissing in pain as more of those bastards found their way into her skin. Somehow, she managed to remain quiet.

There were a ton of them stuck in her trousers, but she didn't care. She could deal with that later. On her feet again, she stayed hidden as best she could behind the massive trunk of the tree she was pressed against.

She held her breath, hearing something. Footfalls. Which direction? She looked to her right, trying to focus. Nothing. To the left. Nothing. Damnit! She ducked down and scurried to another tree, hiding behind it. The problem was, not knowing where the guard had gone, she had no idea if she was hiding or if she'd just moved into plain sight.

CRACK!

She cursed when a bolt landed in the trunk right next to her head. She dove to the ground and began to crawl toward another tree to get behind. She would have done anything to have her bow in that moment. She heard the creaking as the crossbow was being loaded again. She cursed under her breath and decided it was the only time she'd have to make a run for it.

Jumping to her feet, Roishin ignored the pain of her ankle and sprinted as fast as she could, knees pumping high into the air to put as much distance between her and that maniac as she could. She saw a felled tree just up the way, and it was a big one. She'd have to jump it.

Launching herself into the air and pulling her legs up to clear the massive trunk, she cried out, pointed fire hitting her in the side and spreading like a blaze through her entire body. She fell to the ground, crying out again. Her entire right side was nothing but white-hot pain. She placed her hand on it, and it came back with a bloody palm.

An animalistic cry erupted into the morning. As she lay there, Roishin lifted her head to just barely see Elsie run up behind the guard, who was just beginning to reload the crossbow. She was holding a sword and, with a cry, unleashed on the unsuspecting man. He didn't stand a chance and went down hard. With a grunt of exertion, she brought that sword down and impaled him on the ground where he lay.

Breathing hard and looking like a wild Amazon of myth, Elsie dropped her hands from the grip, the sword still jutting out of the man's body. Teeth bared, she looked over at Roishin. Seeming to be pulled out of her rage, the servant shook it off and ran over to

Roishin.

"Oh gods," she whimpered as she threw herself to her knees next to the fallen princess.

Roishin looked up at her, so glad she was there with her. "Please," she managed. "Tell my mamaí that I love her." Tears trailed down her cheeks in pain and fear.

"Shh," Elsie murmured. "No. You're not going to die, Roishin. You cannot."

Roishin gave her a ghost of a smile. "I don't think I have a lot of choice in that." It was getting harder and harder to breathe. She studied Elsie's face, drinking in every feature. "You're so beautiful," she murmured. "I always wanted to tell you that."

Elsie's face softened. "So are you," she whispered in response. Tears began to roll down Elsie's cheeks, making a trail through the splattered blood on her face and smudged dirt from soil-encrusted fingers while picking the plants earlier.

It hit Roishin then, watching those tears fall. She tried to lift her hand, but it was like her body had gone into shock. Nothing worked right. "My tears," she managed to say. "Touch my tears, then go press them to Livia's wound. Save her, Elsie."

The servant studied her for a moment. "Like you did the baby," she said, a statement. At Roishin's nod, Elsie placed her palm against Roishin's face, gently smoothing it over her tear-streaked cheek. When she pressed it against Roishin's wound at her side, Roishin tried to push her away. "Hush."

Roishin gasped, her back arching as it felt like ice-cold fingers dipped into her wound, seeming to numb it. The pain slowly began to fade as her body was overtaken by an energy that made her jerk and gasp. Her eyes rolled back in her head and lips fell open as an almost orgasmic sensation washed through her, making her back arch and toes curl inside her boots.

Her hand was taken and her fingers curled tightly around those that held it. She gasped again as she felt her other hand, of its own accord, move and wrap itself around the crossbow bolt sticking out of her side. She eased it out until it cleared her body, the numbing cold turning to fire hot, then easing into a pleasant warm. A moment later, everything stopped.

She let out a long, slow breath, then lay still. Her eyes closed and she heard a soft sob next to her.

"Roishin?" Elsie asked, her voice filled with fear.

It took a moment, but finally Roishin was able to move. A slow smile spread across her lips. "Wow."

A burst of part sniffle and part laughter escaped Elsie's lips, and she lowered herself to hug Roishin to her. She was crying fully now. It took a moment, but finally Roishin was able to hug her back, the two holding each other tightly.

After a long moment, Elsie lifted her head from where it had been buried in Roishin's neck. Tears were still flowing from her eyes as she looked down at her. "Are you okay?"

Roishin nodded. "Aye." Her eyes popped open. "Livia!"

Elsie helped her to her feet, and remarkably, anything and everything that had gone wrong from the shot to her side to her badly twisted ankle to becoming a princess pincushion—all of it was gone. She felt no pain. It was as if none of it had happened to her.

She took off at a dead run toward where Livia

had fallen. She still lay where she fell, and it seemed she hadn't moved a muscle. Fresh tears fell down Roishin's cheeks as she fell to her knees. Instantly, she ran her fingers through her tears and pressed it into the wound at her back, which no longer even bled.

"Come on," she whispered. "Come on, come on, come on!" She watched, waiting with almost bated breath for what she knew was supposed to happen.

Elsie knelt down beside her. She, too, was crying again. Roishin dropped more tears into her wound. Her face crumbled as she watched.

"It's supposed to work," she cried. "It's supposed to."

Nothing. Absolutely nothing.

She broke down, her face buried in her hands. "I failed her," she sobbed.

"No." Elsie took her in her arms, holding her close. "I think she's been gone too long."

Roishin turned to her, her entire body shaking as she cried.

Chapter Thirty

Hardly able to breathe, Cateline stood there, tears still streaming down her cheeks as her hands pressed together in front of her mouth. Was it safe to go over to her? When Enori glanced back at her from where she knelt by Fallon's head, the look in her eyes told the princess it was time.

Sniffling and using the sleeve of her dress to quickly dry her cheeks, Cateline walked over to where Fallon lay on the floor. Enori's warriors glanced at her before pushing to their feet and stepping away. The walk across the bedchamber felt like she'd walked a hundred miles until finally she reached Fallon, who still lay on the floor.

Her eyes were closed and her chest was heaving, as though trying to catch her breath. She was sweaty, and blood had trailed from her mouth and her nose. She was pale and honestly, if she hadn't been visibly and audibly breathing, Cateline would have thought the worst. Lowering herself, Cateline's eyes never left Fallon's face.

"Fallon?" she said softly, no idea what to expect.

She was so terrified those eyes would open and look at her with the hatred and vitriol they had before, along with the horrible words she'd spat at her. Cateline had known that, if Fallon had been able to reach her, she would have killed her. She didn't fully understand what had happened, but Enori seemed sure that it was over.

Sniffling again, she whispered. "Fallon?"

Slowly, Fallon's eyes opened, and what looked up at Cateline were the beautiful violet eyes Cateline cherished. They were unfocused for a moment, but after a few blinks, they cleared and a look of absolute peace and relief washed over Fallon's battered and bruised face. Clearly in pain, Fallon tried to sit up.

"No." Cateline smiled and moved to her knees, hovering over her. She used the most gentle touches she could as she caressed Fallon's jaw. She looked down into her eyes. The whole world disappeared in that moment, leaving just her and Fallon.

Fallon looked up into her eyes, all the love Cateline knew she felt for her so very bright in those violet depths. "I love you," Fallon murmured.

Cateline smiled, the first real smile she'd had in days. "And I you."

With a heavy sigh of relief, Fallon wrapped her arms around Cateline, pulling her down on top of her. Cateline's eyes closed, her world righting itself. For the first time since all this craziness had begun, she felt that maybe, just *maybe* everything would be okay. After several moments of recentering, Cateline lifted her head and left a careful kiss on Fallon's lips.

Remembering that not only were they not alone but the situation wasn't over, Cateline finally lifted herself up and off Fallon, looking to Enori, who remained close by. "What happened?" she asked, indicating her wife, whose stomach her hand still rested upon.

"*Bāhūthā*," Enori said simply. "He took her over."

Cateline stared at her. It took her a moment to absorb that information and put it into some sort of sense. Nodding, she said, "Okay, why?"

"My guess is," Enori said with a tired sigh as she pushed to her feet. "To get Fallon either to kill herself and take her out of the picture, or to get Fallon to kill all of you."

Horrified, Cateline looked back down to Fallon, who was staring up at the ceiling, so much running through her head if the expression in her troubled eyes was any indication. The princess grabbed her hand, Fallon's fingers automatically wrapping around her own.

"Why?" Cateline asked. "Why would he try and use her for that?"

"Because he can't do it on his own," Enori explained. "Many, many years ago he was cursed, his physical form destroyed." Enori looked to the warrior who still cradled his injured hand. She said some soft words to him. He turned to the couple on the floor and bowed deeply before hurrying from the room, the remaining two warriors staying put.

"Is he going to be okay?" Fallon asked.

"I think so," Enori said. "I sent him to get his hand healed. I'm worried he could lose his fingers if he doesn't."

Fallon's eyes fell closed for a moment. "I'm so sorry."

"There is nothing that happened here today, Fallon, that is your fault."

Fallon nodded, though didn't look any less repentant. She gritted her teeth as once again she tried to sit up. Immediately, one of the warriors was over at her side, using his strength to ease Fallon to her feet. He all but carried her over to the bed and set her down.

"Thank you," she said, holding the man in a warrior's grip at the wrist. She looked up into his eyes as he stood next to the bed. Something passed between them, no doubt a warrior code, Cateline thought, as the man smiled and nodded. He squeezed Fallon's arm before releasing her. Fallon looked to Cateline, who climbed onto the bed to sit next to her. "Where's Isabeau?"

"Back with Collette," Cateline answered. "Where's Roishin?"

"I sent her to find Livia to find herbs to make me feel better." She gave Cateline a sheepish look. "I wanted to get her as far away from me as possible." Fallon looked over at Enori. "Is it over, Enori? Is that bastard gone?"

Enori let out a tired sigh and shook her head. "No. He's out of you, but he will find another vessel until he achieves his goal."

"Taking over Roishin?" Fallon asked.

Again, Enori shook her head. "I don't think he can. If he could, I believe he already would have. I think Roishin is already too powerful. So," she added, indicating Fallon and Cateline, who cradled the warrior's head against her chest. "He's trying to pick off those around her."

"So, what now?" Cateline asked, so afraid of the answer. She was grateful when Fallon wrapped her arm around her waist, pulling her closer to her.

"We have to trap him," Enori said simply.

"I think we already did."

Cateline's head whipped at the sound of her child's voice. She gasped at what she saw. Instantly tears came to her eyes as she hurried over to Roishin, who stood in the open doorway of the bedroom chamber, Elsie at her side.

"Roishin!" She was sobbing by time she reached her.

The girl was bloodied and bruised, hair wild like a mane of midnight around her head and her face pale, making the blood and dirt upon her face stand out in stark relief. But the worst of it was her shirt. It was caked in blood at her side and halfway across her abdomen. The material was torn at what looked to be the site of a grievous wound.

"What happened?" Cateline demanded, turning Roishin so she could look at her wound. "Get Cerdic—"

"No, Mamaí," Roishin said, her voice quiet but firm. She clasped her hand over Cateline's, which was about to pull the garment up. She caught Cateline's eyes with her own, the look in the haunted green depths pinning her. The message was clear: *I'm no longer wounded.*

Cateline gasped, literally staggering backward as the insinuation reached her mother's heart. Strong hands braced her from behind as she nearly fell in her stunned shock of what could have been. She looked to Elsie, noting she looked not a lot better than Roishin. She was also bloody, but it didn't seem she was or had been injured, so much as the blood belonged to somebody else.

"Where is he?" Enori asked softly from just behind Cateline, clearly the one who had caught her.

"He was in a castle guard," Elsie explained softly. "He is dead, but his body keeps twitching. I believe *Bāhūthā* is trapped inside of him."

Steady on her feet, Cateline watched as Enori walked over to Elsie, a pleased look upon her face. She met the young servant's gaze for a long moment before she looked to her two warriors. She said nothing, but they hurried over to her.

Turning back to Elsie, Enori said softly. "You come with us. Let's finish this."

Cateline watched as Elsie and Roishin shared a long look, something passing between them before Elsie turned and followed Enori and the two warriors out of the bedchamber. Roishin looked back to her mother, and as if in silent agreement, the two melted in the other's arms.

Eyes squeezing tightly closed, Cateline held her daughter tightly to her. She buried her face in her hair, breathing her in. No, she didn't know what had happened, but she at least knew Roishin was okay, she was *alive*.

"Mamaí," Roishin said into the hug, her voice thick with emotion.

"What, my love?" Cateline asked, looking into Roishin's face when her head lifted from her mother's shoulder. Cateline brushed back her hair from her stricken face. "What?"

"Livia's dead," Roishin whispered. "I tried to save her," she continued, her words breaking as sobs racked her. "I tried."

Cateline's eyes squeezed shut as she hugged the sobbing girl against her again. Her own tears stung the backs of her eyes, though she tried desperately to keep them back, at least for now. Roishin needed her to be strong. She'd have her own time later to grieve. For now, she was just so relieved and grateful that Fallon and Roishin were still alive.

※ ※ ※ ※

Later that night, Cateline sat by herself in the family chamber. Assured they were safe for the time being, the family hadn't wanted to be apart. So, after getting cleaned up from a horrific set of days, everyone had remained together in Fallon and Cateline's bedchamber. When she'd left ten minutes before, Roishin had been snuggled up with Fallon in the bed, both sound asleep.

Her tears were as heavy as her heart, finally able to deal with the unbelievable grief at what had happened, what could have happened, and what *did* happen to Livia. Her entire body shook with the intensity of her quiet sobs. But five years younger than the princess, Livia had played many roles in the thirteen years she'd been part of their family.

She'd been a lady-in-waiting, younger sister, best friend, confidante, and advisor. She'd been a beloved aunt to Cateline and Fallon's children and an absolute part of their family. A young woman orphaned so very young, she'd found herself bounced from Italy all the way to a Surshan orphanage where the monks had taken pity on her and let her live in a shed as long as she tended the gardens.

Cateline had felt an instant connection with the young girl. Her mind went back to what Enori had told her: the soul remembers love. She hoped against hope that someday, in another time, she and Livia would meet again.

She looked up from her grief-drenched hands when she heard somebody entering the chamber. Elsie passed through the patches of moonlight that filtered in through the windows. She looked ethereal dressed in a white sleep gown with her long, golden hair draped over one shoulder, the rest unseen down her back.

She walked over to the couch where Cateline was curled up. Sitting beside her, she held out her hand, a kerchief in her fingers. Smiling through her tears, not remotely surprised by this young woman's appearance and kindness, she took it.

"*Merci,*" she whispered. She wiped at her eyes and cheeks, even as tears continued to fall. "Did I wake you?"

Elsie shook her head. "No. Woke up from a nightmare." She brought her legs up, tucking them under the material of her sleep dress. She wrapped her arms around her shins as bare toes poked out of the garment where her feet rested on the edge of the cushion. "I saw you were gone." A sad smile reached her lips, but not her eyes. "Wanted to make sure you were all right."

Elsie had joined the family in the bedchamber after returning alone from wherever she'd gone with Enori and the warriors. It hadn't been spoken of. "Are Fallon and Roishin still asleep?" Cateline asked.

Nodding, Elsie said, "Aye. Curled up together in bed." She gave the princess a slightly larger smile. "I think Roishin was so relieved to see that her daidí was okay."

"*Oui.*" She smiled. "They are very close." Cateline reached over and placed one of her hands on Elsie's arm. "You saved her." She met Elsie's gaze. "Didn't you?"

"Today was a team effort, milady," she finally said softly. "We both did what we had to do to survive." They were both quiet for a moment before Elsie continued. "I'm so sorry about Livia, milady. I know Roishin is devastated."

Fresh tears threatened as Cateline nodded. She bit her lip to try to stop the flow. She blew out a breath. "You know, Livia came to us around the age you did. You, just a couple years younger when you arrived." She sniffled, taking a deep, centering breath. "But, you both came to us as very young women, and for the same reason."

"She lost her parents, too?" Elsie asked.

Cateline nodded. "She never fully told me her story, some of which I'm not sure she even knows. But, yes, she ended up here in an orphanage and something about her..." She smiled, remembering the day Fallon had taken her to that orphanage to talk to the monks. "I wanted her under my roof." She smiled, looking over to Elsie. "Fallon made it so," she whispered. "She came to us the same day as Laigen and Garratt. Just sixteen."

Elsie rested her chin upon her cloth-covered knees, staring off into the distance, into a time Cateline wasn't sure she wanted to go. She wondered if it was the events of that very afternoon.

"You remind me a lot of her," Cateline said.

Elsie turned her head so her cheek rested against her knees instead of her chin. In that moment, for the first time, she seemed like her actual age. She was also but sixteen, just becoming a woman, yet still a child. It was so easy to forget that fact sometimes. Cateline reached over and gently brushed golden strands back over her shoulder in a motherly gesture.

"Thank you for protecting Roishin," she said softly. Elsie raised her head and looked away, but not before Cateline saw the tears forming. "Come here."

To Cateline's surprise, Elsie allowed herself to be pulled against the princess and held. Cateline rocked her like she would one of her own daughters—or Livia after she'd been hurt. She combed her fingers through her hair, resting her head against the top of that which rested against her upper chest.

Once the young woman had calmed, her tears coming to an end, she let out a long, contented sigh. Cateline smiled. She wondered how long it had been since Elsie had been held, given the support of a family. She knew she'd had parents that loved her, but being so young when she'd lost them, how long had she felt alone and lost, just like Cateline and Fallon had?

"I want to tell you something," she said quietly, her fingers continuing to enjoy the soft, cool strands of thick, blond hair with her fingers.

"All right," Elsie murmured.

"I know that Fallon and I can never take the place of your parents," Cateline began. "Nor do we want to. But," she added. "You have a family again, Elsie." She gave her a loving squeeze. "You always have a place."

"Thank you, Cateline," Elsie whispered, snuggling in a bit more.

Chapter Thirty-one

Hands clasped behind her back, Fallon slowly made her way around the iron chest. It was about three feet wide, two feet deep, and nearly three feet tall. She stayed out of the way as the sailors were rigging heavy chains around it. She'd paid the captain of the ship handsomely to load it on as cargo and dump it in the deepest part of the ocean.

It had been three days, and her fury was hot. This time, however, it was her own fury, her true anger, and very focused: if that *thing* ever showed itself again, she'd tear its black heart out with her bare hands. It had gone after her, it had gone after Cateline, it had gone after Roishin, and it had killed Livia.

According to Enori, because the body it had invaded died while it was still inside, the bastard was trapped until that body was literally split open to let it out. This, of course, would happen with decomposition. So, before that could happen, the dead soldier had been dumped unceremoniously inside that iron chest.

His body would rot at the bottom of the ocean, right along with *Bāhūthā*. He couldn't be destroyed, but by gods he could be trapped forever. She had no idea what Enori had done, nor why she'd taken Elsie with her to do it, but according to the priestess, an incredibly powerful spell had been used to enchant the trunk, keeping the God of Chaos inside.

"Sire?"

Fallon was pulled out of her thoughts by one of the sailors. "Aye?"

The man held up a huge iron lock. "Would you like the honors, Your Highness?"

"Absolutely," Fallon murmured.

Walking over to the man, she took it from him and then over to the trunk. The chains had been secured tightly. The trunk was already locked with both whatever Enori had done and a lock. She slid the loop through the chain link the sailor indicated, then pushed the mechanism home with a satisfying *click*. She gave it a mighty tug, smiling when it held.

Nodding at the sailor, she stepped back, allowing the men to hook the incredibly heavy chest up to their pulley crane, where it would be heaved up and lowered down into the cargo hold. She glanced over when she saw the captain of the ship step up to her.

"You paid a pretty price to rid yourself of this, sire," he said.

Fallon nodded. "Aye."

"Rival, milord?" the man joked, lightly nudging her shoulder with his own.

She gave him a ghost of a smile. Obviously, the country had not been made aware of what had happened, nor would it ever be. Livia's funeral had been a quiet affair, as she knew that was what she would have wanted. The country had been allowed to pay their respects in their various ways, but overall, it been kept private.

Carthac had given Livia the honor of being entombed with the family in the crypt beneath the cathedral. Fallon, of course, was grateful, as she knew her father had cared deeply for the young woman.

Fallon had little memory of the horrible days her family had suffered through. She'd been told she'd been possessed or some such by the bastard locked in that trunk.

She may not remember it, but all she had to do was look in the mirror to see the bruises, cuts, and what would be yet more scars upon her face.

As she stood there watching, guilt yet again ate at her guts. True understanding of what Fallon had failed to do was still sinking in. She'd failed to protect her family. She had one mission in life, and that was to protect those she loved. She'd failed. Not her wife, nor her children, particularly Roishin, seemed to blame her for what happened, but she blamed herself. How could she ever get over that?

She watched as the trunk was secured, and then the men operating the crane began to slowly lift it. The chain connected from the trunk to the crane went taught, and like the Christian Jesus from the grave, it rose. She followed it, never taking her eyes off it.

Her heart was racing, knowing she was watching the last few moments of this nightmare trickle through the hourglass until finally all the sand was gone. It was time to turn the hourglass over and start anew. It was a new day and a new path her family had to forge.

Livia was gone, dead and in her grave. Roishin would be leaving the following morning, and Fallon honestly had no idea how she was going to handle that one. She'd tried, oh she'd tried, to talk Enori out of it. *Bāhūthā* was gone, so didn't that mean the danger was, too? Didn't that mean her daughter could stay?

No.

Roishin was growing more powerful by the day, and with no way to control it, she'd end up hurting those she loved most. Like I did, Fallon thought bitterly. She was angry. Yes, she was very, very angry. She'd lost the woman that was her closest advisor and the little sister she'd never had, and now she was losing her daughter, too.

"Rot in Hell," she muttered.

☙❧❦❧

Standing outside her door, Fallon closed her eyes, fingers holding tighter to what she'd brought. She took a deep breath, then raised a fist to knock. At the muffled invite from the other side of the door, she turned the handle and pushed the door open. Roishin was doing as Enori had told her to do, which was to pack only the most precious things to her. Everything else would be provided.

Fallon had to look away, as it was a punch to the gut. She used the act of closing the door as an excuse to take another deep breath. *How am I going to let her go?* Centering herself, she turned back around, big smile.

"Hey, you."

Roishin smiled. "Hello."

"Got a minute?"

"Sure."

Fallon raised her hands, revealing two leather ties. At Roishin's questioning look, Fallon explained. "Let's get you your warrior braids, huh?"

Roishin looked from Fallon's hand to her eyes. "Really?"

Nodding, Fallon smiled. "Yup. Have a seat."

Roishin hurriedly grabbed the chair and dragged it to the middle of the floor, plopping down. Fallon saw her brush lying on her desk, which had been moved back into place as Elsie's bed had been returned to her room in the servants' quarters.

"So," Fallon began, gently brushing out the long, dark locks, the exact same color as her own. "Your Uncle Ailfred is the one who gave me my first braids."

"I bet you were a lot younger than I am."

Fallon chuckled. "I was." She gently worked a few tangles out before continuing the long strokes. "But we both earned them, you and I." She set the brush aside as she began to gather the thin ropes of hair she'd use to create the braids.

"How old were you?" Roishin asked, sitting dutifully straight and still.

Fallon smiled. "I was seven."

"So, does that mean I'm a loser at thirteen?"

Fallon chuckled. "No, Roishin, it does not."

They were quiet for a long moment until Roishin spoke again. "Daidí, I want to give Elsie a gift before I go." She paused. "Do you think that's weird?"

"Weird?" At Roishin's small nod, Fallon said, "Not at all. She's been a good personal servant to you, let alone what you two went through together." She held the braided hair with one hand while reaching over to grab the leather tie where she'd set it down by the brush. She began to carefully tie the end of the braid to keep it in place. "You two have gotten close lately," she observed absently.

Roishin didn't say anything for a long moment as Fallon moved to the other side of her to start on the second braid. When she was finished, there would be a braid running down either side of Roishin's head, just like Fallon and Ailfred before her.

Finally, the girl spoke. "Aye." That one word

was quiet, soft.

Fallon said nothing, as she wondered if there would be more coming regarding the beautiful young servant. Truth was, she felt all of them had changed where Elsie was concerned. She knew Cateline certainly had.

"Daidí," Roishin said quietly. "Before you loved mamaí, did you ever love anyone else?"

Very surprised at the question, Fallon shook her head, even though Roishin couldn't see it. "No," she said. "Not like that, not like I love her."

"Were you ever with anyone before her?"

Fallon paused in her braiding, not entirely sure what "with" meant in Roishin's question. "As in, a relationship?"

Roishin shrugged. "That or kissed or anything. I mean, who was your first kiss?"

Oh boy! How on earth was she going to answer this when Roishin knew the woman? She cleared her throat and said, "Well, the first time I kissed somebody, it was to teach me how, Roishin. It wasn't about love or anything like that."

"So," Roishin said, Fallon smiling as she could absolutely see her eyebrows furrowed as she tried to make heads or tails of it, even as she wasn't looking at her daughter's face. "Why did you have to be taught how? By who?"

"Well," Fallon said, clearing her throat again. "As you know, I was thought of as a boy, and as a warrior, certain things are...expected."

Roishin pulled away and looked up at her. "Were you a strumpet?"

A bark of laughter erupted from Fallon's throat. She shook her head. "I was not!" She was still laughing at the indignant look she got as Roishin sat back in the chair and settled in. Fallon had to restart part of the braid as the hair had been pulled right out of her fingers. "I have been with exactly three people in my lifetime," she explained. "And one of those was essentially something I wasn't allowed to say no to."

"Gift from a king?" Roishin challenged.

"Actually, yes." Fallon shook her head, amused. "The other?"

"Why do you want to know this?"

"Why *don't* you want me to know this?" Roishin countered.

Knowing better than to argue a point and make the child even more curious, Fallon sighed. "Fine. The other was a young woman I'd known since I was a child," she explained, opting to keep it vague. "As I was growing up and had to play the role of a young man, she helped me to understand what I had to do." It was only partially the truth, but it would have to suffice. For now, at least.

"So," she asked slowly, the wheels in her mind clearly working. "Mamaí was the only one you loved?"

The smile that came to Fallon's lips was easy. "Aye," she said softly. "I loved the young woman I grew up with, but only ever as a good and loyal friend."

"Is it different?" Roishin asked softly, her own voice holding a wistful tone to it. "To kiss someone you truly love versus somebody you love as a friend?"

"Night and day." She reached for the second leather tie as she finished up the braid. "Roishin, why this curiosity, hmm?" she asked gently.

"What if I told you I had my first kiss?" Roishin asked slowly. "Granted, she was trying to distract me from being taken over by an evil god at the time, but..."

Fallon's movements stopped. "What?" She finished what she was doing then moved around to stand in front of her daughter, who was still seated. "Elsie?" Roishin nodded, looking down at her hands in her lap. Fallon reached down and gently urged her to look up with two fingers under her chin. "What do you think about that?"

"Which part?" Roishin asked. "That it was under duress or that it was Elsie?"

Fallon smiled. "Either one, I suppose." She squatted down in front of her. "Both."

Roishin shrugged. "Well, I hate that it was under those circumstances, because I honestly don't think it would have ever happened otherwise."

Fallon's eyebrows rose. "You wanted it to?" Roishin nodded as she bit her lip nervously. "Sweetheart," she said softly. "Are you attracted to girls? Or, is it about Elsie?"

"I think it's both, honestly."

Fallon nodded. "How do you think Elsie feels?"

"I think she likes me as a person, but I'm sure she sees me as a kid. I mean," she said, looking down at her hands again. "I *am* a kid to her."

"We all grow up, Roishin," Fallon said. "And, whether the two of you end up as anything more than what you are today, you can always look at that first kiss, regardless of the reason it happened, with fondness. Because it was from somebody who cared, and somebody *you* cared about." She smiled. "That alone makes it special."

Roishin met her gaze and held it for a long time. Finally, she nodded and smiled. "Aye. It does."

Before she knew what hit her, Fallon had herself

an armful of curious, feisty, sometimes obstinate, and absolutely precious Roishin. She held her tightly, eyes squeezing shut as she held her for all she was worth.

"This is not goodbye, Daidí," Roishin whispered, her voice thick with emotion.

Fallon smiled. "No." She kissed her cheek loudly before hugging her again. "Not goodbye."

Chapter Thirty-two

S he felt so silly standing there, but she knew she'd regret it for the rest of her life if she didn't. Looking down at her hands, she took a long, deep breath, then raised the fist that wasn't holding anything. After three sharp raps, she waited. She rocked on her heels as she waited, surreptitiously glancing left and right, as it just wouldn't do to have questions.

About to raise her fist again, she was relieved when she heard movement in the room beyond the closed door. It was unlocked and just barely pulled open. A sleepy Elsie peeked out. Roishin smiled.

"Hey," she said quietly. "So sorry to wake you. But, um..." She blew out a breath. "I'm leaving. I wanted to say goodbye."

Dark blond eyebrows drew. "Now? I thought you were leaving on the morrow?"

Roishin gave her a lopsided grin. "Well, it's only two hours before the morrow, but I don't want to put my parents through that."

Elsie disappeared and the door opened wider. Roishin stepped inside and out of the way so Elsie could close the door. The room was very small, just enough room for the narrow bed, a water pitcher and basin, and a trunk for her belongings. In her sleep dress and with her hair down around her shoulders, Elsie looked at her expectantly.

"Again, really sorry for waking you." She felt stupid. Honestly, Elsie probably couldn't care less that she was leaving. Less mess to deal with. Clearing her throat, she said, "Anyway, as I was saying, I don't want to put them through any more. They've been through so much." She looked down at her hands, which were clasped around what she held. "And honestly," she said softly. "I can't handle any more goodbyes."

Roishin was very surprised when she found herself wrapped up in a very tight, very warm hug. She returned it, holding Elsie close. There was very little difference in their height now, Elsie only a couple inches taller. Neither said anything, just held each other. She could feel the soft warmth against her, Elsie's body flush with her own. Her head was cupped where it rested against Elsie's shoulder.

Closing her eyes, Roishin absorbed everything about her. She wanted to memorize it to take with her. She inhaled her scent—her hair, her skin. She focused on how the softness of her sleep dress felt beneath her fingers. And, due to its length, Elsie's hair draped down her back and one of Roishin's hands lay atop it.

Yes, it was as soft as she always wondered it would be. She smiled at that. At least she got to find out. As much as she wanted to stay there all night, she knew she couldn't. Though absolutely loath to, Roishin slowly pulled out of the hug. She looked into Elsie's face, taking one last look at how beautiful she was.

A sad smile crossed her lips. "Well," she said. "I guess at least you won't have to pick up after me anymore."

Elsie smiled. "No, guess not." She cupped the side of Roishin's face. "You go, Roishin," she said softly. "Find out who you are. All the amazing things that make you that."

Roishin nodded, doing her level best to not cry. Again. "So," she said, her nervousness coming back. She brought up her hand, the gold triskelion broach held in her fingers. "I wondered if you'd hold on to this for me," she asked.

Elsie looked into her eyes, then down at the proffered item. She took it in her own fingers, looking at it for a long moment. Finally, she met Roishin's eyes again. "Yes," she whispered.

Roishin blew out a breath of relief. She smiled, nodding. "All right. Good." She chuckled softly. "Thought you'd toss me out on my ear for that one."

Elsie gave her a winning smile and shook her head. "No."

"Well, hopefully you won't for this one, then." She looked at her shyly before reaching inside her cloak and producing what she'd hurried outside to grab. "I know you haven't gotten to go strolling unbidden yet, so hopefully this will bring a smile to your day." She held up the white rose.

The smile that spread across full lips was so incredibly beautiful as Elsie took the rose. She brought it to her nose, eyes closing as she inhaled its fragrance. Finally, she met Roishin's expectant gaze. The slap never came, and Roishin was grateful. In fact, she found herself in another hug, this one tighter, and something a little desperate about it.

"Go," Elsie murmured as she loosened her hold. She cupped Roishin's cheek again and pressed their lips together for a long moment before she turned away from her, though not before Roishin saw the glisten in her eyes.

Roishin's own eyes were stinging again, emotion threatening. Without a word, she turned to the door and pulled it open. One last look over her shoulder, she saw Elsie turned partially away from her, but didn't miss it as her hand came up to wipe at a tear, Roishin's rose hugged to her chest.

Stepping out into the hall, Roishin softly closed the door. She used the sleeve of her shirt to wipe at her eyes as she hurried down the hallway to the stairs that would take her to the third floor, to the family chamber, and finally, to the door.

About the Author

Kim has spent her life in Colorado and can't imagine living anywhere else. She's been writing since she was 9 and stumbled into her first book being published in her mid-20s. She's worked in the film industry as a writer, director and producer, but now enjoys the quiet, happy life of a professional author. She can be reached on Facebook and on her website at, www. kimpritekel.com

IF YOU LIKED THIS BOOK...

Share a review with your friends or post a review on your favorite site like Amazon, Goodreads, Barnes and Noble, or anywhere you purchased the book. Or perhaps share a posting on your social media sites and help spread the word.

Join the Sapphire Newsletter and keep up with all your favorite authors.

Did we mention you get a free book for joining our team?

sign-up at - www.sapphirebooks.com

Check out Kim's other books.

1049 Club - ISBN - 978-1-939062-97-0

Almost two hundred souls, one plane, six survivors, endless heartbreak.

When flight 1049, headed from Buffalo, NY to Italy falls from the sky, a firestorm of drama, pain, angst and sorrow ensues. Can an author, a business owner, a teenager, good ol' boy, veterinarian and ruthless lawyer survive? Better yet, can those left behind?

1049 Club is a story of survival, love, deep regret and miracles. Can the living make peace with the presumed dead? Can the presumed dead make peace with the lives and loves they thought they had before?

Blinded – ISBN – 978-1-943353-53-8

After a horrible explosion sends local television news reporter, Burton Blinde reeling both physically and emotionally, she walks away from her life and the dream job she was about to start at a major news network.

For six long years she hides out in a small mountain town, working at the local library, though is haunted by the life she had, including mysterious messages and gifts she was receiving before her life was turned upside down, a veritable bread crumb trail leading to the unknown.

Unable to resist, Burton begins to follow the clues,

which will lead her into the darkest places of human nature that she may not be able to return from.

Damaged - ISBN - 978-1-939062-45-1

Family. A group of people you are related to by blood or love.

Nora Schaeffer has come home to her family after twenty years working around the world as a photographer for National Geographic. She's welcomed into the open arms of her father and siblings.

Family. A group of people who support you, lift you up when you fall.

Shannon, the youngest of the four Schaeffer siblings, has vanished, leaving her five-year-old daughter, Bella, terrified and alone. To help find Shannon, Nora has no choice but to turn to the dark-haired specter who has haunted her for twenty years. Along the way, she finds her own long-dead heart and uncovers chilling family secrets beyond imagination.

Family. A group of people who will stick together to hide the rotten soul at its core at any cost.

Who will live? Who will die? Who will be the most damaged? And who will learn to love again?

The Gift - ISBN - 978-1-948232-47-0

The dead do speak. You just have to listen. Homicide Detective Catania "Nia" d'Giovanni is the only daughter in a large Italian family of six children. The backbone—a position not applied for nor wanted—she continues to create new glue to hold the dysfunctional group together. For Nia, family time feels more like herding cats than spending time with her brothers and feisty, aging parents.

Her heart has always been in her career with the Pueblo Police Department, especially since it will never be okay with her very Catholic mother to openly give her heart to any woman, until she meets a secretive waitress who has her at, Can I take your order?

And then it begins...

Three murders that are so gruesome, so horrible, they rock the small town to its core. Nia and her partner Oscar are left to piece together a deadly puzzle to find the key to unlock the monster they hunt.

Or, are they the hunted?

As they dissect the murder scenes where not one shred of evidence is left behind, more bodies begin to show up, each cleaner than the last, the shadowy specter that is the killer vanishing without a trace, making the woman Nia loves disappear right along with it.

When there is no evidence to follow, Nia must trust her instincts...or, is she being guided?

The Plan – ISBN – 978-1-948232-43-2

As the dark days of the Dust Bowl came to an end, the

midsection of the United States tried to rebuild and revitalize. In the small, dusty farming town of, Brooke View, Colorado, teenager, Eleanor Landry and her mother were dealing with her father, a self-appointment fire and brimstone preacher to his congregation of two. A plan to survive.

As the dark era of the robber baron comes to an end, giants of industry and innovation emerged with fabulous fortunes manifested in the mansions that dotted the landscape across the country. Lysette Landon, the teen daughter of the wealthiest family in Brooke View, was everything a good, proper girl of privilege should be. Only problem was, she wasn't dreaming of finding a young man to raise a family with. A plan to be free.

One look, one touch, all plans are off.

Secrets deeper and darker than the grave would bring Eleanor and Lysette together, their families connected by a web of lies and broken promises. A plan to escape.

Be careful because, life has other plans...

The Traveler Book One: The Hunted - ISBN - 978-1-948232-91-3

A story so epic one book can't contain it. BOOK ONE:

1977: In the era between flower power and the yuppie, Sonia Lucas is a young wife and mother, just starting out in life. Without warning, a strange presence and dark force enters her life, clouds building...

1917: ...and a storm brewing as the world reeled from the horrific events of World War I just before it was ravaged by a Spanish flu epidemic that would kill millions. Sephora Lloyd is a 16 year old girl lost in the responsibilities of an adult world helping to support herself and her mother. A beautiful young nun-in-training enters her life, bringing love and hope with her. That is, until a force bigger than either of them threatens everything Sephora holds dear.

Four women - three deaths - two words - one house
THE HUNTED

The Traveler Book Two: The Hunter - ISBN - 978-1-948232-93-7

A story so epic one book can't contain it. BOOK TWO:

1890: In the dying days of the Old West, Sally Little runs her booming brothel with the passion and tenacity the business of sex requires. Savvy and indulgent, there's one itch Sally can't let herself scratch. Afraid of hurting the woman she loves, she instead unleashes...

Present Day: ...her renovation crew and fixer upper TV show on a dilapidated mansion that has known nothing but death since a murder there in 1977. Samantha Leyton sees ratings gold in bringing the sagging old house to life, but instead she discovers only she has the power to unlock the mystery that hunted four women across time, leaving death and destruction in its wake. Can she release her sisters who came before her and finally be granted the gift of love that is stronger than any evil?

Four women - Three deaths - two words - one house
THE HUNTER

Finding Faith (Wynter Series Book 1) - ISBN - 978-1-952270-16-1

Faith Fitzgerald thought that if she got an education and became a high-powered attorney in Manhattan, maybe—just maybe—she'd gain the attention and respect of her absentee father. Considering he was the only parent she had left after her mother's suicide when Faith was just a child, she thought that's what it would take.

She was wrong.

What she dreamed would be glamorous and satisfying turned out to be grueling and thankless. Since she wasn't willing to play the game between the sheets, she was forced to stay in the cubicle jungle doing all the heavy lifting while the men got the credit and the rewards.

Deciding she is done, Faith packs up and, with the flip of the bird to the rearview mirror, leaves New York and heads home to Colorado. She has nothing there: no job, nowhere to live, no relationship with her father. Truth is, she barely has a relationship with herself.

On the drive home, she finds herself in Wynter, a tiny mountain town at the foot of the Rockies. Looking more like it belongs in a made-for-TV Christmas movie than on the map, Faith is utterly enchanted. When she tries her luck and buys a raffle ticket at Pop's, Wynter's charming café, her prize is far more than meets the eye—or the heart.

Enter Wyatt, a feisty, sexy southerner and waitress at Pop's, who just happens to be married to a local sheriff's deputy. All is not as it appears with the All-American boy and his Georgia peach.

A colorful cast of unforgettable and charming characters will teach the jaded attorney that sometimes to find yourself all you have to do is go back to the basics...and have a little Faith.

Taking Liberty (Wynter Series Book 2) - ISBN- 978-1-952270-24-6

A victim of a massive corporate downsize, Liberty Faulkner suddenly finds herself without a job, without a home, and without a plan. Though certainly not part of her vision, Libby decides that the familiar is the safest path back to her life goals. In this case, the devil she knows is home: the tiny mountain town of Wynter, Colorado, a close-knit place where everybody knows everybody and everybody's business. Seems like the perfect place for the twenty-five-year-old to start over and figure out who she is without being noticed...not.

Sergeant Grace Montez escaped her dead-end job and toxic relationship in New Mexico and moved to Wynter to help build their police department from scratch. Now an established figurehead in the community, she's got her professional life dialed in

and even mentors new recruits on the force. After a
challenging childhood and lifetime of abandonment
and disappointment, Grace hasn't been interested in
another relationship—especially because no one has
caught her eye since a certain quirky college student
who used to make her caramel macchiato at the local
coffee shop moved away three years ago.

Now that quirky college student has returned as the
beautiful, mature woman Libby has become. Can Grace
keep her distance, or will she finally take liberties with
what is being offered?

Justice Won (Wynter Series Book 3) - ISBN - 978-1-
952270-36-9

In 1890, seventeen-year-old Justice Kilkoyne and her
mother, Ninny, are one bad decision away from living on the streets of Azrael, Pennsylvania. Ninny's
propensity for the bottle has left Justice to play the
adult, her androgynous good looks helping her pass as
a young man to gain employment and keep them—if
just barely—above water.

Determined to find a better life for them, Justice saves
every penny to get them on a train headed west to
the sunshine of California. Before they can leave, the
bigotry of one shopkeeper sends Justice on the run,
chased by the police for a crime she didn't commit and
straight into the unwitting arms of a stunning young
prostitute, who, after an unexpected connection,
becomes Justice's Angel.

The day arrives to leave Pennsylvania for good. As

Justice and Ninny get settled, they're surprised by the appearance of Angel, also wanting to start anew. When the trip is violently interrupted in Colorado, Angel just may be lost to Justice forever.

Can Justice find a new life when she makes her way to the fledgling mining town of Wynter, Colorado? Can her heart ever be whole again?

Curtain Call - ISBN - 978-1-952270-42-0

What do you do when you come from a long line of dancers that spans the globe and generations, yet you can't tell your right foot from your left? You fall in love with a dancer, of course!

Gray Rickman is an awkward seventeen-year-old when she first sets eyes on Christian Scott at the dance studio/theater Gray's parents own and run in Denver, Colorado.

Though only a handful of years older than Gray, Christian carries herself with poise and wisdom far beyond her years. A woman of few words, she speaks volumes with her body.

Before Gray even really knows what her type is, Christian stars in endless daydreams and even fulfills a couple of her fantasies before vanishing out of thin air, leaving Gray in an empty bed with nothing but bittersweet memories and broken dreams.

With no choice but to move on, Gray attempts love, even moving with her college girlfriend to New York

City to pursue a career in journalism. But her standard has been set, the bar way too high for any other woman to reach or clear. It's an unexpected encounter in an obvious place when Gray sets eyes on her dancer again. Will the bright lights of Broadway illuminate the way back to the woman of her dreams? Or will they blind her to any other possibility of happiness?

Break a leg, Gray. The Great White Way calls.

Encore Performance - ISBN - 978-1-952270-52-9

Grey Rickman, a journalist for The New York Times, is offered the opportunity of a lifetime and a huge boost to her career—ghostwriting a memoir for one of the world's most beloved actors. She is deeply in love with her girlfriend, dancer Christian Scott, and her world couldn't be better.

Christian, though proud of Grey and all that she's accomplished, is facing her own career dilemma. All she's ever wanted to do is perform and create, her body her kinetic canvas. But, in one of the few industries where youth matters above all else, her time is coming to make decisions that no woman in her mid-thirties should have to make: is it time to retire?

As the career of one begins to explode into the stratosphere and the other's implodes after a career-ending injury that makes any retirement discussion irrelevant, Grey and Christian begin to drift apart. Changing priorities and newly built walls lead to fears and accusations, further tearing at the fabric of the love they've worked years to create.

Will cooler heads prevail to warm up the hearts of the deeply passionate couple in time to create a new dream for their second act?

Swann Song - ISBN - 978-1-952270-63-5

Christine Swann is a world-famous singer/songwriter and lesbian icon, known for her edgy style and heart-pounding songs. Gorgeous, rich and miserable. Her music has always been her life, her escape from an unimaginable childhood, and choices no thirteen-year-old should have to make.

Now, pushing thirty, she wants out. From all of it.

Willow Bowman lives in the farmhouse her beloved grandmother left her, with her husband. A pediatric nurse and small-town girl, she relishes in the safety of her marriage that keeps difficult questions at bay and keeps her life quiet and peaceful, because that makes sense to her.

Until one night when Willow is driving home and is about to cross the old, rickety Dittman Bridge not far from the farmhouse, and she sees a figure jump off into the cold waters below.

The moment she jumps in and pulls the woman dressed in leather pants out, both their lives change forever.

Keeping Hope (Wynter Series Book 4) - ISBN - 978-1-952270-78-9

Twenty-four-year-old Hope DeSilva has been released from a three-year stint in a Georgia prison. After returning to her family property in a tiny Georgia town, she decides she's had enough of the poverty, violence, and progound family dysfunction. It's time to get out on her own. She buys a $400 car and heads to find work out west.

After the car breaks down in Colorado, she's given a ride into a mountain town called Wynter where she runs into brash, aggressive police officer Samantha Gains, who has not one ounce of patience or sympathy for a felon in her black-and-white world of right or wrong, good or bad.

But, running from her own family trauma and inexplicably bewitched by the young newcomer Hope, Samantha begins to realize that maybe her strict worldview isn't as simple as it seems. When a freak accident brings the two women together, it will take both of them letting go of their pasts to truly move on.

Take another trip to Wynter and revisit old friends as they work their magic to help Hope and Samantha find their footing—and ultimately bring them home.

She Who Would be King - ISBN - 978-1-952270-89-5

Cateline is the seventeen-year-old daughter of a nobleman in fourteenth-century France. It's a time when children aren't seen as those to be loved and cherished, but instead are used as pawns and bargaining chips on the chessboard of control and privilege.

She is married off to a prince in the country of Sursha, a Gaelic-speaking island nation near Ireland. Fergus, her betrothed, is next in line to take over once beloved King Carthac dies. Or is he?

Fallon, the youngest royal child and only girl, has been raised as one of the king's sons her entire life, for reasons she has never fully understood. A natural fighter, she was raised to be a warrior and head the Crown's Elite Guard assigned to protect her boorish brother Fergus.

Forced to fill in for her brother in an unexpected way, an instant attraction between Fallon and Cateline forms. In a game of thrones filled with deception and betrayal, even the most secret love can mean death.

Control - ISBN - 978-1-959929-01-7

Keller Mitchum has already lived a lifetime in eighteen years. Fully responsible for her five-year-old sister Parker, Keller has seen and experienced things in life that should exist in the most intense fictional plot. Wise beyond her years, she will do absolutely anything to keep Parker safe.

Garrison Davies is a twenty-three-year-old pilot in Massachusetts, working with her father in a small, family-owned cargo business. Independent, feisty, and brilliant at what she does, she makes little time for anything outside of her beloved planes and dogs. Her simple and structured world is turned on its head when a difficult situation lands two unexpected guests into her life and her house.

Garrison tries to make a safe space for Keller and Parker, only partially aware of the horrors they come from. As time passes, it becomes clear that it's not only the past that keeps the two sisters at arm's length. Can Garrison break through Keller's defenses and help her regain control?

Other books from Sapphire Authors

Out of the Ashes - ISBN - 978-1-952270-84-0

When unusual seismic activity is detected on Mount St. Helens, volcanologist Nova "Cano" Kane, along with a team from the United States Geological Survey, is sent to investigate. The year is 1980, and there hasn't been a large-scale eruption on the mountain in over one hundred years.

Dr. Allison "Allie" Albright is a prominent professor at the University of Washington where the seismic activity is being tracked. As more scientists pour into Seattle, she braces for the possible return of Cano.

Neither Allie nor Cano has fully recovered from their breakup four years earlier. Both live with the pain and regret of how their relationship ended. Maybe it's best to leave it in the past and focus on the job at hand.

They must battle the limits of predictive science, the shortsightedness of bureaucracy, and the bias of the media, while fighting their complicated feelings for each other. As Mount St. Helens continues to churn, so too does their attraction.
Which will erupt first—the volcano or their feelings for each other?

The Serenity Nearby – ISBN – 978-1-952270-65-9

Veronica Hockmeier's relationship with her girlfriend/ PhD supervisor is on the rocks. A graduate student has died by suicide in her English Department. And her eating disorder has returned with a vengeance. All Veronica wants to do is get out of town for a weekend, and when her paper is accepted at an academic conference on Emily Dickinson, in Dickinson's hometown of Amherst, Massachusetts, Veronica takes this as a good sign.

On the way there, she is greeted with calamity after calamity: an accident on the road, a person from her past, and what appears to be the ghost of a graduate student in her hotel room. When a friendly hotel worker named Bo Wu shows her some kindness, Veronica can't help but fall for the tall woman with a winning smile—even if she does have a creepy collection of items dead patrons have left behind.

When Veronica's passport goes missing and another body turns up at the hotel, she becomes trapped in a nightmare she can't escape from—not without Bo's help.

Dusty Road Home – ISBN – 978-1-952270-72-7

Melanie Crenshaw has fallen off the proverbial map. Notoriously private on a good day, the world-famous mystery author has gone dark to avoid any public blowback or scandal from her latest failed relationship. Seeking quiet and solace, she retreats to her rural hometown, hoping isolation will be just the atmosphere she needs to finish her novel. But going back home is never as easy as it sounds, especially when a nosy reporter starts sniffing around.

Pulitzer-winning investigative journalist Pilar Stein

has seen people at their worst—and has the scars to prove it. After taking time off to heal from a particularly brutal assignment, she's back in the saddle and ready to reclaim her place among the elite of hard-hitting reporters. Unfortunately, her re-entry story—a profile on elusive author Melanie Crenshaw who has suddenly disappeared—seems to lack the teeth necessary to catapult her back to the top of her game.

Appearances are deceiving, of course, and Pilar soon discovers that what she deems a simple fluff piece might well lead to the scoop of a generation…just not the one she expected.

As Melanie fights to maintain her privacy while Pilar takes a backhoe to her past, the two women find themselves torn between their own professional convictions and their growing attraction to each other. And no matter which road they take, it's going to be a bumpy ride.

You Can't Outrun Your Roots – ISBN – 978-1-952270-82-6

What if instead of meeting someone new, you reconnected with someone from your past?

As Southern as fried chicken and peach cobbler, free spirit Gloria Robinson spent her lifetime building a successful permaculture farm on the tired dirt of former cotton fields in South Carolina. Now widowed, Gloria is certain she'll never find someone new, not in this town. She wouldn't even know how to try. Politically, she fears her years of effort for social justice are slipping backward. She's becoming weary, but she's digging in her heels.

Living in Washington D.C., perpetually single, party girl Anna May Walker floats through life disconnected from her roots in the South. Self-focused, she often ponders how she wronged Gloria in high school. When Anna May's father dies, she heads home to lure her mother to move near her in a retirement community.

Avoiding each other in a small town is impossible, particularly when Anna May's boss unwittingly assigns her to write a story about Gloria's farm. After decades apart, will the old sparks be enough to restart a fire between them?

First comes Marriage: Morgantown - Book One - ISBN - 978-1-952270- 80-2

Take one CEO, one pink-haired alien, a secret marriage, vengeful aliens, unexplained deaths, and a bitter sister out for revenge, and two women's lives will never be the same.

As CEO of MartinTech, Brynn Martin is at the top of her professional game. Her personal life is another matter, but she's not in a hurry to break her single status. All that changes on a Tuesday morning when a bombshell is dropped.

At sixteen, Micah Legon fled her abusive family and home world of Vubloxia. Now, at twenty-nine, she's content and settled in her life, running a cleanup business with her siblings. Then one morning, she gets a phone call that changes everything.

A chance encounter six years ago in Las Vegas at a "Meet an Alien" convention comes back to haunt both women. While Micah remembers the day with fondness, Brynn remembers nothing. After meeting again, both women come to an agreement. However, nothing is ever that simple.

Micah makes it her mission to break through Brynn's tough exterior. Brynn makes it her mission to keep Micah at arm's length. Nothing will stop either woman from getting what she wants. The trouble is convincing the other that her plan is the right one.

www.ingramcontent.com/pod-product-compliance
Lightning Source LLC
Chambersburg PA
CBHW030636020726
47493CB00006B/1737